save
my
daughter

BOOKS BY SAM VICKERY

My Only Child
One Last Second
The Promise
One More Tomorrow
Keep It Secret
The Things You Cannot See
Where There's Smoke

NOVELLAS
What You Never Knew

save my daughter

SAM VICKERY

Bookouture

Published by Bookouture in 2021

An imprint of Storyfire Ltd.
Carmelite House
50 Victoria Embankment
London EC4Y 0DZ

www.bookouture.com

ISBN: 978-1-80019-426-7
eBook ISBN: 978-1-80019-425-0

For my daughter, Aurora. My joy, my little shadow, my love.
You make me smile a thousand times a day. This one is for you.

PROLOGUE

I never planned it, though I know that's exactly what people will think. They'll watch with one eye on the news as they sip their morning coffee, tutting under their breath, condemning me without stopping to question what they're hearing – or whether it's even true.

I know how it works. How people's lives are picked to pieces by vultures in their determination to create a villain. They'll say I bided my time, waited for the perfect opportunity to make my move, betrayed my best friend in the world; that my whole life was a lie leading up to this one pivotal moment. I know the whispers that will follow me everywhere I go. The hateful glances. Doors slammed shut in my face.

But the picture they'll paint of me is nothing but a lie. I never intended to break her trust. Never even considered it, even after discovering the secrets she'd held back from me. What she'd done.

I loved her, loved them all. I would never have hurt them.

What I did was a shock, even to me. I never planned it, but in the end, I don't suppose the intent mattered. It was my actions that counted. And those I couldn't excuse.

CHAPTER ONE

Lily

The smell of candyfloss and fried foods filled the sultry August air, making my mouth water despite the picnic we'd eaten only an hour before. I adjusted the constricting waistband of my cotton sundress as it swished around my calves, a light breeze teasing every now and then, offering a moment of relief from the heat before disappearing into the crowd. I'd known what we were getting into before agreeing to come today, been perfectly aware that the place would be packed with families, children hyped up on sugar or having a heat-induced meltdown, but once the idea had come to me, I'd latched on to it with conviction. It must have been three years since we'd last had a day out to a theme park, and it was long overdue.

Jon took my hand, our eyes meeting for a moment as he pointed towards the dragon-themed roller coaster. I nodded, slipping my palm from his, ignoring the crease that appeared between his eyebrows and wiping the damp sheen of sweat from my hand on my dress.

Last time we'd come, William had only been five, Maisy three, and we'd spent the majority of the day watching the parrot shows, hanging around the merry-go-round and the toddler area. I remembered how Jon had been called up to the stage in the tiny arena, where he'd had a large, intimidating macaw placed on his shoulder. How the children in the audience had roared with laughter when the parrot had relieved its bowels down the back of his T-shirt. The complimentary vouchers we'd been given by the flustered twenty-something-year-old guy who'd been leading the show, though Jon had taken it all on the chin and laughed along with the audience. It seemed like a lifetime ago now.

I closed my eyes, breathing in the summer air, letting the screams and laughter wash over me. I wished we could go back to that day.

'Mummy, look at the bear!'

I opened my eyes to find Jon watching me, his mouth twisted in that familiar look of concern. Maisy was tugging at my arm, half awestruck, half terrified as the huge bear mascot interacted with children nearby, making exaggerated movements and dishing out hugs.

'Do you want me to take you over to see him?' I asked, reaching for her hand, enjoying the fact that for once she didn't pull hers away.

She shook her head. 'I don't think I want to. He's really big. And his eyes are scary.'

'It's not real, silly,' William said, coming to stand at my other side, his fingers encircling mine. He squeezed tightly, waiting for me to look down at him, ensuring he had my full attention before continuing. 'It's just a man in a suit. Or maybe a woman. Whoever it is, they must be really, really hot.'

Hannah nodded in agreement as she shifted Ella in the baby carrier. I smiled at my best friend holding my three-month-old daughter with all the clumsy ineptitude she'd had with my first two. My breasts twinged, signalling that it would soon be time for another feed, and I glanced at the sleeping face of my baby girl, her head resting against Hannah's over-washed pale pink T-shirt, dribble pooling in a wide circle on the cotton.

'I don't think they stay in those suits for more than ten or fifteen minutes,' Hannah said over the top of Ella's head. 'Can't have bears collapsing in the park, can they?' she added with a wink. The look on William's face told me he intended to watch and find out for himself.

'Come on,' Jon said, hoisting Maisy onto his hip, despite the fact that at six, she was nearly too big to be carried by her daddy. 'Let's just go and have a look from a distance. You don't have to speak to him if you don't want.'

She nodded bravely, though her little hand snaked over his shoulder and gripped the back of his shirt in a vice-like hold.

William looked up at me again. 'Come on, Mummy,' he said, tugging at my hand.

'You go, sweetie. I'll stay here with Auntie Hannah and Ella. We'll go on the ride once you've had a look at the bear.'

'The *man*, you mean.' His eyes followed Jon, but he hesitated.

'Go on, William,' I said, smiling. 'It's only for a second. Go with Daddy.'

He shuffled his feet, watching Jon getting further away, then suddenly let go of my hand, rushing after him, his desire to get a closer look at the mascot overriding his need to be constantly by my side.

Hannah offered a smile, adjusting Ella's cotton sunhat, shielding her face from the afternoon sun. 'There goes your little shadow. Quick, bask in your freedom, it won't last long,' she teased.

I raised an eyebrow, shaking out my arms. 'Ah, the bliss of not having someone permanently attached to you. He's been more intense than ever lately, can't stand it if Maisy so much as holds my hand. He really gets jealous.'

She nodded. 'Yeah, I noticed. Maisy doesn't seem fazed though.'

'She wouldn't be, would she? She's in her own world. Today's been the most animated I've seen her in months.' I stared after her, going over the same repetitive worries I always drove myself mad with. Maisy was a dreamer, an unusually independent child who never seemed to need, or even want, my attention or input in her life. Even as a tiny baby she'd been content in her own company, and though I tried to be there for her, to play or chat or just spend quality time with her, I always felt her pulling away, her desire to get back to her own space, where she could lose herself in books or daydream uninterrupted, creating a chasm between us that I couldn't seem to navigate my way across. But I didn't stop trying. That had to count for something.

William, on the other hand, was so dependent on me I often wondered how he'd ever cope in the future. He needed me by his side every moment of the day, and any effort on my part to put a little distance between us only served to make him more anxious and hold on even tighter. I sometimes wondered if Maisy's independence was an unconscious consequence, a reaction to her brother's neediness. If somehow she instinctively knew she could never compete for my attention in the same way William could so didn't even try.

'I'd love to find more opportunities to bond with her without William hovering over us,' I said, sighing heavily as I watched Jon move closer to the mascot, Maisy bravely slipping out of his hold to peer curiously at the man in the bear suit. I shrugged, not wanting to spoil the day but needing to voice my fears out loud. 'There are times when I feel like I'm getting there and then other times when I feel like I hardly know her,' I confessed. 'It's not right. My own daughter and most of the time I couldn't even pretend to guess at what's going on in that mind of hers.' I shook my head. 'At least she's come out of her shell a bit today. We really needed this.'

'She looks like she's having fun. It's lovely to see her getting involved,' Hannah said. She looked down at Ella, and my stomach clenched. I felt like I had so much going on, so many balls in the air, and I had no idea how to keep all of them from clattering to the ground. I never seemed to get the balance right, and with Ella's unexpected arrival, everything had become so much more difficult.

I swallowed back my sadness and forced my mouth into a smile, determined to make the best of things. 'Thanks for coming with us today, Han,' I said, squeezing the top of her arm affectionately. I knew a trip to a busy theme park was probably the last thing she wanted to spend her Saturday doing. She worked so hard during the week and her weekends were precious to her – time to recharge her batteries in the kind of luxury I could only imagine. She liked to go for an early-morning swim at the leisure centre, or book herself in for a deep tissue massage, or just spend the whole day eating chocolate and watching Netflix. I had no right to be jealous of her freedom, nor her exciting career as a homeware designer, but that didn't stop me feeling envious sometimes when she was flying off to Milan to run her fingers through fabric samples between boozy lunches and meetings with the heads of any number of swanky department stores while I was stuck at home, mediating arguments between William and Maisy and trying for the thousandth time to explain the point of learning the correct spellings when everyone had access to a spellchecker nowadays. Hannah always insisted that her life wasn't nearly as glamorous as it sounded, but it was a damn sight more glamorous than teaching times tables while cramming down a slice of cold toast, baby dribble drying on my chest.

It wasn't that I'd swap lives with her if I had the option. I'd been lucky, blessed with two planned children and little Ella, our surprise addition. I knew I should be grateful for the memories we'd created together as a family. But sometimes, it was hard.

Hannah had all the stresses and challenges that came with a busy career, but she didn't have the responsibility of people's lives on her shoulders. I hated to let those dark thoughts creep in, but sometimes, when I was up for the umpteenth time in the night to feed or change or soothe one of the children – Ella and William for the most part – when I was pulled in a thousand different directions and feeling like I was failing in everything I did, as a wife, a mother, *a woman* even, I wondered what life would have been like if I had chosen a different path. Been like her.

I had hoped to keep working after we had William – that had always been the plan. My job back then hadn't been anything special; when I got pregnant, I was only doing filing for a law firm, but just being in that environment, surrounded by the buzz of people working hard, passionate about their cases, their clients, made me want to retrain and join them. I'd intended to keep working part-time and study for a law degree in the evenings, but I hadn't bargained for how intense William's needs would be. At the time, it had made sense to adapt our plans and have Maisy just two years later, the idea being to wait until William was in school before diving back into my career goals, but it hadn't panned out.

William just couldn't settle at school; every time I managed to leave him with his teacher, I'd barely make it through the front door before I got the inevitable phone call asking me to come back and collect him. He just wouldn't accept being there. We tried everything, from waiting it out and hoping he'd settle to changing teachers and then, finally, me going into class with him for three weeks, having to leave Maisy with my less-than-keen parents so I could support him, but it wasn't a long-term solution, and it didn't seem to matter whether I stayed or not – he never did relax in that environment.

It just didn't work for him; he hated the noise, the confusion of all the children talking over each other, the lessons he didn't have any interest in. The longer we persevered with it, the more I could see my sweet little boy becoming a shadow, trying to make himself small – to disappear. If I tried to leave him there, he would scream until he passed out, terrifying everyone around him, then wake up and start all over again. His fingernails were broken, the tips of his fingers splintered from holding on to the door frame when the teaching assistant tried to carry him inside each morning. At school, he wouldn't eat. He never spoke, except to shout *no*. He wouldn't pick up a pencil, barely looked me in the eye, and his teacher might as well have been invisible for all the attention he gave her. I could see his trust in me fading each day as I woke him up and manhandled him into his school uniform. He hated it, and I knew we couldn't go on.

Jon had been the one to tentatively suggest keeping him at home, educating him myself, and as soon as he mentioned it, I'd felt a sense of absolute relief wash over me. It just made sense. The moment William stepped through the front door to our home, he once again became the rambunctious boy only we got to see. There was no end to his talking, his questions, his curiosity, and I knew his reluctance to learn had nothing to do with a lack of intelligence. Home education might work, and it would mean I could be around for Maisy too, not constantly tearing myself between his needs and hers. Not missing out on those precious early years. It was a sensible option, I could see it working, and I knew I would enjoy the challenge of teaching him myself, but it didn't come without sacrifices. It meant putting my career on hold once again.

Jon's income as a TV researcher, primarily for environmental documentaries, was paying our bills, our mortgage, and back then he had just been offered a huge promotion, a long-term role for a cutting-edge series on climate change, which I knew he was desperate to take. He already travelled a fair amount, and the step up to the new role would mean even more international trips. It would have been impossible for him to quit if we wanted to manage financially, and I knew how much he wanted that job. It wouldn't have been fair of me to ask him to walk away from it after pursuing it for so long, just so I could have a chance at trying something I wasn't even certain I wanted, and so it fell to me to home-educate the children.

I was relieved to see the happiness return to my son. The moment I told him he didn't have to go back to school, his face had split into a smile, his eyes filling with tears as he clung with small, sticky fists to my jumper, making me repeat my words, swear to him that I wouldn't change my mind. It was a sacrifice I was happy to make. What mother wouldn't if she had the option? But that didn't mean I didn't occasionally get a pang of jealousy, a 'what if' moment, when I looked at Hannah's life and saw how different it was from my own.

I watched Maisy's face light up now as the mascot leaned towards her, animated in a way I rarely saw. Today was exactly what we all needed. Quality time together and a chance to make some memories. 'Is she still asleep?' I asked, peering over Hannah's shoulder, trying to see Ella's face.

'Absolutely conked. Must be the heat. Do you want to feed her?'

I shook my head. 'Do you mind holding on to her a bit longer so I can go on the roller coaster with Jon and the kids?'

Hannah glanced down at Ella and shrugged. 'I don't see why not.'

'Thanks, Han, you're a gem. There's a couple of bottles in the changing bag if she wakes up, but I doubt she will.

I glanced away, hoping I wasn't taking advantage of her generosity. It wasn't exactly an exciting day out for her, but she'd promised she didn't mind when I asked her to come, knowing how tricky the rides would be with Ella in tow. I wasn't ready to leave her with a babysitter for the day, and besides, Hannah seemed only too happy to help. She was always willing to take Ella for a cuddle in a way she hadn't been with the other two, and I was grateful that I often had an extra pair of hands to help out. It was really important to me to show Maisy and William that they hadn't lost me to their new sibling. I hadn't missed the resentful glances William had thrown Ella's way, and Maisy had barely acknowledged her, choosing to spend even less time downstairs with us since she was born. I wanted to show them I was still fun. I could still make time for them too.

'You sure you don't mind?' I frowned, wondering if she was okay. If she might have had a bad date, or a disagreement with her boss. She wasn't usually so quiet, but it was hardly the right time for a heart to heart. I'd have to make a pot of tea and grill her later on.

'Course not. We'll be fine. Go. Have fun,' she insisted, reaching for the changing bag I was holding and slinging it over her shoulder. 'I'll wait in the shade over there.'

I nodded as Jon and the kids made it back to us. 'He *was* a man!' Maisy said, grinning in a way that made my heart swell. 'Daddy saw too, didn't you, Daddy? If you looked closely through the nets over the eyes, you could see his real face!'

'Well he didn't trick *you*, did he?' I grinned, my eyes meeting Jon's briefly. 'Auntie Hannah's going to take care of Ellie-Belly for us so we can go on that big ride. That is, if you're brave enough?' I teased, tickling William's tummy, making him squeal with delight.

'I am!' he said, his hand finding mine, clasping on tight. He dragged me towards the queue and I glanced over my shoulder, watching Jon and Maisy following close behind.

We packed in together behind the row of parents and children and I let myself be carried along with the crowd, the excitement of giddy children palpable around me. Jon smiled as we moved through the barriers, the four of us slipping into the row of suspended seats. I hoisted Maisy up into one, glad that despite its hair-raising appearance, the ride would be pretty tame. I wasn't looking forward to the teen years, when I'd have to go on the far speedier rides. I'd never been a fan of that awful feeling of falling.

I checked Maisy was buckled in, though I knew the attendant would do it too, then did the same for William. 'Hurry up, Mummy,' he said, his eyes filled with worry. 'What if it starts without you?'

'It wouldn't, darling. They have to press a button – it's not automatic.' All the same, I hopped into the seat at the end of the row, my feet dangling above the ground beneath. I strapped myself in and nodded to Jon. 'Make sure yours is done up,' I told him.

'Yes, Mum,' he said, grinning, and William burst into peals of delighted laughter.

I craned my head round the edge of the seat and looked past the queue to the spot where I'd left Hannah and Ella. 'I can't see them,' I muttered. 'Jon, did you see where they went?'

'Probably gone to get a drink or something.'

'Maybe,' I murmured, fidgeting in my seat to get another look. The attendant came past, pushing down the security bar with strong hands. 'Wait, I'm not ready, I—'

'Mum's scared,' William said, a tremor of nerves making his voice unsteady. I knew he looked to me for confidence.

'No,' I said, shaking my head, still trying to peer around the wide edge of the bucket seat. 'I'm... I'm—' But I didn't get to finish my sentence. The ride sprang into action, shooting us forward, stealing the words from my lips. I couldn't explain the sudden coldness that swept through my body, the metallic tang of fear on my tongue that had nothing to do with the jolting motion of the roller coaster, but I suddenly had a desperate need to get off and get back to my baby girl. I couldn't explain how, but I was suddenly sure something had happened. Something was wrong.

I paid no attention to the laughs and squeals coming from around me, the dips and whirls of the ride, my hair whipping my face as I frantically scanned the ground below, desperate to catch a glimpse of Hannah. At last the roller coaster made it back to the place it had started, only to shoot off again, to my crushing disappointment. I felt sick with terror as we repeated the dives. Jon shouted for joy, while William and Maisy giggled and screamed, adrenaline and excitement lighting up their faces. My fingers dug into the thick rubber covering my harness and I wanted to scream too. I *had* to get off. I had to.

The ride finally screeched to a stop and I jumped out of my chair, unclipping William and Maisy myself before anyone else had even got down. 'Quickly, come on.'

'What is it?' Jon asked, following after me, his eyes still alight with joy. 'Are you okay, Lils?'

'No… no…' I muttered, surging forward through the maze of fences to get to the exit, my hands clasped tightly around each of my children's. There were so many people, so much noise. I forced a path through the heaving mass of bodies, ignoring the disgruntled comments as I pushed roughly past, my eyes searching frantically among them.

'Mummy!' Maisy whined. 'Let go. You're hurting me.'

'Lily? What's going on?' Jon frowned, taking Maisy's hand from my own. He grabbed my arm as I made to rush on. 'Lily! Stop!'

'She's gone,' I whispered, seeing the spot in which Hannah had promised to wait. Frantically I scanned the empty bench, the bin overflowing with ice-cream wrappers and cardboard coffee cups. A foil packet fluttered from its tentative position where it had been haphazardly shoved into the mass of litter, catching in the light breeze and skittering across the hot paving stones. I couldn't seem to take my eyes off it, the flash of gold glinting in the sun. 'She's gone,' I said again, this time, my voice growing loud with the panic that was bubbling up like lava within my belly, burning a hole through my insides.

'So?' Jon shrugged. 'I'm sure she'll be back in a sec. It's hot, Lils, she's probably gone to get an ice lolly. Or a cold beer, if I know Hannah. She'll be here any minute.'

I looked up at his confused face, knowing his words were perfectly logical, yet certain he was wrong. It didn't make sense, but somehow, I knew. My gut was screaming at me. I just knew.

Hannah had taken my child, and she wasn't coming back.

CHAPTER TWO

Hannah

Lily let William guide her towards the queue for the dragon-themed roller coaster and I watched as she looked back over her shoulder, seeing the brief uncomfortable eye contact between her and Jon. She couldn't hold his gaze anymore. Didn't seem able to let herself get too close to him. I couldn't pinpoint when that had started, but once I'd begun to look, watching the two of them with more awareness, the truth had been there, plain to see.

The baby carrier chafed against my shoulders through the thin cotton of my T-shirt, and I shifted my position, leaning my weight on one foot and then the other, unable to get comfortable. My grey linen shorts felt tight and itchy against my thighs, and I wished I'd worn something else rather than fishing these out of the back of my wardrobe. They'd fitted just fine the last time I'd had them on, but clearly I'd gained weight since last summer. I watched as Lily and her family moved to the front of the line and wondered how the woman who had been my best friend for seventeen years could have become such a stranger to me.

We'd met when we were both just eighteen, at a group camping trip my parents had been taking me to since I was tiny. It was the annual camp for members of the Sandy Shores sailing club, a chance to share stories and catch up without the lure of the sea to distract them, and my parents, being figureheads of the club, never missed it.

As a child, it had been exciting to pack my little bag of belongings and sit in the back of the car, fizzing with excitement about the two weeks ahead of me. Our family was always the first to arrive, and I would climb trees and build dens and generally get in the way of my parents as they swore under their breath trying to navigate the tent, until one by one the other families would arrive and soon I would have a tribe of playmates to fill my days with. Those days seemed endless. We would splash in the river, play frisbee, toast marshmallows. We would make rope swings and stay out long after sunset, never tired, always begging for just half an hour more.

As an only child, those annual trips had been the happiest days of my life. I'd longed for them to continue just like that, to go on forever, but as the years passed, families moved away or dropped out of the sailing club. New ones arrived with children who were too young for me to play with. The friends I had made grew older, chose to stay with grandparents or school friends rather than spend their free time in the woods. Slowly the little tribe I'd treasured so dearly dwindled to nothing, and by the time I reached the age of fifteen, I was the only person under forty still attending. The energy of the trip had changed from hot dogs and songs around the fire to dull political debates between brandy-swilling parents. It was no longer something to look forward to but something to endure. I never considered not going, partly because my parents insisted on it and partly from a sense of nostalgia. I still carried the hope that one day I'd be pitching my tent and would look up to find the smiling faces of those friends who had made my childhood memorable.

Which was probably why, the year I turned eighteen, when I saw the pretty teenage girl standing awkwardly near the campfire, her hands clasped together as if she were afraid of the nature surrounding her, I'd dropped my book on the ground and rushed up to introduce myself, forgetting in my excitement that I was no longer eight years old and a different approach might have been better. My confidence had faltered when I saw the carefully applied eyeliner, the perfect nails. My own were short and dirty, my cropped blonde hair unbrushed, but as I searched for words, Lily had broken into a wide, warm smile and I'd felt the tension unravel inside my belly, sure that I wanted to know this girl.

We had formed an instant bond, intensified by the fact that for two whole weeks there was nobody else to talk to, nobody competing for her friendship. I was sure she would have been surrounded by attention had we met anywhere but out in the woods, and I was grateful to have her to myself, to have a chance at being her friend. Night after night we'd sat under the thick canvas of stars, talking about everything: our old schools, our families, past boyfriends – I'd had two, neither one serious; she'd been with the same boy for three years, and when she talked about him, her eyes lit up. I told her how excited I was to be starting at Bournemouth University the coming autumn, and she explained that her family had just moved thirty minutes down the coast to Mudeford, hence them joining our sailing club. Before that, they'd been a stone's throw away in Barton-on-Sea, but her parents, she'd explained, got bored and never liked to stay in the same place for too long.

In all the years that had passed since that first meeting, her parents had never settled for long. Even the lure of grandchildren hadn't been enough to clip their wings. Two years ago, they'd packed up and moved back to Whitehaven in the Lake District, the town where they'd met and grown up, saying they wanted to be near Lily's grandparents and have a change of scenery. I knew Lily had been sad to see them go, but she and Jon were settled in Bournemouth, and there would have been no point in following them up there – it would only be a matter of time before they moved again anyway. Jon's parents had sold up and downsized to a little Cornish cottage just before William was born, and though he'd never been particularly close to them, I knew that he and Lily felt the isolation and lack of family support more than they'd expected to. I'd worried back then that they might leave me behind, go off in search of a community, but as the years had passed and they'd stayed put, I'd stopped worrying.

I smiled, remembering that first camp together – the hope that for once in my life I'd found someone who didn't see me as just someone to pass the time with, but something more. As out of place as Lily had seemed in the woods, when she talked about the sea, she came alive, and I knew I'd found a kindred spirit. She'd been sailing all her life and knew as much about it as I did, if not more. We shared secrets and laughed until we couldn't breathe, and at the end of that trip, we'd promised we would stay friends. I hoped she meant it, but something inside me told me it was too much to wish for. She'd be busy with her own life, her real friends.

When she'd called the day after we arrived home, inviting me to the cinema, my heart had leaped. I'd never managed to keep a friend, always been left behind for someone better, prettier, more interesting, so the fact that she had kept her promise had meant the world to me. From then on, we'd been as close as sisters. We'd shared our deepest secrets, our hopes and dreams. She'd introduced me to Jon and somehow made me feel included – never the third wheel, never out of place. I'd liked him right away, relieved by his warm, friendly welcome and his quick-to-laugh nature.

We'd never fallen out and we'd never lied to each other, but somehow in recent years, the trust that had formed the bedrock of our friendship had been shattered, and as I watched Lily buckling herself into the ride now, all I could see was a stranger.

Ella stirred and I bent my head, kissing her downy forehead, breathing in the scent of her. It was impossible to understand how any mother could be as blessed as Lily was and not appreciate what she had. If she only knew how lucky she was. What

I would give to just… I swallowed back the rush of emotion, refusing to fall victim to a fantasy, wrapping my arms around the baby carrier, the warmth of Ella's tiny body nestled against me, calming somehow.

She was the most beautiful baby. Dark expressive eyes. Full rosebud lips. Fluffy chestnut hair. She was so calm, so sweet. If only… I closed my eyes for just a second, shaking away the awful thought, then opened them and looked down at her little eyelids fluttering in sleep, almost translucent. Her half-moon fingernails so tiny, her palm resting open against my chest. I could feel the longing spreading through my limbs, a feeling of absolute need. Maternal. Powerful. Completely overwhelming. It wasn't fair. It wasn't fair. It wasn't fucking fair.

I bit down on my bottom lip, trying not to give in to the tears that were determined to break free. My throat felt swollen, a lump wedged deep inside, painful and throbbing in my struggle not to cry.

'Oh, Mummy! Look at the tiny baby!' a little girl squealed, pointing up at Ella. I glanced to the left, surprised to find her watching me.

Her mother smiled, her eyes warm as they met mine. 'How old is she?'

'Three months,' I managed, my voice choked and unfamiliar.

Her smile grew wider. 'Such a precious age. Enjoy it – it flies by.' She glanced down at her daughter with misty eyes.

'I will,' I said, nodding, allowing myself the pretence for just a moment, letting the warmth of the lie cocoon me like a protective blanket. 'I will,' I whispered again, looking down at Ella once more.

I turned back to watch the roller coaster, the attendant moving along the rows of chairs, checking the harnesses. Then, on stiff, robotic limbs, I turned slowly, walking in the opposite direction. I could hear a ringing in my ears, the slap of my sandals on the hot tarmac as my footsteps grew faster and faster still, crystal clarity and dream-like confusion mingling and clashing all around me. I followed the path, not letting myself stop, think, question. I saw the sign for the entrance to the park and walked purposefully towards it, not slowing my pace or making eye contact with anyone.

I pushed through the crowd, past the souvenir shop filled with brightly coloured teddies, toys and sweets, my hands firm across Ella's back, the thick strap of the changing bag cutting into my shoulder. A shuttle bus heading for the taxi rank was in the lay-by, its engine ticking over as if preparing to leave. I stepped up into the cool interior and bought a ticket, slipping into a seat on the far side.

My heart was pounding, my palms slick with sweat, my stomach churning. I clenched my jaw, my arms forming a cage around the baby, and stared out of the window, my mind blank, curiously empty.

The bus doors closed with a hiss and then we were pulling away from the theme park. I let out the breath I'd been holding and stared dead ahead, not allowing myself to think about what I'd just done.

CHAPTER THREE

Then

I grasped the mug of coffee between my palms, knowing I wouldn't drink it but glad of its warmth. Maisy sat beside me at the Formica-covered kitchen table, her head bowed over an exercise book as she silently worked on her writing practice. A deck of flash cards was spread across the tablecloth, and I watched with quiet pleasure as she stretched out her little hand, choosing one. 'Kuh, ah, tuh,' she murmured softly, her brow creasing in a way that made me think of Jon. 'Kuh, ah, tuh… cat!' she announced quietly to herself. She picked up her pencil, adjusting her grasp carefully before dipping her head to write a shaky C.

I wanted to say something, to praise her for how hard she was working, but I was afraid to interrupt her when she looked so busy. She didn't want my input; she was completely focused and it was fascinating to watch.

I pressed my palms tighter against my mug, swallowing back a wave of sadness as I heard Lily coming back down the hall. A drop of moisture slipped unbidden from the corner of my eye and I wiped it roughly away, then pasted on a serene smile. Lily bustled into the kitchen, a plastic laundry basket with a large crack down one side of it tucked beneath her arm.

'So?' she asked, squatting down to shove handfuls of dirty laundry into the washing machine. 'How did you manage to wangle a Friday afternoon out of the office? Don't you have shedloads of work to do?'

I fiddled with my coaster, not looking up as I offered a vague answer. I'd been glad to see that my boss, Eloise, was out at meetings all day. I wouldn't have pushed my luck with taking the time off otherwise. 'Nothing that won't wait until Monday.'

Lily straightened up, pressing a few buttons until the washing machine roared into action with a metallic-sounding crunch. 'That's on its last legs,' she sighed.

'Mummy!' William's voice drifted in from the living room.

'In a little while, sweetie.' She shook her head. 'He wants me to read to him again. He's obsessed with this dragon series, and they're too hard for him to read by himself. I wish I'd never bought the books. I'll have lost my voice by the time I make it through them all.' She picked up her own mug from the kitchen counter and took a gulp. 'Ah, blessed caffeine. I swear, without coffee I'd never make it through the day. He's had me up since five this morning.'

'Must be tough.'

She shrugged, not bothering to answer. 'Are you still going to Rome next week?'

I nodded. 'Yep. Just for three days. I'm meeting with a new supplier.'

'You're so lucky, Hannah. I wish *we* could get away.'

'It's just work. There won't be time for sightseeing or anything like that.'

'But still, it's something. A change of scenery. And you might meet a nice Italian man and I can live vicariously through you when you tell me all about it.' She took another sip of her coffee and closed her eyes. When she opened them, she looked sad. 'I thought we might be better off when Jon took that promotion. He's working all hours and we hardly see him, but as it turns out, with me not working, we're barely making ends meet, God knows why. He said we can't go away at all this year. I was only asking for Devon. A little cottage or something. It's not like I'm expecting Rome.'

'I told you – it isn't a holiday.'

She shook her head, putting down her coffee. 'Sorry, I'm moaning. Long day is all.' She rubbed her fingers into her eye sockets.

Maisy placed her pencil down on the table and I glanced over at her book, seeing the long list of words she'd tried so hard on. 'Mummy, I've finished,' she said softly, looking up at Lily. I didn't miss the hopeful expression that flashed briefly across her little face, the way she knotted her fingers in her lap as she waited for Lily to give her approval.

Lily walked around the counter towards us.

'Mummy!' William appeared in the kitchen doorway. 'It's later now. You said you would read another chapter.'

Lily nodded. 'I know, I know. Go and sit down then. I'll be right there, okay?' She leaned across the table, glancing briefly at Maisy's book. 'Good, darling. The Bs could be a bit neater,' she said. I cringed silently at her criticism, feeling the sting of her words. 'Pop it away and we'll do some more tomorrow,' she finished, turning away without waiting and following after William.

Maisy pressed her lips together, looking down at the page. She gave a tiny, almost imperceptible sigh, then closed the book and stood silently, dropping it into the drawer. I watched, wanting to say something, to reassure her that her mother didn't mean to be so offhand, that she was of course proud of her, but what could I say? It wasn't my place. It was meaningless coming from me. All the same, I wanted to find some way to let her know I'd noticed her hard work; to comfort her with a kind word or two.

I glanced down at my coffee cup, my mind racing, and a moment later I heard her footsteps on the stairs, followed by the soft open and close of her bedroom door. I stared at the empty doorway and felt my heart sink, knowing that not for the first time, I'd missed my opportunity to make a difference. How many times had I watched Lily gloss over Maisy's feelings, her attention focused so intently on William that there was no room for anyone else? It hurt to see the rejection on Maisy's face, and though I tried to block it out, I couldn't help but be reminded of my own childhood.

Each time I saw Maisy retreat silently, her head bowed, her shoulders slumped, I thought of the little girl I had once been, being sent to my room so my parents could have some time alone, listening through the floorboards as they laughed and talked without me, knowing I was unwelcome in their private little twosome. I always felt like my parents never wanted me, choosing social engagements or time together over nights in with me. And when I learned that I was an accident, that feeling made sense. I knew how it felt to be seen as a chore, to know that my very existence was enough to cause resentment in the people who should have wanted me most. I remembered vividly the deep sting of cutting words or their complete disinterest, which they never even tried to disguise, as I'd tried to draw their attention my way, if only for a fleeting moment. The way I would keep my bedroom as tidy as possible to show them how good I was, having heard them comment on the messiness of my cousins', though they never once praised me for it. The dance classes I took because they enjoyed going to the ballet, though they never once came to one of my performances.

When I realised I could get a kind word or two tossed my way for high marks in a test at school, I clung to that path, working harder, becoming more and more driven, desperate for acceptance, acknowledgement, a glimpse of their pride, though as the years passed, I'd had to strive harder and harder still to get those tiny gems, flippant remarks that kept me pushing forward, sure that eventually they would be impressed, that the next step, the next achievement would finally grab their attention and hold it. That they'd start to spend more time with me, less time at work or at the club as a result. All I wanted was to be seen, to feel that they cared, but it had never happened. And when Mum had died, my dad had pulled away even further, seeking comfort in his sailing, his golf, his gardening and his friends, refusing even now to let me in.

Watching Maisy was a painful reminder of those feelings I had squashed down, unable to confront them head-on. They were too confusing, and I preferred to block them out, but Maisy was reliving them in front of me, and her pain reignited my own. I wanted to make it better for her, but I could never seem to find the words to tell her what I knew she needed to hear. Perhaps because I understood it would mean so little coming from me. Lily was too blind to see that her daughter was crying out for more. And she was failing her.

CHAPTER FOUR

Lily

Now

I paced back and forth in front of the bench where I'd hoped to find Hannah. My body trembled, adrenaline rushing through my blood, and I longed to move, to go somewhere, find my baby, but Jon had told me to stay put while he went to look for them, and I was afraid to leave, to not be here when he returned. There was a chance I'd got it wrong. That it was just me being silly, my hormones going haywire or something, but even as I tried to convince myself that this was nothing but an overreaction on my part, I felt my heart beat faster and knew it wasn't true.

William and Maisy sat side by side on the bench, Maisy staring off silently into the distance, William looking sulky and giving off dramatic huffs every now and then to demonstrate his dissatisfaction with how the day was panning out. I ignored his scowling face, scanning the crowd for Jon. I should have made him stay with the kids so *I* could go and look for her. He hadn't appeared to be in a hurry, didn't seem to understand the severity of the situation. My phone, sweaty in my palm, remained silent, and I pressed call on Hannah's number again, holding my breath then groaning in frustration as it went straight to voicemail without ringing.

'Mummy, I want to go on another ride now. This is boring!' William complained, his little arms folded, his brow creased.

I didn't bother to reply, though I knew my silence would only serve to stoke his frustrations. He hated to have his words go unanswered, but an impending meltdown from William was the least of my worries right now.

Where was Jon? Had something happened? I could taste fear on my tongue, the emotion alien and out of place against the backdrop of blue skies, happy faces and cheery repetitive music coming from the speakers nearby. I wanted to scream, to press pause and make them all listen. To stand up on the bench and demand that they stop the rides. Stop the music. Help me find my baby girl before it was too late.

I shouldn't have agreed to just wait here and leave it to Jon. With every second that passed, my daughter was being taken another step away from me. I had to find her now. I couldn't bear the stillness, the inaction. I spun, making an impulsive decision. 'Kids, come on. We have to—'

'Lily!'

I turned from the bench, my heart thudding erratically, to see Jon, his bald head turning pink under the sun, his black T-shirt clinging to his shoulders in the heat. My relief at seeing him turned instantly cold in my stomach as I saw he was alone. 'You didn't find them.'

He shook his head. 'Did you try her phone?'

'Of course I did! I'm not an idiot!' I snapped.

He stepped back, his eyes instantly clouding with hurt. He was so sensitive these days, and I often forgot myself and had to backtrack.

'Sorry,' I said quickly, stepping towards him, bridging the gap, my hands clasped tightly in front of me, my fingernail worrying at the skin around my cuticle. 'I'm sorry. I just…'

He nodded, not needing me to say anything else, his wounded expression clearing in an instant. 'You don't think she could have had an allergic reaction?' he asked under his breath, glancing over to the children to make sure they hadn't heard him. I didn't have to ask why he was keeping his voice down. Not after last time. Hannah had a serious allergy to nuts, and I doubted the kids had got over the trauma of what had happened at Christmas two years previously when she'd eaten one of my great-aunt's home-made mince pies.

Aunt June had sworn there were no nuts in the pies, only to remember too late the almond milk she'd added to the mixture. The effect was almost instantaneous. Within two minutes Hannah's lips had swollen, and before she could even reach her EpiPen in her handbag, she had collapsed head first onto the dining-room floor, taking the tablecloth and half the buffet with her. It had taken two EpiPens, an ambulance ride and three days in hospital to get her back on her feet. And neither Maisy nor William had eaten Great Aunt June's food since.

Jon wouldn't want to remind them of an event we'd all rather forget. 'Do you think she might have eaten something?' he whispered. 'Been rushed off in an ambulance while we were on the ride?'

I stared at him, wondering why the possibility hadn't even crossed my mind. Could it have happened so quickly? Was it even possible? Surely we'd have seen something? 'Ask,' I said, making up my mind. 'We need to go to the park security team. Now.'

Jon nodded, and I saw the strain around his eyes that he tried so hard to hide. Casting my gaze downward so as to avoid his pained expression, I turned to the children. 'Come on, we have to go now.' I grabbed William's hand as Jon took Maisy's, and glad to be moving, doing something at last, I surged forward through the crowd, ignoring William's questions about what was happening, when we were going on the log flume, why he had to wait for an ice cream, because he was really hungry and none of this was fair. I bit my tongue, focusing on moving forward.

The security office was near the front of the park and the door was open as we approached. I pushed inside the room that was barely more than a cubicle, and two men, both a good ten years younger than me, paused in their conversation, looking up expectantly. 'My daughter,' I gasped.

'Lost child?'

'No. Well, yes, but—'

'Don't worry, love. Happens all the time. Kids get distracted and wander off.'

I shook my head, frustrated. Jon put his hand on my shoulder, squeezing lightly. 'No,' I snapped, slamming my palm down on the desk. 'You aren't listening. My daughter, my newborn baby, is missing. She was with my friend and I—' I choked back a sob, pressing my hands to my face.

Jon stepped past me, clearing his throat. 'Our friend has her,' he explained. 'We can't find her, can't get hold of her. What we want to know is has an ambulance been called in the past half hour? You see, the woman who has our baby has a severe nut allergy and—'

'No ambulance been today, mate,' the guard interrupted, shaking his head. His words brought me no comfort. They weren't a surprise. I heard a pained cry and realised it had come from me.

Jon gave a short nod and turned from the man. Grasping my elbow, he steered me towards the door, out of their earshot. 'Wait in those seats there,' he instructed Maisy and William, pointing to a row of red plastic chairs lined up along one wall. William gave a groan, but both of them did as they were told. Jon looked back down at me, his hand still grasping my elbow as if I might fall or suddenly run. 'Lils,' he muttered. 'Why are you so worried? It's *Hannah*. Our friend. What's she going to do?'

I shook my head, aware of the silent stares coming from behind us as the security guards watched our interaction with unconcealed curiosity. 'I don't know,' I admitted. 'But I feel scared, Jon. I can't explain it, but I do. Why isn't she here? Why would she just go with our baby? I… I think she's taken her.'

'Taken?'

I nodded, fear pulsing through my body as I admitted the truth out loud. My body seemed to know something was amiss already. I had to hold her, had to find her. Where could she be? Why had Hannah gone without waiting for us? I closed my eyes, picturing my tiny vulnerable daughter, and wanted to scream.

'Mummy, your dress is wet,' William announced loudly.

I opened my eyes, glancing down at the damp patch that was beginning to spread across the cotton as my milk let down.

'You really mean it; you're genuinely worried, aren't you?' Jon murmured, his hand sliding down my forearm, grasping my wrist gently, waiting for me to look at him.

'Yes.' I pulled my phone from the pocket of my dress and unlocked it for what seemed like the thousandth time in the last five minutes, needing to call her again, to try and get through to her. A text flashed up on the screen and my heart froze in my chest as I saw Hannah's name, the moisture evaporating from my mouth as I let myself feel hope. I'd made a mistake – of course I had! She'd obviously gone off somewhere to cool down, and like an idiot, I'd overreacted. I would have to distract the kids with sweets and a look round the souvenir shop before we went to meet her so they would have something to talk about other than the monumental scene I'd caused. I cringed, embarrassed at how quickly I'd jumped to the wrong conclusion, and with shaking fingers opened the message. A cry escaped my lips as I read the bewildering words, my hopes smashed to pieces in an instant.

Silently, I held the phone towards Jon, who read the text under his breath. 'I'm sorry but I had to do it, Lily. Ella needs more than you're capable of giving. You don't deserve her.'

His face snapped up to mine and I suddenly saw his expression change, his eyes narrowed and dangerous. It was frightening to witness the moment he realised I'd been right. That Ella had been stolen out from under us by the person we trusted most.

And what did Hannah mean, I didn't deserve her? How could she say such a thing?

Jon turned back to the two security guards. 'I need your help. Our friend was looking after our newborn baby, and when we came off the ride, the two of them were gone. I've searched the cafés and toilets. Her phone is off. She's gone, and' – he glanced back at me, his brow creasing – 'my wife just received this message.'

He held the phone out for them to read it, and I wanted to stop him, to protect myself from their scrutiny. I didn't understand what Hannah meant, but anyone reading those words would jump to their own conclusions. They would think I was a bad mother, when all I ever strived for was to do right by my children.

Jon continued to speak quickly, his voice filled with a confident authority I rarely heard unless he was on a work call. 'We believe she's abducted our baby. I need you to help us search for them. Use your cameras or something.'

The guards exchanged a meaningful glance, and the taller of the two lifted the handset of the phone on the desk.

'What are you doing?' Jon asked, watching him.

'Calling the police. It's protocol.'

'It might not be necessary – she could still be in the park, and if your security team is quick…' Jon faltered, and I saw his reluctance to accept the truth of what Hannah had done. I didn't blame him. I couldn't grasp it either.

The guard didn't bother to give a reply as he spoke quickly down the line. The first one, the one who'd looked at me with a condescending smile on his face not two minutes before, was saying something into his radio, words tumbling from his mouth as he rose to stand, his shoulders stiff as if ready for battle. I felt the whole atmosphere transform in a matter of seconds. They were no longer joking and laughing, looking at me as though I was a hysterical mother whose child had got distracted by the candyfloss machine. They were going through their mental checklists, putting their training into practice, setting the ball rolling on a search, and suddenly it all felt so much more terrifying than before. It felt real.

My world started to spin, and I was only half aware of William and Maisy arguing over what 'abducted' meant. Jon's trembling hands were clamped around my phone as he searched for photographs of Hannah and Ella to show the security guard. I saw how pale his skin was beneath the shadows under his eyes, the muscles around his mouth tight...

I wanted to do something to help, but I didn't know how. I was desperate to move, to tear the whole fucking park apart to get back to my baby girl, but there was no point. They would be far from here by now. Where would Hannah have taken her? I needed to think, to tell them where to look, but my head was buzzing with a thousand conflicting thoughts and none of them made any sense. I walked on shaky legs to the open door of the hut, blinking as the bright sunlight hit me, gasping in deep breaths of air to ward off the panic that was filling my chest, fogging my vision.

This wasn't how today was supposed to have turned out. This wasn't what we needed, what I'd pictured. We'd been hanging on to the idea of a happy family by the skin of our teeth, and now it had started to crumble and I could do nothing to slow the process. I didn't know how to stop the erosion of my family, where to even begin. I glanced back at Jon and felt a tear slip down my cheek as I gripped the frame of the door and dug my fingernails into the wood, forcing myself not to run.

CHAPTER FIVE

Hannah

Then

I gripped the ballpoint pen, scribbling down notes as my boss fired off information about the new department store we'd secured a contract with in Prague, listening as she rolled off the dates of the meetings I had to fly over for, the expectations of the new partnership. Her voice was husky, her words to the point. Eloise never wasted time with unnecessary detail or chat, preferring to keep her meetings short so she was free to get back to her to-do lists. I liked that about her. I'd had bosses before who could waste a whole afternoon going back and forth over inconsequential questions, who would call a meeting for something that could have been decided in a five-minute email conversation, and it was obvious to everyone who had to sit there feigning interest over the plate of complimentary pastries that it was more about them enjoying the sound of their own voice than it ever was about the work in question.

Eloise was fifteen years my senior and exactly the kind of powerful, driven, career-minded woman I'd anticipated following in the footsteps of up until very recently. She was a commanding woman, confident and self-assured in her ability to make quick decisions and lead a team of forty designers and buyers, but despite her efficient nature, she was also kind and fair.

There had been so many occasions in my first few years at the company where I'd made a mistake, or messed up somehow, when she could have embarrassed me or used me to make an example to the rest of the team, but she'd never taken the opportunity. In my first year working with her, I'd once added an extra zero to a fabric order, and ten thousand bolts of Persian silk had been delivered, rather than the expected thousand. Eloise had simply raised an eyebrow, placed a hand on my shoulder and told me to call round our contacts and offer it at discount, then she'd taken me to lunch on her expense account and told me a few of her own blunders, which had made me feel instantly like less of an incompetent fool. She wasn't a friend – we rarely discussed personal topics – but she was a good boss and a fair woman, and I enjoyed working with her.

It was funny to think that I'd been so certain I would follow in her footsteps, keep climbing the ladder until I'd reached the absolute top of my game. I'd had a plan laid out that I knew would take me another ten to fifteen years to achieve, and I had been content with that, knowing that striving for that goal would give me the sense of purpose and drive I'd always sought in life. It was all I'd ever thought I wanted, but I could remember the exact moment I realised I wasn't going to tick that achievement off my list, and happily, it was a choice I made with no outside input.

It was about four months ago – two years after I'd got the promotion to my current position as senior buyer and designer – and a promotion had come up for junior manager of department. I was primed to go for it, and though there were a few others on the team who had a chance, I was almost certain I would be the one to snap up the coveted role. It had been part of my plan from the start: two years in this role, then move to management and work my way up the ladder until I reached the dizzying heights of CEO. There was no reason for me not to succeed. I knew it was going to take a monumental level of work and commitment on my part, but that had never stopped me before. But this time, something did. As I'd stared down at the application form, twiddling my pen like a baton between my fingers, I'd had the sudden realisation that despite my carefully constructed game plan, I didn't want this job. And I didn't want the one above it either.

I'd worked hard to get where I was, and now I was in the comfortable yet challenging position of having a job that on a daily basis made me feel lucky. I loved my role. I loved the travel, though I never let on to Lily quite how fun those trips were – the raucous dinners we had at the end of the working day, the tapas and wine the group shared at little restaurants down cobbled alleyways, or looking out over the Seine, watching the sparkling lights of Paris twinkle on the midnight-black surface of the water. I loved the variety in my life. The chance to meet new people. The time I spent working in the office, losing myself in fresh designs for hours on end. The pay was generous and I had a fantastic boss who I respected. Why would I want to leave it behind for something I wasn't sure I even wanted anymore?

The new job would come with much longer working hours and no travel, and rather than designing homeware myself, I would be given the task of approving – or rejecting – the designs that were put on my desk. No more personal creativity. No more spontaneity, feeling the fabrics with my own hands in the places they were created, coming up with a vision for a new design inspired by some piece I'd seen in a tiny furniture store in Naples. All for a better title and a bigger chunk of cash. Was it worth it?

I'd spent an hour thinking about it, and that was all I had needed. I'd taken Eloise aside and told her I wouldn't be going for the position after all, and I'd seen something akin to respect in her expression when I'd explained my reasons why. She'd insisted on taking me out for coffee and a chat, and I'd been sure she was going to try and change my mind, but she'd surprised me, sitting back in the cosy armchair in the corner of the cramped coffee shop and fixing me with a curious little smile as she finished off her macchiato in one gulp. 'It takes a lot of drive to keep moving forward. But it takes courage to stay still. To appreciate what you have. You've made a big decision today, Hannah, and it wasn't based on ego or empty goals, but on your own happiness. It's brave of you. Sometimes I wish I'd made time to re-evaluate my own path before charging down it like a greyhound at the races. Well done for doing what's right for you.'

I'd been taken aback and quietly touched at her words, though a pang of sadness that they'd come from her and not my mother had soured the moment ever so slightly. From that moment, I'd never doubted my decision, even when it was announced that my teammate Lewis had got the promotion.

A few weeks on from stepping back, I'd begun to realise something. Without the focus of the ever-changing career path to keep me occupied, for the first time since I could remember, I had space in my mind to create new goals. To start figuring out what I *did* want now that I'd begun to establish what I didn't. I'd never considered any other option for myself than the fulfilling career, the powerful role. I didn't want to get married or even to have a long-term partner, much preferring the simplicity of the occasional casual boyfriend, who I could choose to see at my own convenience. I valued my freedom and my independence too much to give it up for anyone. But though a man wasn't on my wish list, there was something I realised I would enjoy. Being a mother. Having a little family to call my own.

I loved being fun Auntie Hannah to Lily's kids, but to have a child of my own… The first time the thought had popped into my mind, I'd swept it aside as nonsense. I had never wanted kids. I wasn't maternal. My childhood struggles of trying and subsequently failing to get some scrap of attention from my self-obsessed parents had left no room for dreams of a family of my own. I'd wanted tangible successes to present to them.

Certificates, awards, promotions – the things I knew they valued and admired. Children, in their view, didn't make the cut, as I'd learned the hard way.

I'd never strayed from my path in all these years, always working that bit harder, giving that little piece more of myself away to get where I wanted to be. I reasoned that it was probably just my biological clock starting to interfere – I was thirty-four and I knew as well as anyone the tricks a woman's hormones could play at this time of life. I didn't have the space or the patience to raise a child. I would be terrible at it. After all, I'd learned nothing from my own parents to guide me. But despite my misgivings, as the days slipped by, I'd kept thinking of ways I might make it work.

Perhaps it was the passing of my mother the previous year – knowing that I was still clawing my way up a ladder for a dollop of praise I could no longer hope to receive – that had opened my eyes to how I was living my life. I'd become almost robotic in my need to meet my goals, never questioning what I was doing or why.

The first step to waking up and taking back control, I realised, had been in turning down that promotion, something I would never have had the courage or desire to do when my mother was still living. I'd had an unwelcome epiphany in the months following her funeral. I'd been trying everything to get close to my dad – cooking meals to take over to him, calling and visiting and having my heart broken again and again by his coldness. I was driving home one afternoon, having had the door closed in my face, my father turning me away so he could share his grief with his friends, his peers, rather than his only daughter, and it was as if a light bulb switched on in my head, shining a glaring beam on the reality of my situation.

I was working myself to the bone in order to please a woman who was no longer here and a man who clearly didn't want me in his life. In that moment, as I finally accepted that

I was never going to have the relationship I craved with my parents and I needed to stop chasing an empty dream, a world of possibility seemed to open up. And turning my back on that promotion, taking that first step to break those ingrained patterns, seemed to have sparked more ideas than I could have possibly imagined.

I had been brave and made a choice for my professional life I never would have made when my mum was still around. And now, I realised, I *could* be a mother if I wanted to. I could make my own rules, decide on what I really wanted without the need to please a woman who, I knew, would never have cared about me no matter what I achieved. If I really wanted this, there were ways to make it work.

I could get a nanny. I earned more than enough to afford one. I could take advantage of the fantastic twelve-month maternity package the company offered. I could cut down some of my international travel, or maybe even take the baby and nanny along for the adventure. Why not? Other women made it work. Why shouldn't I?

The seed of an idea had sprouted and grown, until soon there was no question in my mind. I wanted it all. The dazzling career *and* the family.

And, I thought now, my secret warming my insides as I nodded at Eloise, jotting down the details for my trip to Prague, if my predictions were right, I might already be on the way to getting my wish. I hadn't planned to have unprotected sex with Luke after the tipsy night out two weeks earlier, but it had happened. We'd been caught up in the moment, and when I'd realised I'd run out of condoms, neither of us had wanted to stop and we'd recklessly decided to take the risk. I hadn't expected it to happen, but now my period, always so regular I could set my calendar by it, was two days late. And rather than feeling frightened or regretful, I felt excited. This could be it.

I couldn't wait to see Lily's face when I told her the news. I hadn't told her that my opinions on motherhood had changed. I wanted it to be a happy surprise, and I was sure she'd be completely stunned when I confessed that I was ready to dive head first into this new dream.

'So, you'll meet twice. The first time to tour the factory and see samples, the second at the Four Seasons to discuss the costs. The usual set-up, you know the drill. I've spoken with Radek on the phone. Good guy. You'll like him,' Eloise said, leaning back in her chair.

'Great. I'm looking forward to meeting him.'

Eloise didn't have to voice her dismissal. I knew better than to hang around making small talk when we both had plenty of work to be getting on with. I rose from my chair, and as I stood, I felt my stomach sink at the familiar, unwelcome trickling sensation between my thighs. I kept my face clean of any expression as I walked from her office, making straight for the ladies' toilets and hurriedly shutting myself inside a cubicle, yanking up my skirt and pulling down my underwear.

I stared in silent disappointment at the spot of claret seeping into the white cotton, feeling strangely tearful, though I never usually cried. I'd been so sure. Sure enough to make pencil markings on my calendar at home this morning, planning out when the baby would be due, when the best date to take maternity leave was and how soon I'd have to give up flying. I knew from Lily that you couldn't fly in your third trimester, not that she'd ever needed to worry about that.

I sighed, unravelling the toilet roll to clean up and then getting a fresh batch to wipe my eyes with. It wasn't that I wanted it to be Luke's baby. I didn't have strong feelings for him, and like the other men I'd dated, I was under no illusions that he was *the one*. In fact, I was pretty sure he was seeing someone else behind my back, and I'd been preparing myself for the inevitable conversation where we decided to go our separate ways. I didn't mind. But how simple it could have been if we had conceived a child that night. He needn't even be involved if he didn't want to be. And I doubted he did.

I flushed the chain, coming out to wash my hands and reapply my mascara, and fixed my reflection with a determined stare. I'd been through many disappointments in my life, as any woman with an ambitious dream and the courage to take risks had. I'd failed and been knocked back, but I'd picked myself up and kept trying. This would be no different. I would get there; it just might be trickier than I'd initially hoped. I swallowed back the tears that hovered so close beneath the surface and, with my head held high, walked back to my desk, back to my work.

CHAPTER SIX

Now

I felt like every single person on the bus could sense what I'd done, like their eyes were burning into my back, judging me – condemning me. I felt sick to my stomach, and yet there was a sense of energy buzzing through my veins, propelling me forward as I watched Ella sleep. The bus pulled into the taxi rank and I stood up before it had even stopped, wrapping my arm protectively around Ella in the sling and holding tight to her changing bag. The moment the doors hissed open, I stepped out onto the pavement. I was hit with a blast of hot air, the sun still scorching above me, and I instantly missed the air-conditioned interior of the vehicle, but at least I could escape the claustrophobia of being confined.

I walked purposefully, as if I knew where I was going. As if I had a plan. I could feel Ella beginning to wriggle and knew I didn't have long before she would wake. What then? What would I do? A fresh wave of fear washed over me and I paused in the shaded exterior of a little newsagent's, panic coursing through me. I felt all at once nauseous and faint, and I gripped the wall, trying to regain my balance. What was I doing? I should go back, I should—

'Can I help you, miss?'

I looked behind me, seeing a large man taking up the entire doorway of the newsagent's. His blue T-shirt, stretched tight over his round belly, was damp with perspiration, and his unshaven chin was pink beneath the light-brown scruff. He looked at me expectantly, his blue eyes small and piercing in the wide expanse of his face.

'No, I'm fine,' I muttered hurriedly. 'Just hot, that's all.'

He looked me up and down, pausing when he saw the sleeping baby on my front. His expression softened slightly, but he said nothing and I had no wish to continue standing there like an idiot with him watching my every move. Pushing aside my panic, I glanced around and saw the row of taxis idling at the edge of the road, not far behind me. Without offering any parting words to the shopkeeper, I turned towards the cars, striding towards them, my ears ringing, my mouth dry and gluey. I had almost reached them when I saw the sign for the train station. I paused. Would that be better? Less traceable?

'Fuck, Hannah… what are you doing?' I muttered under my breath. I dithered on the spot for a few seconds and then, making up my mind, made for the first taxi in the row, opening the door and sighing in relief as I felt the cool blast of the air conditioner. The driver, a middle-aged Asian man with thick black hair sprouting from the one ear I could see, glanced at me in the rear-view mirror, his finger hovering over his satnav. 'Where to?' he asked in a heavily accented voice.

I leaned back against the leather seat, adjusting Ella, fishing a thin blanket from her changing bag to cover her bare legs against the sudden cool air, stalling for time as I realised I didn't have a clue what the answer to his question was. 'Madam?' he pushed. 'You want to go somewhere?'

I stared down at Ella, knowing what I should do. If I took her back now, I could make up some excuse. They didn't have to know the extent of what I'd nearly done. God, I thought, squeezing my eyes shut in horror. I'd sent that awful text as the bus drove away. What had I been thinking? I bit my lip, wishing I hadn't been so hasty. It had felt right in the moment to tell Lily why I'd taken her child, and if I was honest with myself, I knew I still meant it now. Lily *didn't* deserve Ella. If I hadn't sent the message, I wouldn't have trusted that she would even consider the fact that it was her own faults that had led us to this point. I had to be sure she understood. But still, was I the right person to make that choice? I opened my eyes, drumming my fingertips nervously against my thigh, indecision making my stomach churn.

There was still time to fix this. I could give her back to Lily and Jon and make out like this was all some big misunderstanding. Blame it on heat stroke or something. A prank, taken too far. I could keep on pretending everything was okay.

But it wasn't. It hadn't been for a long time. And looking at the sweet, innocent child snuffling against my chest, I knew it wouldn't be fair to her to turn back now. I was doing this for a reason. To give her the life she deserved. I breathed in deeply, making up my mind as I looked up to meet the driver's frustrated glare.

'Do you want me to take you somewhere?' he asked again, his tone impatient.

'Yes,' I said, nodding. 'I do.'

CHAPTER SEVEN

Lily

William's body was moulded to mine and I wrapped my arms around him as tight as he would allow, a fierce need to keep him safe making me cling to him. I wished Maisy would sit with me too, but when I'd tried to pull her close, she'd shuffled out of my grasp, heading over to the squashy sofa on the opposite side of the room where a widescreen television was playing some animated movie I half recognised. We'd been led to this little room not far from the security office, offered tea and coffee as if we were casual visitors who'd just popped round for some reason far more benign than a kidnapped daughter, and then abandoned here while the security team went to meet the police.

I'd argued, wanting to go with them, or at least to go back out to the park and search, though I knew it was fruitless, but Jon had put his arm round me, murmuring reassurances against my hair, and I hadn't had the heart to fight him off.

I'd watched the two young men go, leaving us here in this stuffy stark white room, the view from the window consisting of nothing but a couple of enormous wheelie bins and a concrete wall, and now we were trapped waiting, each minute lasting a lifetime as strangers who had no stake in our plight were left to fix our lives for us. How could I trust them with something so important? Wasn't it *our* job to find Hannah and get Ella back? Shouldn't *we* be the ones who kept looking rather than sitting here uselessly, letting our baby girl get further from our grasp with each passing minute? I closed my eyes, squashing down an urge to scream, and took a shuddering breath.

William rubbed his hand up and down my back in a soothing motion. He always did that when I was ill, or suffering with a migraine. He would ask Jon to help him make me a cup of tea, and then carefully carry it to where I was resting, sitting quietly beside me and just stroking my back or playing with my hair. Letting me know he cared.

'Mummy?' he asked now, and I opened my eyes to look at him, determined not to drag him and Maisy into my terror. I had to put on a brave face for their sake. 'Is Ella coming back?' he asked softly, twiddling with a loose thread on my dress, his gaze fixed on his fingers, conspicuously avoiding my eyes.

'Of course she is,' I answered automatically, not daring to question whether that was the answer he'd hoped to hear. Just because he hadn't yet bonded with her didn't mean he didn't love her. That he hoped she was gone for good. He sighed, resting his head on my lap, trying to angle his body so that he could see the TV whilst staying close to me.

'Here.'

I looked up to find Jon standing above me. He held out a cold bottle of water and I took it, gripping it tightly in my palms. 'Thanks. Sit down, will you?'

He glanced towards the door without moving. 'I don't understand, Lily. I don't get why she'd take Ella. She's not exactly the maternal type, is she? What does she want with her? And what the hell did she mean, you don't deserve her? You're an incredible mother; surely she knows how much you do for our kids? I can't believe she would ever think something like that!'

His voice was shaky, and I saw the fear beginning to cloud his features, the tightness around his lips, the wide pupils that seemed to drill into mine. I glanced at his hands, noticing the way his fingers trembled, his body almost swaying with exhaustion. He was reaching the point I'd been at an hour ago, and as much as I was grateful that he was finally grasping the severity of the situation, I hated to see him so shaken. I'd never been able to cope with hurting him, letting him down. I'd only ever wanted to see him smile. In the past year or so, that had become increasingly challenging to maintain.

'I don't know why she would say that.' I shrugged, aware of William's steady breathing as he stared at the TV, pretending not to listen to us talking. 'I thought she was my best friend, but what she's done… I don't understand any of this, Jon. All I know is that we have to get Ella back. We have to start looking.'

The panic at knowing Ella was somewhere I couldn't reach her was making my hands sweaty, nausea churning in my belly. I didn't want to think about that text. How deep those words had cut, jabbing at my deepest fears. What mother didn't, at some point, think they weren't good enough, weren't up to the job of raising their children? What woman didn't feel like they were drowning sometimes, failing at every turn, missing those special moments, going through the motions when it was all too overwhelming? I'd felt like I wasn't enough more times than I could count, silently berating myself for getting it wrong, messing it up, but to hear those words from Hannah was something I'd never expected. If I wasn't so afraid, I'd be heartbroken right now.

Jon opened his mouth to speak, then closed it as the door banged open. William's body tensed on my lap, his rigid shoulder digging into my thigh as we watched four uniformed police officers file into the room, followed by the burly security guard who'd tried to brush me off to begin with. He looked anything but jokey now. He faced Jon with a grim nod. 'There are ten PCs scanning the park, we've closed the main entrance, and any staff who were on or near the gate at the time of the abduction are being questioned.'

My stomach flipped painfully at the word as my arm slid tighter around William, though he made no attempt to release himself from my hold.

'These officers would like to ask you some questions, but first we can show you the CCTV footage of the approximate time you believe your daughter and your friend disappeared.'

He glanced over to where Maisy was watching the television and strode across to it, pressing eject on the DVD player. Maisy shot me a hurt look, and I ushered William off my lap so I could move closer to the screen. He gave a disgruntled moan, but his fear of the police helped contain his irritation, and he sat down on my vacated seat, folding his arms with a pointed tut. Jon followed me, as did the group of severe-looking police constables. The security guard slid a DVD into the player and pressed play.

'It's the entrance, Mummy,' William said from behind me, unable to hold back from sharing information when he knew something.

'That's right,' said a female officer, stepping forward. 'I'm PC Canton.'

She held out a hand and I shook it automatically, thinking how strange it was to keep up the social niceties at a time like this. But I didn't want to be rude. I needed her help.

She nodded towards the screen. 'We'd like you to watch the footage and tell us if you spot your friend. It will help narrow down the moment she left, and may enable us to track her movements. We already have constables en route to the local bus and taxi ranks, but at this point, the more information we can gather, the better.'

I nodded, staring at the screen, watching the happy, smiling faces of families leaving the park after a long day; a toddler having a meltdown, no doubt brought on by too much sun and excitement; a little girl staring up at the sky, watching the balloon that had slipped from her grasp disappear into the atmosphere. A staff member dressed as a princess was bending down, having her photograph taken with two small children, and behind her, I saw a familiar short haircut, a walk I recognised: Hannah striding straight out of the exit, on her chest the black and purple patterned baby sling containing my precious daughter.

'Ella,' I whispered, reaching out with my fingertips as if I could touch her, grasp hold of her. I should never have let her go. I snapped my head to look back at PC Canton. 'That's her. That's my baby.'

The security guard pressed pause as they all crowded in front of me to get a closer look. Only the side of Hannah's cheek was visible. I needed to see her eyes, see the expression on her face as she stole my world out from under me. I wanted her to look ashamed, guilty, to know that there was some shred of human decency left in her, some tiny piece of the woman who'd been my best friend for nearly twenty years.

'How could she do this to us?' I whispered, staring at the screen, my mouth dry. Jon's hand slipped into mine and I didn't pull back. Not this time.

'That's very helpful,' PC Canton said, nodding some silent instruction to her colleague, who moved towards the door, talking quickly into his radio.

I watched, wondering why they were all still here, why nobody was doing anything. I turned back to PC Canton, hoping that she would explain their plan to bring Ella back. Jon was bent over a table, scribbling down Hannah's address, her phone number, as she asked him a set of mundane questions that seemed irrelevant. We'd already been through everything we knew with the security guard – this was just time-wasting. I stepped closer, folding my arms tightly across my sweat-dampened cotton dress. The material felt heavy against my skin, itchy and constricting, and the drying milk staining my chest was beginning to smell sour in the heat, bringing with it a rising nausea. The room was stifling, one lone ceiling fan moving in languid circles, having next to no impact on the sweltering temperature. I pinched the side of my arm, feeling the tension build within me. 'I should go to Hannah's flat,' I said. 'Maybe she—'

'We'll do that,' PC Canton said, cutting me off. 'You can rest assured, we'll leave no stone unturned.'

'But I—'

The door opened and I turned to look, my heart in my mouth. I was half expecting to see Hannah's sheepish face peep through the doorway; I would have given anything to see that right now. Instead, a slender woman in a smart grey trouser suit with a shiny chestnut bob strode in. PC Canton quickly relayed to her what we'd seen on the CCTV footage. She nodded and approached the table where Jon and I were waiting, me with a sense of increasing impatience.

'Mr and Mrs Jones, I'm DCI Roberts,' she said in a brisk but friendly tone. Her eyes met mine, soft and sympathetic, and I suddenly felt like I might cry. She held my gaze. 'I know you've spoken to my colleague already, but can I ask you some questions?'

Twenty minutes later, having relayed the entire timeline to DCI Roberts, showing her the text Hannah had sent, telling her repeatedly that no, we hadn't had any suspicions that there was anything wrong prior to today, and no, we didn't have the slightest idea where she'd taken Ella or what she meant by her accusation that I didn't deserve her, the woman rose from the folding plastic chair at the little square table and gave a short nod. 'We'll be in touch as soon as we have more information. Thank you for your help. I know it seems overwhelming, but the more information we can gather at this early stage, the more likely we'll apprehend her quickly.'

I stood too, glancing at my phone on the table, though it hadn't rung the entire time. 'What do we do now?'

'Go home and wait. We'll be in touch the moment we have information. I know it's hard, but there's really nothing else you can do right now.'

'What?' William exclaimed from his place on the sofa where the children's DVD had been restarted. 'But I want to go on the log flume! You said we could, Mummy! You promised!'

The security guard shook his head. 'Sorry, mate, but the park's closed now. All the rides are shut. You'll have to come back another day.'

William shrank back, suddenly shy at being addressed by the big man, and I dipped my head, grateful that I'd been saved from having to talk my son down. I didn't have it in me to deal with a meltdown on top of everything else right now.

'But we can't go home without Ella and Hannah, Mummy,' Maisy said, frowning. 'When they come back, they won't know where we are. They'll be lost.'

I glanced at Jon and he looked as stumped as I was. What could we say to explain that Hannah might not bring Ella back? How could we even begin to articulate what was happening in a way Maisy and William could grasp when we ourselves could hardly understand what was happening or why? Right now, I didn't want to discuss it with them. I just wanted to keep them close, safe with me.

The police filed out of the room and I turned to Jon, stepping close so that only he could hear me. 'Do you really think we should go home? It feels wrong,' I said.

'I don't see what else we can do. We can't stay here. They're locking up.'

I sighed, knowing he was right, yet not ready to leave. I felt as though walking out of the park without my child was conceding defeat. Giving up on her. How could we just go home and wait when we didn't even know if she was okay? It wasn't like we were waiting for a call from the airport about a lost suitcase. This was our daughter, our newborn baby, and she was out there somewhere where we couldn't get to her. I couldn't bear it.

'I'll call my mum – maybe she can get a flight and then she can stay with the kids while we go out and look.' My dad, I knew, was away on a sailing trip and wouldn't be back until early next week. I sighed, shaking my head. 'But she'd have to drive to Manchester, and that's hours away. Even if she gets one right away, it's going to be ages before she can get here.' I frowned, wishing more than ever that I had family close by I could lean on. I hated the feeling of isolation that came with having our relatives so far from us, Jon's down in Cornwall, mine six hours to the north in Cumbria. We'd always consoled ourselves that at least we knew we had Hannah to support us if ever we had an emergency. How ridiculous that seemed now.

'Come on,' Jon said softly. 'You can call from the car. I'm sure she'll come.' He took my hand, leading me to the door, calling for the kids to follow. Something in his voice made them come without an argument for once, and as we walked in silence towards the car park, I felt William's fingers knot around my free hand. Maisy walked beside Jon, looking down at her feet, her little shoulders slumped.

We reached the car, one of the few remaining on the tarmac, and Jon took the keys from the pocket of his cargo trousers, opening the doors, letting the heat that had built inside dissipate a little. The children clambered inside, rolling down the windows, complaining about the hot metal of their seat belts, the bar of chocolate that had been left to melt on the dashboard. I stood at the rear door, making sure Maisy was strapped in properly. I couldn't help but stare past her, my gaze fixed sickeningly on the empty baby seat on the far side, Ella's soft elephant toy dangling from the handle above it, her spare dummy lying in the curve of the seat, as if waiting for her to come back.

Behind it, in the back of the beat-up old seven-seater we'd purchased the previous summer for occasions such as today, Hannah's cardigan was slung over the seat where she'd left it. Just this morning I'd stood in this spot, laughing with her, cramming in chocolate-chip cookies we'd bought at the petrol station and talking with the children about all the rides they wanted to go on. How could I have missed the danger lurking just ahead of me? She'd taken the bottle of sun cream from my hand, applying it to Maisy as I did William's. She was the woman I trusted most in the world. My best friend. How could everything have changed so quickly?

Jon put his hand on my shoulder and moved me towards the passenger door, guiding me inside the car. I knew I should refuse. I always drove. It had been an unspoken arrangement between us for a long time now, even during my pregnancy. Jon suffered with cramps in his legs, which would strike out of the blue, and sitting in traffic with his foot pressed to the clutch was one of the times it hit him hardest. But today, I didn't argue. I honestly didn't think I could make it home without crashing the car. A pulse thudded behind my left eyeball, the muscle surrounding it twitching erratically, my temples throbbing with pent-up tension, something I usually only experienced when I was overtired. I couldn't drive. I felt like my skin was crawling with need. The act of forcing myself to sit down, strap myself in and not leap from the car as Jon turned the key in the ignition was almost impossible.

I turned my face from the theme park, knowing I'd never return to this place, and pictured Hannah walking out of the exit with my daughter. And for the first time since we'd met, I felt the corroding bitterness of hatred saturating the image of the woman I'd always held so dear.

CHAPTER EIGHT

Then

I listened through the open upstairs window, hearing William and Jon talking as they refilled the birdfeeder with seed. William was regaling Jon with the facts he'd learned in his new British wildlife book, explaining how the females of many garden varieties, such as the great tits and sparrows who regularly visited our little garden, did not mate for life. 'In fact,' he said knowledgeably, his voice serious, glad to have a captive audience in his daddy, 'the females are known to have multiple partners, and male blue tits will often raise chicks that aren't their own. I'm glad you and Mummy don't do that. I'd hate to have that many brothers and sisters.'

I heard Jon laugh and moved quietly away from the window. Maisy was playing in her bedroom and I made sure not to disturb her as I passed her door, heading for the bathroom. I locked the door, then climbed up to stand on the edge of the bath, reaching for the package I'd squashed on top of the cabinet earlier that morning. It was hidden behind the bleach and the spare bubble bath, and I pulled it out, my heart thumping erratically. Listening again for sounds of someone approaching, I clasped the paper bag in my hand; hearing nothing, I opened it slowly and pulled the box out.

It was hardly the first time I'd done a pregnancy test, but this was the first time I'd spent the three weeks prior to taking it hoping to God that I was mistaken. That it would be negative. I couldn't have a baby. Not now. I just couldn't.

I'd waited and waited for my period to come, and when it hadn't, I'd come up with a thousand reasons to explain why. I was having an early menopause. I'd got my dates mixed up. I was too stressed, or maybe too skinny. The weight had dropped off me in the last two months, and I knew it was anything but healthy, but I couldn't seem to help it. Food was the last thing on my mind these days. There was probably a perfectly reasonable explanation for the missed period. There had to be, because there was no way I could bring another child into our family now.

I could just picture Jon's face if I had to break *that* news. The confusion that would cloud his face as what I was trying to say dawned on him, followed by the inevitable denial. It just couldn't happen. I would not be forced into having that conversation.

Even so, I knew I could no longer keep putting off the next step. Sooner or later, I had to know for sure.

I opened the box, staring at the plastic wand, glancing at the instructions, my mind fuzzy about how to use it. I flipped up the toilet lid and sat down, still listening hard, sure that I wouldn't have long. I never managed to sneak away for more than five minutes' peace before William came searching for me. For a child as uncomfortable around big groups of people as he was, he was surprisingly incapable of being alone. He always needed to be talking, and though I loved him dearly, sometimes it made my head spin and I longed to escape, just for a little while.

When I'd finished, I rested the test on top of its box on the edge of the sink, flushing the chain and washing my hands. A queasy, unsettled churning had started up in my stomach, and I forced myself to believe that it was entirely due to the fear coursing through me, not the first flutterings of morning sickness. I perched on the edge of the bath, then stood almost instantly, unable to keep still, tapping my foot on the old flaking lino, folding and unfolding my arms. A knock reverberated through the echoey room, and I jumped, lurching forward, my hand wrapping around the test as if to hide it, before I remembered I'd locked the door.

'Mummy, are you in there?'

I closed my eyes, feeling a sudden burst of irritation, followed by instant worry that pregnancy hormones were affecting my typically endless supply of patience. *Ridiculous.*

'Yes, William, I am. And I'd appreciate five minutes' peace if you don't mind,' I said pointedly.

'She's doing a poo!' William yelled. 'Daddy wanted me to ask if you want pasta or rice with dinner.'

'Whatever you like. I don't mind. Go and help him, okay?'

'Okay.' His voice was loud, muffled, and I realised he was pressing his lips to the crack between the door and the frame.

'William, please! Just give me a few minutes. Go downstairs now.'

'Fine.' I heard him huff, then mutter something less than polite under his breath, but his footsteps retreated along the landing, clattering heavily down the stairs, and the sound of him amusing Jon with far too much detail about my 'terrible bowel situation' carried from the kitchen below. Great, that was all I needed.

Wasting no time, I sat down on the edge of the bath again and turned the test to inspect it. The world seemed to pause for just a fragment of a second as I saw the unmistakable result. Two dark blue lines; no ambiguity, no doubt. It was positive.

'No,' I whispered, feeling tears prick at my eyes, my throat constricting against the wave of emotion, the fear. 'God, no.'

I had known it all along, I realised now. With both William and Maisy, I'd felt the change within me the moment I conceived. Hannah had laughed at me the morning following William's conception when I'd told her I was certain I was pregnant and it felt like a boy, but I'd known. I had felt my body shifting, readying itself for what was to come. I'd sensed him there, sure that from now on, wherever I went, I wouldn't be alone. I'd known it then, and if I'd let myself entertain the possibility, I would have known it now. I closed my eyes, and with sudden clarity, I realised I knew the night I'd conceived this baby. What had I done?

'Lils? Are you all right?' Jon's voice called up the stairs. Hurriedly I shoved the test back into the box, then wrapped it in the paper bag and climbed up on the edge of the bath to stash it away. I pinched my cheeks, flushed the chain for effect and threw open the door. Jon was standing at the bottom of the stairs looking uncertain, and I swept down them, brushing past him without pausing.

'I'm fine,' I snapped, not turning to look at him as he followed me into the kitchen looking concerned. 'Can't I even go to the bloody toilet without having to answer twenty bloody questions? Is it really that hard for you to do the dinner without me having to micromanage every step of the way for you?' I pulled out a pan from the cupboard above the counter and slammed it down hard, the noise harsh and shocking.

William stared at me from his seat at the table, where he was peeling mushrooms, Jon stood frozen in the doorway. I felt the anger leave me in a rush, swiftly replaced by an overwhelming desire to cry. I couldn't. I had no right to fall apart now. I'd brought this on myself.

'I'm sorry…' I released my grip on the saucepan handle, turning to Jon. 'It's just—'

He shook his head, brushing away my apology, his face full of an understanding I didn't deserve. 'I know, sweetheart. I get it. It's okay,' he said softly as he stepped forward, pulling me close against his chest. 'You have enough on your plate already. I just remembered you saying you wanted to save something in the larder for tomorrow's dinner, but I couldn't remember if it was the rice or the pasta.'

'It was the rice,' I mumbled now, feeling stupid for flying off the handle. 'I wanted to make chilli.' I let him hold me, though I didn't deserve his comfort. He smelled of cut grass and sunshine, his cotton T-shirt stretched tight around his broad chest, soft against my cheek. I let myself sink into his warmth and tried to recall the last time we'd held each other this way, but I couldn't conjure up an image.

I closed my eyes, still shocked at the realisation that I was pregnant again. There were so many reasons this couldn't happen. William wouldn't cope. Maisy would fade into the background of our family even more. I would never be able to go back to work, to even consider taking a night class, or training for a career for the future. I would be back to square one. And right now, I couldn't say for sure if I would have to do this without Jon's support. I couldn't expect him to raise this baby. It was all wrong, the worst possible timing.

I blinked back my tears, determined not to give in to them in front of him, pulling back from his arms to pour water into the kettle, my shoulders stiffening, my defences coming up, hoping he would take the hint and give me some space to think. I'd brought this problem on myself. I would just have to deal with it.

CHAPTER NINE

Hannah

'So, I broke up with Luke.'

'Luke?' Lily dumped the frying pan covered in the remains of the scrambled eggs we'd eaten for breakfast into the washing-up bowl full of hot soapy water, dipping her hand into it as she fished around for the plastic brush. Breakfast had been as hectic as it always was on a Saturday morning, with the kids declaring that Jon's eggs were better than Lily's. I secretly agreed, swallowing down the burned bits before coming to her defence. She hadn't seemed to notice their complaints, nor my suggestion that she shouldn't have to cook on a Saturday and next week we should go to Mark's Café as we always used to. It had been months since we'd had a proper brunch, one where we could talk and relax without Lily rushing around like a distracted bumblebee on a mission. She never seemed to slow down anymore, and I found myself feeling increasingly drained after spending time with her, as if I'd absorbed her stress as my own. I'd love her just to sit down and chat, but she never even seemed to look me in the eye anymore, let alone take on board what I was saying.

She did now, however, turning from the task of scrubbing the pan with a screwed-up expression. 'Do I know a Luke?'

I took a sip of my coffee, trying not to feel irritated that the man I'd been seeing for close to three months hadn't even made it across the barrier of her radar.

'From the dating app Jon's friend suggested?' I prompted. When she still looked blank, I shook my head. 'Blonde. Tall. Big beard. Came to see that live band at the local with us last month, and took me to Paris for our third date. *Luke!* For heaven's sake, Lil, it's like you're in your own world!' I added, feeling more hurt than I wanted to let on.

'Oh, Luke, yes, of course,' she said slowly, frowning as if she were searching the very depths of her mind for a picture of him. I got the feeling she didn't have the faintest idea who I was referring to and was only trying to placate me. I picked up a corner of cold toast from one of the children's plates, nibbling at the edge before dropping it back down. Lily turned back to the sink. 'Sorry to hear it didn't work out. Any particular reason?'

I sighed. I knew it was hardly the first time I'd told her about one of my casual relationships coming to an end, but I always listened to her problems, her little stories about the kids, her worries about Maisy and her frustration with William. I had always been there for her, but more and more these days it felt as if she was only ever half present when it came to listening to me. I wanted to tell her the real reason that Luke and I had stopped seeing each other. That I'd been so upset after discovering that I wasn't carrying his child that I hadn't been able to face him since. That I was suddenly so consumed with my new-found desire to have a baby that I hadn't spared a thought for anything else, and when I'd seen on social media that he was out with another woman, getting quite friendly as far as I could tell from the photos, I hadn't even bothered to call and confront him. He didn't matter. I didn't care.

I wanted to tell Lily about my hopes of having a child of my own. I had been thinking of how I should broach the subject, how shocked she would be to hear that after all these years of being one hundred per cent focused on my career, I'd suddenly done a complete one-eighty and decided I was ready for the one thing I'd never even considered. Motherhood. Just the word made my insides glow with a warmth and excitement that made me want to shout from the rooftops. But unlike the news about Luke, this really meant something to me, and if I was going to tell her, I wasn't prepared to divulge it to a half-present audience. I wanted her to look at me, *hear* me. To see just how important this was to me so that she wouldn't brush it off as some silly fad on my part. I wanted her to be my best friend, a task that seemed increasingly difficult for her lately.

I waited in silence for her to ask more about Luke. To show an interest that would open the door to the deeper topics I wanted to delve into. Instead she grabbed a tea towel, picking up the plates I'd washed from the draining board one by one and placing them in a pile on the counter. I heard William's high-pitched laugh and looked out through the open back door to the garden to see Jon lying flat on his back, his stocky arms and legs stretched out above him, William balancing precariously over him, hands outstretched as if in flight. Lily was watching through the window, a deep frown etched on her forehead. 'What the hell is he doing?' she muttered. 'Does he think he's still a teenager? He's going to hurt himself.'

'Oh, don't be such a spoilsport, Lil. I think it's sweet that he's so good with the kids. He's always playing with William and trying to find things to do with Maisy. You're lucky. You realise that, right?'

'What? Oh, yeah, lucky. Of course. Lucky me.' She threw down the tea towel just as the letter box clanged. 'Maisy, get the post!' she yelled, pressing her hands to her eyes.

I watched her closely. 'Are you okay?' I asked, my voice soft, inviting her to share whatever had her so agitated.

Her head snapped up, our eyes meeting, and for just a moment, I saw a flash of something in her eyes that made me worry. Lily had always been so light-hearted and carefree, such a glass-half-full kind of person, but the expression she wore now was unfamiliar – pained almost. She tore her gaze away as Maisy padded in carrying a handful of envelopes.

'I'm okay, thanks,' she said, rifling through the stack of post, avoiding eye contact again. 'Just tired is all. William's been getting up at five these past few weeks, and you know, when he's up, I'm up. That's the rule.' She gave a hollow laugh, but I didn't join in as I might normally have done.

'If you're sure?' I pushed.

'Yep.' She paused in her rifling through the letters, staring wide-eyed at a white envelope as if she'd unearthed something venomous. I couldn't see the writing and didn't have a chance to before she bundled all the post together and pulled open the kitchen drawer, shoving the stack inside. I wanted to ask again if there was anything going on, besides the tiredness, but she immediately moved to the back door, calling for William to calm down and go and do his times tables.

A moment later, Jon came in looking flushed and bewildered. 'On the weekend, love? Give the boy a break.'

'He needs to practise, and I thought you might need rescuing from all the rough and tumble.' She gave a tight smile.

'He's fine. *I'm* fine. Don't worry so much, Lils, there's nothing to be gained from it.' He wrapped her in a hug, flashing me a wink over her shoulder, and I wondered if she *did* realise how lucky she was. She had a hands-on husband who clearly still adored her after all these years, two gorgeous children and a home filled with love. If only she could stop and take it in once in a while, count her blessings rather than rushing from task to task, she might see how good she had it.

I turned my face away as Jon pressed a kiss to her forehead and sighed. Clearly there would be no deep and meaningful chat between me and Lily today. The topic of Luke had been completely forgotten already, and it was clear that she wasn't in the right headspace to give me her full attention. Telling her my baby plans would have to wait. For now, it would remain my little secret.

CHAPTER TEN

Lily

Now

The rainbow-striped knitted booties were the first thing I saw, still sitting on the kitchen table where they'd been left. Hannah had brought them over this morning – a little gift for Ella, she'd said – and I'd been touched that she'd thought of her. Hannah, while lovely to the children, had never been the type to go shopping for gifts and trinkets for them. The booties had, as it turned out, been far too big, but we'd laughed about it and I'd hugged her, promising I'd let her know when Ella grew into them. How things had changed in such a few short hours, I thought now, swiping them off the table with the back of my hand, then kicking them in the direction of the bin, not wanting to have to touch them. Did she know this morning what she was going to do? Was she already looking at Ella and thinking of stealing her from me and Jon?

I placed my hands down on the table, leaning heavily into it, breathing hard. I'd called my mum as soon as we got on the road and she'd called me back fifteen minutes later. My heart had sunk when she told me she hadn't been able to get a flight at such short notice, but she'd heard the fear in my voice and insisted on driving down. It would be dark by the time she made it here; she was almost sixty and driving alone. I had tried to backtrack, talk her out of coming once she'd told me her plan, but she'd insisted, and now I was torn between a desperate need to see her and my terror that she might crash. I wished she at least had Dad with her to share the driving. I closed my eyes, thinking of Mum, Hannah, Ella, and let my memories travel to the day my precious third baby had entered the world, changing everything.

I gave a low, guttural scream that seemed to come from so far within me I knew I would never access that place again. The sound was animal, pure instinct and yet familiar too. I rolled to my side and felt soft glove-covered hands pressing on my ankle, lifting, manoeuvring.

'That's it, Lily,' the gentle female voice said now. 'Just one more push and she'll be here.'

I glanced up at Jon, seeing him sway slightly, the sudden image of him crashing to the ground filling my mind. It had been a long night, eight hours of active labour, and I could see the sun rising through the window of the maternity unit. He looked dead on his feet and I felt guilty that I'd had to drag him out of bed to bring me here. Could he keep going? Could I? He brushed my hair away from my sweat-soaked cheek and our eyes met, a thousand messages passing between us. 'Are you okay?' I whispered.

He broke into a smile, though it wasn't enough to hide the exhaustion in his eyes, the sallow pallor of his cheeks. He'd stood by my side for my first two labours, caring, cajoling, encouraging, and this time had been no different.

'Trust you to worry more about me than yourself. I'm fine,' he insisted, his hand finding mine, squeezing tight. 'Concentrate on you, babe. You're on the home stretch.'

'She certainly is,' the midwife said, her head peering up at us from the foot of the bed. 'Do you feel another—'

She broke off as a primal sound escaped from my lips, my head falling back against the pillows as my body pushed down without my command or involvement. It worked instinctively, with no need for thought or instruction. I felt the pressure inside me shift, the sharp burning sting that I remembered vividly from the last two times I'd been through this. The head was crowning. Jon's hand was around mine, but I pulled back, gripping my pillow hard, not wanting to hurt him as I let myself go, giving in to the sensations, the overwhelming feeling of my baby entering the world. The last part always made me feel sick, and I tensed for just a moment, not ready to feel it, yet unable to stop it.

'Relax, Lily, you're doing so well. Let it happen,' the midwife said, her voice still low and quiet.

I liked her. She hadn't treated the event like an opportunity to cheerlead. She was exactly what I needed. Calm, gentle and unobtrusive. I took a deep shuddering breath and relaxed. It happened almost instantly, the sliding sensation of the body slipping from my own, freeing itself, leaving me suddenly empty and shaken in its absence. I fought off the familiar urge to vomit, taking deep shaky breaths, my grip on the pillow releasing as the pain left me.

'You did it, babe! You were brilliant!' Jon announced, kissing me full on the lips, then turning to look at the new tiny person in the room. I eased myself up off the pillows and leaned forward, reaching out to lift the baby from the mattress with careful movements. 'Oh, Jon,' I exclaimed, my vision blurred as tears filled my eyes. 'Oh, look at her, Jon, look!'

'She's perfect.'

'Careful, she has a short cord,' the midwife warned, coming around the side of the bed, helping me to lift her to my bare chest and settle her against me. There was no pain now. Just the absolute bliss of knowing that this child was made from my own body, that she was a part of me and I would do anything to protect her and keep her safe. It was shocking to believe that I might not have let this happen. That I could have let my fears take over and force me into a decision that would have ended her life before it even began. I might never have known who she was. Never have got to see her tiny fingers and toes, breathed in the smell of her downy head. I would

always have carried that wonder with me, the unknown child who might have been. I knew, even now, that the choice I'd made in the end wasn't a simple one. It came with a price. But looking at her, so perfect, so very innocent, there was no doubt in my mind that it had been the right one.

Jon wrapped an arm round me, smiling. 'She's probably going to be our last,' he said softly. 'At least you won't have to go through that again.'

I shook my head, not wanting to face the truth of his words, feeling the tears trickle from the corners of my eyes. He brushed them away with his fingertip. 'Thank you,' I whispered. 'For giving me the courage to keep going.'

He nodded. 'Thank you for giving me another beautiful daughter. I'm a lucky man.' Our eyes met and I found I couldn't hold his gaze. I turned my head to look at my new daughter, determined to keep my focus on her. I would lose my mind if I didn't.

I blinked, torn from the memories that called to me, where I could lose myself for a blissful moment of respite, and heard footsteps entering the kitchen behind me, then a sigh as Jon took in the scene, looking at the discarded booties on the floor, my grip white-knuckled on the edge of the table, as if I could stop myself from falling into the black hole of despair surrounding me. Wordlessly he walked around me, picking the booties up and dropping them into the bin. 'I suppose they have lost a bit of their beauty now, haven't they?' he said wryly.

I didn't answer.

'The kids are asking about dinner,' he said, glancing at the clock. I looked up, surprised to see that it was coming up for 6 p.m. It felt like it should be later, like Ella had been missing for days, not a couple of hours. Too long.

The sound of William emptying his toy box out onto the living-room floor crashed through the house, and I swallowed down the urge to shout at him to tidy it up, moving robotically to the fridge, opening it and pulling out mince, mushrooms, vegetables. It felt wrong to be preparing a meal, going through the motions of my normal routine when I should be doing so much more. Where was she? Was she crying for me? I swayed on my feet, trying to picture her, to imagine her wailing for me, and felt the hot trickle of milk spread across the front of my dress, my breasts tingling as if calling to her, needing her here. I leaned my head against the fridge door, feeling Jon's gaze on me. I knew he wanted to comfort me but was unsure how to. He moved towards me, and I realised he was going to try and hug me.

'No.' I shook my head, held out my palm, a warning. 'Don't. I can't let myself fall apart. It wouldn't be fair.'

'To who?'

Ella. You. The children. I turned away, ripping open the packets of vegetables, pulling the knife from the block. The sound alerted the cat. The *bloody* cat. I heard the rush of paws running down the stairs, the loud meow as the black-and-white ball of fluff ran into the kitchen, pressing against my ankles, winding between them, almost tripping me over. 'No, Fluffy!' I snapped.

When Jon had suggested getting a kitten for Maisy during the second trimester of my pregnancy, a companion to help her feel safe and to confide in when she wouldn't talk to us, I'd been ambivalent. I had never particularly considered myself a cat person, but I had nothing against them either, and I had to admit, it sounded like a good idea. I was hoping the kitten would become a friend to Maisy – sleep in her bed, be with her when she couldn't bring herself to spend time with the rest of us. It had seemed like the perfect solution. But it hadn't turned out anything like we'd hoped.

Jon had procured the kitten from a friend of a friend who was looking to rehome him, and he was already six months old when he came to us. Maisy had named him Fluffy, bouncing with excitement and far more animated than we were used to. We had been full of hope, but it had quickly become apparent they weren't going to have the kind of relationship we'd dreamed of. Within days, I felt like we'd made a mistake, but Jon had wanted to push on, give their bond a chance to develop, time for the trust to build. It never happened, and when we realised what a difficult cat we'd managed to find, we knew that we'd never be able to rehome him. We didn't have the heart to put him in a rescue.

He meowed incessantly – before feeding, after feeding, when he was in the house, when he was in the garden. He tore up the furniture, and within a week of being with us, he'd scratched Maisy twice, completely unprovoked, terrifying her and destroying our hopes of them becoming close. He remained fiercely independent, far preferring to go off exploring outside to sitting on a lap, and when he came back in the early hours of the morning, often with a mouse between his teeth, he made so much noise that I worried he'd wake the neighbours. I couldn't be sure if his behaviour was normal for a cat, but I'd quickly decided I was definitely not a cat person and made damn certain he never got close to Ella, terrified that he would hurt her if given the chance.

I threw the mince and veg into a pan, pouring in a jar of sauce, then turned to fill Fluffy's bowl, despite the fact that he still had biscuits left over from the morning. I scraped the wet food into the dish and watched as he walked over and stared down at it with an expression of disgust before turning back to me, meowing again.

'Oh, for God's sake, eat it or get out! Either way just shut up, will you!' I yelled, slamming my palm down on the counter and closing my eyes, fighting the tears that simmered just beneath the surface. The cat continued his pitiful whining, completely unfazed by my outburst, and I scooped him up and deposited him outside the back door, closing it tightly. His complaints could still be heard through the glass, but I ignored him.

Jon stood silently, and I knew he was at as much of a loss as I was about what to do, how to fill the seconds, the minutes that seemed never-ending. Even so, his lack of activity irritated me, and a buzz of concentrated energy pulsed through my body that felt volatile and dangerous.

'Stir the dinner, will you? I have to change. The milk—' I broke off, pointing to my dress, the sour liquid once more drying in dark patches across the yellow cotton. I opened the cupboard above the worktop and pulled out my hand pump, knowing I couldn't put off expressing any longer. It didn't feel right, doing it without Ella here to drink the spoils, but I could feel the lumpy hot throb of my breasts, the full heaviness turning painful, and knew that if I didn't do it now, there would likely be mastitis to deal with. I didn't need *that* on top of everything else.

Jon stepped forward, seeming relieved to have been given a task. 'I'll finish up here. You go and sort yourself out. Hop in the shower if you like. I'll serve the kids their dinner.'

I gripped the pump and dipped my head, not meeting his eye. 'Thanks.' I left the room without lingering, moving quietly past the door to the living room so as not to alert William to my presence. I just needed a moment alone. A few minutes without police firing questions at me, without Jon looking like a wounded puppy, and without William clambering all over me.

I walked into the bedroom, steeling myself against the sight of Ella's Babygro on the bed, her teething rattle lying across my pillow. I looked away, stripped off the damp dress and bra and perched on the edge of the bed, positioning the pump against my swollen nipple and pressing down gently. A hiss escaped through my teeth as I felt the pressure of the milk beginning to flow, but the pain only lasted half a minute before I felt it begin to dissipate, the milk coming easier as I massaged my breast, dreading the thought of repeating the action on the other side once I'd finished this one. The departure of the pain made space for my mind to wander though, and I couldn't stop my thoughts from going to Hannah.

There was no denying that in the past year or so, our friendship had changed somewhat, and not for the better. Life was so busy now – both hers and mine – and the long, deep chats we'd once had over a bottle of wine when the kids were in bed and Jon was making himself scarce seemed to be something we'd long since let go of. There was a distance between us these days, one I'd known deep down I should try and address, but I'd never had the time, the energy to get into it.

I knew there were things I hadn't told her about my own life that had created a chasm between us. Secrets I was unable to divulge. It had been difficult for me to hold back from the person I'd always shared every little detail of my life with, but we weren't teenagers anymore. We had responsibilities, people who needed protecting from the things that could hurt them. I couldn't always confide my deepest truths to her. But I hadn't considered that she might not be sharing *her* problems with me. Had she been quietly pulling back from our friendship as I'd been consumed with my own thoughts and worries? Had something fundamental broken in the foundations of our friendship without my ever having realised it? If so, what secrets had she held back from me?

I moved the pump to the other breast, trying to remember the last time we'd spoken about anything important, anything that couldn't be considered idle small talk, something we'd both always claimed to despise. I couldn't think of a single conversation. It was clear to me though, that one thing was certain: Hannah wasn't the woman I'd thought she was.

I finished expressing and placed the pump on the dressing table, then walked into the bathroom and found a flannel to wipe away the milk residue and sweat that had accumulated on my body. I threw it into the sink and went back to the bedroom for fresh clothes, stopping dead as I heard the sudden shrill ring of the house phone from downstairs. My mind racing, I yanked my clothes from the wardrobe, pulling on a pair of cropped trousers and a white cotton T-shirt, trying to listen to Jon's muffled voice as he talked to the caller but deciphering nothing. I ran barefoot down the stairs, waiting impatiently behind him as he finished speaking. He offered a stiff thanks and placed the handset down, his hand coming to his forehead as he closed his eyes, sighing deeply.

'Jon?' I said, trying to keep my voice measured, though I wanted to scream in my impatience. 'Who was it? What's happened?'

'That was DCI Roberts,' he said, turning towards me, rubbing at his face with a rough hand. 'She said there's no sign of Hannah at her flat, no answer, and the windows are all dark.'

'Didn't they go in to check?'

'Apparently they can't, not without a warrant. I asked if that was their plan and she was pretty vague. It sounds like they want to concentrate on tracking her first. They're searching airports, train stations. Going through CCTV footage. They're doing all they can, babe. We have to be grateful for that.'

I shook my head. 'It's not enough, Jon. This is *Ella*. She's out there somewhere, and the longer we wait, the harder it becomes to find her.'

'Hannah wouldn't hurt her, Lily. She just wouldn't.'

'I wouldn't believe it possible either. But then I would never have thought her capable of kidnapping, so how can we be sure of anything now?' I folded my arms tightly, feeling chilly despite the balmy evening.

Jon's shoulders seemed to slump and I hated that this was so hard for him to accept, but there was no time to skirt around the truth, no way to sugar-coat what Hannah had done.

'She won't hurt her, Lils,' he repeated, though he didn't look as if he wholly believed his own words.

'Maybe not. But she's not just going to bring her back now, is she?' I countered. 'She's got my daughter and she's going to take her far away where we won't ever find her. I know it, Jon. And I won't let that happen. Ella needs us; she needs to be here – this is her home; this is where she belongs!' I broke off, shaking, and bit down on my thumbnail, glancing over my shoulder at the door. 'I can't do this; I can't just stay here. If the police won't search the flat, then *I* will. I'm sick of waiting for a bunch of strangers to find my daughter. I need to do something, anything to help. I have to go and look for her, Jon.'

'Are you sure that's a good idea? What do you expect to find?'

I shrugged. 'I don't know. But I have to try.' I glanced at my watch, realising that my mum would still be hours away. I knew it wasn't fair to make Jon stay put, but until she arrived, one of us had to stay here to take care of William and Maisy, and I would go out of my mind if it was me.

'Will you put the kids to bed for me?' I asked, meeting his eyes briefly then looking away, not waiting to see the concern in his expression. 'I won't say goodbye or William will have a meltdown about me going. It will be easier if I just disappear quietly.'

He glanced over his shoulder, then looked back at me, resigned to my plan, though I could tell he wished I would stay with him. 'We'll be fine. And if this is something you feel you have to do, then go. Take your phone and I'll call the moment I hear anything, okay?'

I nodded, slipping my feet into my flip-flops and grabbing the car keys from the hook by the door, riffling through the bunch to check the spare key to Hannah's flat was still there.

Jon stepped forward, his arms opening, and I darted back, shaking my head. 'Not yet... I can't... I have to be strong. For *her.*' I glanced down at my hands and saw how they were shaking. I *always* have to be strong, I thought, squeezing the keys in my palm. I turned before he could argue, relieved to finally have something to do that might make a difference.

I had to find an answer, a clue, *anything* to help me get my daughter back.

CHAPTER ELEVEN

Hannah

I muttered my thanks as the elderly gentleman held open the door for me to pass through and glanced over at the reception desk, seeing it manned by a young woman with neat blonde hair and a faraway expression. There were people sitting about on the sofas, some with suitcases by their feet, guests heading for the restaurant on the opposite side of the atrium, and I was reminded of the last meal I'd had here, when I'd stayed the night after a business meeting ran long and I'd had a few too many glasses of wine to fancy the train back home to the coast.

I'd been reaching the end of a long, fulfilling project back then, designing a new range of living-room decor – lampshades, rugs, cushion covers – with some of the most vibrant people I'd ever had the pleasure of working with, for one of the oldest and most highly regarded stores in the country. The mood had been light and free, the brunt of the work having already been decided on, and we'd taken advantage of the delicious Michelin-star meal paid for by the swanky department store and laughed loud and hard into the night. Now, my mood couldn't have been more different.

I'd been panicked and confused about where to go after having left the theme park, and though several crazy ideas had popped into my head about getting a flight, going somewhere far away, I didn't have my passport, nor one for Ella, and there was no way to make it work. I craved a sense of familiarity to stabilise myself, and on a whim, I'd directed the taxi driver to the five-star hotel on the rural outskirts of Salisbury. We were less than an hour's drive from home, but it might as well have been a million miles. The distance I'd created in my friendship today was vast and wholly insurmountable.

I straightened my back, trying to look the part, and walked purposefully to the desk, glancing around to see if anyone was looking at me – if they knew what I'd done. I felt exposed, desperate to get upstairs and hide away where I could think straight without feeling so conspicuous. The girl at the desk smiled languidly at me.

'Hi,' I said, my voice not nearly as shrill as I'd expected. I patted Ella's back, ignoring the sore spot where the changing bag strap had rubbed my skin raw in the short time I'd been wearing it. 'Do you have any rooms available?'

'Do you have a booking?'

'No, I don't. I…' I tried to think of a reason someone might arrive at 7 p.m. at a hotel in the countryside with a newborn baby and no booking and no luggage, and drew a blank.

The girl's eyes met mine and she smiled. 'Had to get away from the husband for a bit? Good idea. A night away will make him stew, and he'll be grovelling at your feet by the time you go back. You're not the first woman to do it,' she added with a grin.

I was half stunned by her lack of professionalism, making such personal remarks about my fictitious husband, sure that she would be sacked on the spot if her supervisor had heard her little speech, yet the relief at having her fill in the blanks on my behalf and clearly take my side in the imaginary argument with my fake husband was undeniable. 'Yes,' I agreed quietly. 'I needed some space. Shouldn't be more than one night.'

'Good for you. Let me see what I can do.' She drummed her fingertips on the computer keyboard, clicking her tongue. 'As a rule, we don't accept children under three – they aren't exactly known for being quiet during the night – but in your case, I'm going to bend the rules and squeeze you in on a quiet floor.'

'Thank you,' I breathed, wanting to kick myself for not having thought about Ella being too young. Lily would have. She would have known straight away and thought of somewhere far more appropriate to spend the night with a child in tow. One of those cheap family hotels Jon always chose to take them to. They were usually on some busy road or roundabout, opposite a sprawling retail park where they could pick up cheap meal deals from the supermarket to take back to the room for dinner. It had never been my idea of a good holiday. Lily frequently voiced her complaints to me about the fact that since having the children, they never went abroad anymore, and I knew she resented the fact that she couldn't even go somewhere a bit nicer in England. She was always leaving brochures for country cottages and spa weekends around as a not-so-subtle hint to Jon, but he never seemed to pick up on it. I bet she would have loved it here.

The girl tapped a few more buttons. 'Right, that's the one. First floor, end of the corridor, and tonight you'll have no one above or below you. The room next door is vacant too. It's not a garden view – those are the ones everyone always requests – but it's comfortable and has a spa bath and a balcony. Would you like me to book you in?'

'Oh, yes, yes please, that sounds perfect,' I gushed, my gratitude making me far more effusive than usual.

'Lovely. Can I have your name and address. And how would you like to pay?'

'It's—' I broke off, catching myself before I gave myself away. Surely by now there would be people looking for me. Maybe they'd even called the police. Of course they would have done. What parent wouldn't? Even Lily would have called by now. I tried to imagine how she might be reacting to the sudden disappearance of her daughter, and couldn't.

I looked up to see the girl waiting expectantly. 'It's Louise Farmer. Mrs Louise Farmer,' I said, offering the name of one of my colleagues who'd recently invited me to her wedding. I rattled off her address from memory, hoping I'd got it right. 'And I'll be paying in cash. I don't want my husband to know where I've been.' I winked conspiratorially and she tapped her nose.

'Keep him guessing,' she said, grinning. 'It's the best way.'

The room was just as I remembered from before, though last time I'd not been shuffled off to the far corner of the building. I'd had a gorgeous garden view then and a bigger balcony. After the works dinner, I'd slipped through the door of my room out onto the quiet, private terrace. I'd wrapped myself in a blanket, sipping a mug of hot tea and gazing up at the clear view of the stars, uninterrupted by street lights, thinking how much I loved my life. I'd still had hope then that I might be able to get everything I wanted. The baby I dreamed of. I was sure it was simply a matter of patience and perseverance, just as every challenge in my life had been.

Now I slipped the changing bag over my shoulder, tossing it onto the opulent king-size bed, groaning as I undid the straps of the baby carrier and carefully eased Ella out of it. My neck was tight, the muscles tense from hours of carrying her, and I stretched it from side to side, then placed Ella on the bed, allowing her to wriggle her legs. I was so used to seeing her either feeding from Lily or snoozing peacefully that it had come as a shock when she'd started bawling loudly in the taxi. It had started as a pitiful whimper and I knew right away that I should do something, respond somehow, but I wasn't confident enough with the baby sling to start whipping her out in the back of the taxi. I might not be able to get her back in, and tiny as she was, five minutes of carrying her, along with the full-to-bursting bag, would have had my arms shaking.

So I'd kept her against my body, wondering what it was she needed, trying to talk to her, calm her with songs and pats. She'd become increasingly agitated, and I'd seen the disapproval of the taxi driver as he watched the mess I was making of it in his rear-view mirror, feeling more and more panicky as her howls grew louder. Eventually she'd seemed to run out of steam, and with trembling, pitiful sobs she'd closed her eyes and gone back to sleep. I could see now that her nappy was sodden, desperately needing a change, and I was sure she must be wanting a feed too. Lily had said she'd packed two bottles, just in case, but what I would do when those ran out, I had no idea. I hadn't thought about it, and now I realised that was going to be a big problem. The family hotel opposite the retail park was sounding more appealing by the moment. I wondered if I could ask one of the staff to go and find a shop and buy me some formula for her. Would she even take it? Lily only ever fed her herself or gave her expressed milk. What if she wouldn't accept something different?

I went to the door, slipping the Do Not Disturb sign on the outside handle before closing and locking it, feeling a momentary sense of relief that at least for now, we were out of sight. No one would think to look for us here. Robotically, I went to Ella, pulling open the poppers of her little vest, stripping off the wet nappy. I fished around inside the changing bag for wipes and a fresh nappy, realising as I left her bare-bottomed on the bed that I was playing a very dangerous game. I hurriedly grabbed what I needed and was grateful to have made it in time before she left a present on the bed. I threw the wet bundle into the bathroom bin and washed my hands, then rummaged through the bag again to find a bottle of milk. Ella squirmed, giving little grunts of dissatisfaction, and I kicked off my shoes and scooped her up.

Propping the pillows against the headboard, I climbed up onto the bed and leaned back against them, stretching my legs out on the comfortable mattress and positioning Ella against me; then, resting my arm on a thick pillow, I eased the teat into her mouth. She needed no further encouragement, sucking ravenously at it.

I picked up the remote from the bedside table and turned on the television, flicking to the news channels, wondering if I was about to see my own face plastered on the screen. I watched, my stomach tense and queasy, as Ella worked on her bottle, but there was nothing about me... us. At least, not yet.

I turned the television off and picked up the hotel phone, hoping to get the same helpful girl at reception. She answered on the first ring and I explained the formula predicament to her. She brushed away my stumbling apologies and told me she would have someone bring me a tin within the hour. I placed the receiver down feeling grateful and relieved. There was a reason this hotel was so highly regarded. With the feeding issue potentially resolved, I should have been able to relax a little. There was no chance anyone would find us here. I'd used cash in the taxi, a false name at the desk. I was just another woman with a baby. There was no police raid coming for me, not tonight.

But it didn't matter. I should have felt happy. I had what I wanted, and I knew I'd taken Ella from a mother who had never appreciated her, from the moment she knew of her existence. Lily had been a good mother to begin with, but in the past few years, it seemed her own wants had come before her children and their needs. I shouldn't have felt guilt or shame for taking Ella from a home like that.

And yet somehow, looking down at her as she gripped my finger, her eyes wide as she focused on the ceiling, rosebud mouth working away on the milk her mother had provided for her, that was exactly what I felt. Guilt. Shame. Fear. Because today I had done something that would never be forgiven, and there was no way to escape the consequences of that.

CHAPTER TWELVE

Then

I squinted at the computer screen, sipping the unpalatable chamomile tea and swallowing reluctantly before placing the cup down on my desk as I resolved to find a better replacement for my morning double espresso. I'd been trying to make little changes to my diet and lifestyle to increase my chances of getting pregnant when the time came, and to make sure my body didn't go into shock if I suddenly went cold turkey on all my vices. I'd cut down to one glass of wine a night, from three, and I was making a real effort to keep track of the caffeine I consumed. I'd been shocked to realise how much I usually needed just to be able to function and had found the mornings a challenge since switching to a single mug of instant, the buzz that usually carried me through to lunch conspicuously absent.

I'd allowed myself a lie-in this morning, rare for a Friday, but I'd worked sixty hours already this week and was determined to have a proper rest over the weekend – another of my pregnancy prep goals. I'd had a slow breakfast, a jog along the seafront, and now I sat at my home desk in the bright sunny room overlooking the leafy shared garden below, scouring the internet for the answers I needed.

I didn't know why it had taken me so long to seriously consider the idea of going down the sperm donor route. I supposed it was the fact that part of it felt strange, unnatural somehow. To have a baby without ever meeting the father… It was a concept I wasn't sure I was completely on board with, but the more I had thought about it, the more I realised how much it would suit me. There would be no father figure hanging around in the background, offering unwanted advice or taking me to court over my parenting choices or to get access rights. I didn't want a man in my life, interfering with how I raised his child, taking them away from me for weekends and holidays. I wanted a full-time family of my own, and I wasn't prepared to compromise on that. This solution wiped out those complications. It would be simple.

I closed a couple of tabs, focusing on the web page for the most professional-looking clinic, reading the information and nodding along. It was so clear and unjudgemental. I loved the fact that I lived in a time when a woman was free to make this choice. That I could keep the career I had worked so hard for and embark on parenthood as a single woman with a man I would never have to meet. It was quite incredible to think about how far we'd come since my grandmother's days. I could just imagine what her expression would have looked like if she'd been alive to hear my plans.

Grandma Rosa had lived in a constant conflict between her fascination about how different and free my life was in comparison to how hers had been at the same age, and disapproval that things had gone too far and we'd lost more than we'd gained in having so much choice. I could imagine how she might have made some of the same choices for herself if she was my age now though. We were more similar than she'd realised, and I could see how easily the drive she'd turned into being a great mother and housewife, cooking everything from scratch, making all my mum's clothes and many of mine when I was small, could have translated into the modern world. She would have been a woman to be reckoned with, I was sure of it.

I scrolled to the bottom of the web page and clicked on the box to make an appointment, filling in my details and fizzing with excitement at the prospect of what would come next. I couldn't wait. Making up my mind, I stood, rushing down the hallway with a burst of energy, grabbed my keys and coat, and pulled open the front door. The time had come to share my plan with Lily. This was too exciting to hide any longer.

The road outside Lily's was packed, and a car I didn't recognise was parked in the driveway behind Lily and Jon's. I was about to pull into a side road when I saw a vehicle vacate a space just ahead of me and slipped into it, wondering who Lily's visitor was and if Jon had taken the train in to work today. I craned my neck to get a view of the visiting car, a red Honda Civic that looked like it had seen better days. My fingers hovered over the keys, still in the ignition, as I wondered if I should go home and come back later.

There was no reason to think I would be interrupting anything – Lily and Jon didn't have any family locally who might just drop in for a visit, and I knew Lily had struggled to make friends at the home education groups she often took the children to. It wasn't that she wasn't sociable and friendly, but she'd told me that William still struggled when in the company of his peers, and though it was hard to imagine, Lily insisted she wasn't able to leave his side to chat to the other parents. It was something she regularly complained about, her lack of mummy friends and her need for more adult conversation in her week, especially when Jon was away and I was working late and couldn't visit.

I sat staring at the unfamiliar car, my hands clasped tightly on the steering wheel. It didn't make sense to feel tense and uneasy, but something was stopping me getting out. I wondered why my mind had instantly jumped to the most suspicious avenues. There was no denying that Lily had been acting strangely recently. That she'd carried an air of secrecy about her – dodging questions, changing the subject, pulling back from me in a way I neither understood or expected from her. But, I reasoned, keeping things to herself didn't mean she was doing something wrong. I didn't know why my instincts kept trying to push me towards a conclusion I didn't want to draw. Lily was a good person and I was letting my imagination run wild.

I pulled the keys from the ignition and stepped out onto the pavement, looking left and right as I waited for a gap in the traffic. I was just about to cross when my eye was caught by the sight of Lily's front door opening. A man – handsome, dark-haired, much taller than Jon and dressed smartly in a suit – stepped out, followed closely by Lily. I watched, wondering who he was, moving back to let a car go past, rather than cross over. I felt a strong urge to keep out of sight, though I couldn't explain why. Lily placed a hand on the man's arm, looking up at him as she spoke. She gave a nod as he leaned forward, speaking words I couldn't hear, and I caught her expression. It was filled with sadness, regret almost. The man put his hands on her shoulders, then pulled her into a hug, and I saw her arms wrap around him. The hug lasted longer than it should have. It made me uncomfortable, and I couldn't stop my mind from going to Jon. What would he say if he saw his wife doing this?

Lily finally pulled back, glancing over her shoulder into the house, then said something else to the man, and they shared a look that made me feel that they knew one another deeply, that they had shared something intimate. There was an understanding between them that was obvious, even from where I stood half hidden behind the car across the street. This wasn't a salesman or a casual acquaintance. I saw the warmth in Lily's expression as he moved back – affection, trust, the kind of look she usually saved for Jon – and my stomach plummeted, a wave of sickening dread washing over me as I considered the possibility that she was keeping something huge from me. I shook away the thought, chiding myself, sure that there must be some reasonable explanation, though my gut screamed the opposite.

The man gave a nod, touching Lily's arm one last time, then walked to his car and climbed in, waving as he pulled out of the drive and headed down the road in the opposite direction from where I stood. Lily put her hands to her face, clearly trying to rein in her emotions. I'd seen the familiar gesture a thousand times before when she was trying not to cry – after a tough week with the kids or getting a bit of bad news. I remembered just last year how she'd stood in her kitchen, her lip wobbling, hands moving to cover her face when she'd got a call from Jon in Argentina, apologising and explaining that instead of coming home that week, he'd be away another fortnight. William hadn't been sleeping and Lily had just been telling me how much she wished Jon would hurry up and come home so she didn't have to cope with everything by herself. She missed him, she had said. Was that what she was feeling now, as her companion drove away? Was she wishing *he* could stay? That she didn't have to wave him off? I didn't dare to guess at an answer to that. She pressed her fingertips to her eyes, taking a deep breath, then went back inside, closing the door.

I stood on the pavement feeling bewildered. Who was he? What was his relationship to Lily? I tried to place his face, wondering if I might have seen him somewhere before – their wedding, their anniversary party, to which Lily and Jon's extended family had travelled from all over the country to celebrate – but I couldn't summon a memory of him.

Slowly, I crossed the road and headed up the driveway, knocking at the door. Lily's footsteps approached quickly and she flung it open, looking flustered and surprised to see me.

'Han, what are you doing here?' She stepped back automatically, letting me pass her, then followed me into the living room.

'Just popped by to say hello. How are you?' I asked, smiling warmly, hoping that she might tell me what the hell was going on so I didn't have to push for answers to questions I wasn't sure how to broach.

'I'm okay. Busy as always – you know how it is.' She shrugged, her fingers combing through her hair, and I looked closer, half wondering if I'd see the truth written on her face: a smudge of lipstick, or perhaps a missed button on her dress. But as per usual, Lily wasn't wearing lipstick, and her dress was fine. I felt like a hunting dog stuck on the scent of the wrong trail and reminded myself not to jump to conclusions, though it was easier said than done after what I'd just witnessed.

'Where are the kids?' I asked, noting the tidy carpet, free from toys, the coffee table empty of mugs that might suggest an innocent chat over coffee.

'Both upstairs, playing in Maisy's room. William is being very magnanimous for a change, sharing his best toys with her, so they seem to be getting on for once. Either that or they're plotting something,' she said, lowering herself onto the sofa. I took the armchair opposite.

'Nice.' I dropped my bag on the carpet and leaned into the soft cushions. Lily's house was far from my taste when it came to decor, the furniture battered and worn in a well-loved, entirely non-vintage fashion that smacked of hand-me-downs and boot sales, but despite its lack of precision and style, I had always loved the softness of the rooms. The warmth that made the ramshackle house and cluttered bookshelves feel like a proper home. I ran a finger over the threadbare arm of the chair, feeling the old embroidery, stained red from when Maisy had spilled a bottle of food colouring over the fabric. 'Have you been out with them this morning? No home education groups on?'

'There's a science one that I wanted to take Maisy to, but William didn't want to go and it's proving impossible to convince him to try it. I'm hoping I can take her next week when Jon's not working so I can sit down with her to do the activity without William complaining and begging to come home the whole time. So much easier to leave him here to play where he's comfortable.'

I nodded. 'Worth a try. It's a shame to have her miss out just because he isn't keen. Must be so tough trying to balance both their needs.'

'That's an understatement.'

I nodded again, holding my tongue, noticing the way she glanced around the room, far from relaxed. I wanted to let the silence grow, give her the chance to speak first, but when she didn't, I felt uncomfortable and my curiosity got the better of me. 'I saw a man leaving as I was looking for a space to park just now. Friend of Jon's, was he?' I asked, keeping my voice casual, though I didn't take my eyes off her face as I watched for answers in her expression.

'Man?' She shook her head as if she didn't understand, but her face flushed scarlet and she looked away. In an instant the sinking nausea returned to my stomach. Her reaction was exactly what I didn't want to see. I'd been holding on to a scrap of hope that she might have some reasonable explanation for the visitor, that he was someone she wouldn't feel the need to hide from me, but her response spoke volumes, and I felt my whole body tense as I saw her shut down, her shoulders stiff, her eyes not meeting mine.

'The suited and booted one I just saw leaving in the red Honda?' I pushed, willing her to tell me, to be honest about whatever she was hiding. It hurt to think of her keeping secrets from me, though I knew I'd been holding back some of my own lately. But I had come here with the intention of sharing mine. I'd been waiting for the right moment, and with the kids occupied and the two of us finally alone, now seemed like the perfect opportunity. I'd only waited this long because it had been so hard to get her full attention. But despite the chance we had now, Lily was still holding back. I could feel the distance between us and I didn't understand what was going on.

'Oh... oh, him. He's just, well, you're going to think I'm being a bit over the top, but he's a tutor. For the kids, you know? He's been teaching them a bit extra in maths and science. It's hard work, this home education stuff, and William has been falling a bit behind with some of his work. And like I said, getting them out to groups hasn't been going well. I thought it might take some of the pressure off.'

'A tutor?' I repeated. 'And Jon's okay with that? You're always saying he worries about money.'

'Yes, he does, you're right.' She hesitated, pressing her lips together. 'But education is important, and though it doesn't come cheap, it's worth it. Besides, it's only temporary. Just to catch up on a few bits. Do you want a coffee?' she offered, already on her feet and heading for the kitchen.

I stared at her, feeling dizzy at the speed with which she'd changed the subject, unsure how to steer her back and dig deeper into what was really going on. I was sure she was making it all up on the spot, the signs impossible to ignore as her cheeks flushed red and her hands moved restlessly by her sides the way they always did when she was nervous. But why should she be nervous unless she was hiding something from me?

I pressed my lips together, looking deep into her eyes, willing her to be honest, to see that I had caught her in the lie, that I didn't buy her story, but she remained silent. Feeling frustrated and unsure how to proceed, I decided to let it go for the moment. 'Do you have anything herbal?' I asked as she paused unwillingly by the door, clearly keen to escape my scrutiny for a bit.

She frowned. 'Why?'

'Just on a bit of a health kick. Some of the women at work are doing it, and I thought it might be a good idea. My poor body needs a detox,' I lied, feeling suddenly unsure about confiding my baby plans to her.

'I'll see what I can find. Jon likes some of the infusions – ginger and lemon, is that the kind of thing you mean?'

I nodded, watching her leave.

There was no way the man I'd seen was a maths tutor. He was far too smart, he'd carried no briefcase or folders, and besides, hadn't Lily said that Maisy and William were upstairs playing? Surely they would have been down here clearing up the table if they'd just had a lesson. And you didn't go in for a long embrace with the kids' tutor. I'd seen the look in Lily's eyes. The emotion that had passed between them. Her story didn't make any sense.

She came back and I caught the aroma of spicy ginger as she placed a mug in front of me. 'Jon working in the office this week?' I asked casually.

'Oh, he's away on location this week. Back Sunday night. This project he's working on. You know Jon – he gets so into these documentaries. I'm glad he's found a career he loves so much. Like you,' she said. Her voice was shrill, her words rambling, and her smile didn't meet her eyes as she fidgeted with the cushions, plumping them up, switching their positions.

Watching her made me feel tense – uneasy. I didn't know what was going on, but if I wasn't convinced when I arrived here, I certainly was now. Lily was hiding something from me. And if that man was visiting her when the kids were tucked away upstairs and Jon was out of the country on business, there was only one reason I could think of.

Lily was having an affair.

CHAPTER THIRTEEN

Lily

I pulled into the little car park by the beach, scanning it for Hannah's car and spotting it on the far side. She got out as I backed into the space beside her, and the moment the engine cut, the kids were bounding out of their seats, flinging open the doors.

'Careful, Maisy!' I yelled as the edge of her door narrowly missed the car on the other side of us. I sighed as she skipped away without a backwards glance and got out, grabbing my bag and putting on a pair of sunglasses before walking round the back of the car to greet Hannah. The kids were already all over her, and I smiled when Maisy didn't shrink away from the hug she was offered. Hannah nodded with interest as William told her about his latest obsession – tigers and their hunting styles – and I patted Hannah on the arm, leaving them batting wildlife facts back and forth while I went to get a ticket.

It had been a difficult morning, and I had spent a good part of it crying, but I needed to push down those emotions now and be strong. I wanted to get Hannah's advice about the unexpected positive pregnancy test, and I hoped that after today I'd feel less guilt and finally have some clarity about what to do. I'd been thrown when she'd turned up unannounced at my door the previous week, and though part of me had wanted to blurt everything out to her, I hadn't been able to even consider broaching the subject of my pregnancy, sure that all the secrets I wasn't able to share would spill out alongside my confession. I had shut down, and Hannah had left after a brief, uncomfortable chat consisting of muted small talk and dodged questions. I'd got the impression she was annoyed with me, but then, I'd reasoned, she had no idea what I was hiding and had no reason to go digging. I was creating drama where there was none. I was nervous about telling her about the pregnancy test today, it having been so long since we'd had a conversation about anything so important, so emotional, but I'd had time to prepare and felt strong enough to broach the subject without falling apart and telling her everything I'd been keeping from her.

Hannah glanced up from William, her eyes meeting mine just for a second as I walked back to the car before she looked away again.

'Hey,' I said, making an effort to smile. 'Shall we go?'

William cheered and Maisy picked up her bucket and spade. The car park was hot and dusty, but as we walked down the path to the beach, we were treated to a light, blissfully refreshing breeze. The beach was quiet and calm, although William did his best to put an end to that, yelling at the top of his lungs as he ran in circles around us. I laid out towels on the hot sand, relishing the feeling of it running through my fingers, the sound of the sea breaking in soft waves against the shore.

Seagulls circled overhead, their beady eyes casting hopeful glances in our direction, and the smell of salt and sun cream filled my nose. There was a sense of peace that always came in being by the sea, a calming energy that seemed to numb my fears, if only for a little while. I loved it more than anywhere else in the world. And it was one of the few places I could come where I would get a break from William's relentless demands. I saw the same joy in him here too, the sense of freedom, a wild independence that only ever seemed to surface here.

He stripped off his shorts and T-shirt, down to the striped swim shorts he'd put on earlier, and with a shout of joy rushed down the beach to the shoreline, splashing into the water without hesitation. Maisy took her dress off, sedately dropping it on top of my bag, then picked up her bucket and spade and followed in the same direction, quiet and dreamy as she stared out at the horizon. I flopped on top of a towel with a sigh, kicking off my shoes and patting the spot beside me. Hannah sat down, knees folded beneath her chin, and I smiled. 'I feel like it's been ages since we had a chance to have a proper chat. The kids are so full-on these days, it's hard to keep a thought straight in my head.'

She nodded, opening her beach bag and pulling out a bottle of water, glugging back half of it in one go. The temperature was perfect, just how I liked it. Twenty-eight degrees, but with the lightest breeze so it didn't feel stifling. Jon would have hated it here today. He preferred snow and thick jumpers to heat waves.

'So, how are you?' I asked when Hannah had put her water bottle down.

She shrugged. 'Not bad. Work's good.'

'Seeing anyone at the moment?' I realised it had been a while since I'd heard about any dates she'd been on. I loved hearing about the people she met on online matchmaking sites, laughing as she told me all the strange things that happened. I'd worried about her at first, not wanting her to go and meet strangers alone, but Hannah had her head screwed on right, and never took any unnecessary risks or put herself in danger, and I'd soon learned to relax and live vicariously through her hilarious stories. I couldn't think of the last time she'd told me one though. She hadn't mentioned a man since Luke, and I knew that had ended, though I couldn't recall the reason why.

I knew I was partly to blame for not being in the know about the ins and outs of her dating life. I was usually the first to broach the subject, keen to hear all the details, but I knew my mind had been elsewhere lately and I probably hadn't been making enough effort to ask about the latest developments. Hannah never seemed to mind though, just as I didn't when the shoe was on the other foot. I loved that we had the kind of strong foundations to our friendship that we could go a few months without living in each other's pockets. We always came back to each other in the end. When she'd first started her new job, I'd barely seen her for months at a time, but in the brief moments we were able to grab, it was never hard to fall back into our comfortable habits, reigniting in-jokes and sharing news without bitterness or resentment. It was one of those friendships that was special, rare, and I was glad we finally had a chance to catch up properly now. I wanted to know what I'd missed in her life while I'd been busy with my own stuff.

'Not right now,' she answered. 'I don't have the time for dating lately.' She gazed out towards the sea, watching the children playing, and I frowned. She never usually held back so much, never gave me these little one-sentence replies.

I followed her gaze. 'They were supposed to start sailing lessons this week, but Jon's cancelled them. Says we can't afford it and we'll have to wait and see if they can start next year instead. Even then, he didn't sound optimistic. I was so disappointed for them – I want them to have the same experiences that I had at their age. Learning independence, freedom, understanding the water, feeling it move beneath you. I can't imagine how different my life would have been without all that.'

I filtered a handful of sand through my fingers, pressing my toes beneath the surface of the hot glassy top layer, savouring the coolness, trying to focus on it as William's shrieks of joy bounced on the breeze.

'I know he's been tightening his belt recently, but it seems like he's not willing to spend money on anything. It's getting frustrating. I want them to have memories, things to hold on to… and it's not like you can take your money with you,' I added, feeling a sudden rush of sadness that made me clear my throat and look away.

'They *are* making memories,' Hannah said, turning to look at me. 'Don't you remember being that age? The sailing lessons were great, but it's the little things like this that stay with you. A day at the beach is priceless. I wouldn't worry about it. If you want them to learn to sail, they can always do it in the future, but playing like this, the freedom they have right now, no worries, no responsibilities – you can't get better than that, Lily.'

'You might be right.' I smiled.

I wanted to ask more about *her*, find out if there was anything going on in her life, but I found that I was afraid to – she seemed so hot and cold. I realised that there must be more going on for her than she was saying. I could only assume it was the pressures of her work weighing heavy on her. She took on so much, and though I knew she loved her job, I understood better than anyone how you could love your life and yet be worn down by it; need to escape and switch off at times. I understood the chains that came with committing to a vocation, the desire to be someone else, if only for a brief interlude.

I bit my lip, waiting, wanting to give Hannah the opportunity to fill the silence with her own worries, but she continued to stare out to sea, and I could feel the tension start to form between us as the silence grew. It was clear that she wasn't in the mood to confide her own problems. Instead, I decided to ask for the advice I so desperately needed. It was why I'd invited her to come out with us today. I wanted to talk to her without the kids listening or Jon hovering in the background.

'Han… there's actually something I need to tell you, something that's been going on and I haven't known what to do.'

She turned towards me and reached for my hand. Her expression was full of an openness that took me aback. It was as if she'd been waiting for me to say something all along. I felt a sudden wave of nausea wash over me as I wondered if she knew, but I shook off the thought as soon as it had arrived. There was no way she could. I'd been too careful. Her eyes were intense as she spoke. 'Lil, you know you can tell me anything.'

I nodded. 'I… I'm pregnant. And please don't hate me for this, but…' I shook my head, closing my eyes, the sound of the ocean filling my mind. 'I don't think I can keep the baby.' I admitted it so softly it was barely a whisper, as if saying it quietly could mute the pain of what I was telling her. 'I didn't plan for it to happen, and the timing is awful.'

Hannah loosened her grasp on my hand, pulling hers away, and I glanced up at her blanched face, seeing the shock in her eyes. She took a breath. 'What does Jon say?'

'I haven't told him. I don't want to worry him.'

She shook her head, looking down at her knees, and I wished she would hug me and tell me it was going to be okay. Offer advice like I'd expected her to. Be the friend I needed right now. But what she said surprised me beyond belief.

'Is it his?'

'What?' I replied, my voice shrill as I stared open-mouthed at her, shocked that she would ask such a question.

'Is it Jon's baby?'

I clasped my hands together, our eyes meeting. 'Why would you ask me that? Of course it's Jon's!'

'Is there anything you would like to tell me, Lily? Anything *else*, I mean.'

I shook my head, wishing I *could* share more with her, that I could tell her the secrets that kept me awake through the night, that made me sick with terror if I let myself think of them. I wished I could confide in her, lean on her, but I didn't have that choice.

I stood up, kicking the sand off the tops of my feet and shielding my eyes with the back of my arm, looking over to my children. 'Isn't my being pregnant enough?' I asked, wishing I hadn't told her. 'I just don't know what to do, Hannah. I wish I did.'

I bit my lip, trying not to cry, but I could feel the tears, treacherous and unstoppable as they blurred my vision, and I didn't want to let them fall in front of her.

'I'm going to check on the children,' I said, stepping off the towel onto the hot sand. I walked away, shoulders stiff, my throat thick with a ball of emotion I couldn't let out.

'Tell Jon,' Hannah called after me. 'You have to tell him.'

I nodded, though I didn't turn to look at her. I walked down to the sea and waited for the calm it always offered to descend over me, but this time, it didn't come.

CHAPTER FOURTEEN

Hannah

I stared after Lily as she walked down the beach, back poker straight, head held high, and wondered how she could have changed so much from that girl I'd made friends with at camp all those years before. What had happened between us to make her lie, make her hide so much from me? I'd been with her when she'd taken a pregnancy test for the very first time, when she'd fallen pregnant with William. I'd held her hand as we waited for the longest two minutes of my life, and then seen the play of emotions that ran across her face as we flipped it over to see the result. She'd been simultaneously excited, terrified, jumping for joy and worried about how she would manage – whether she'd be a good mother – but I'd never doubted her. Not then. She'd been open in her fears, and it had brought us closer as I'd convinced her she could do it and she would not let this baby down.

I'd been in Paris when she took the second test, that time for Maisy, but she'd called me from the bathroom in tears and I could hear how happy she was, how excited for the future she sounded. The difference in her now was undeniable. This time, there was no joy. No fizz of anticipation to meet the little person currently growing and developing inside her body. Nothing but terror and regret, and I could guess why.

Jon had hardly been home for a month, busy with his latest wildlife documentary, and the last few times I'd seen the two of them together, I hadn't missed the difference in their interactions. They had always been the kind of couple who liked to touch, to reassure and seek comfort in each other. They had never made me feel uncomfortable with their affection – it was sweet and loving rather than overt: holding hands any time we went for a walk, a touch of a shoulder, an arm snaking round a waist. It had been my normal for so long – perhaps that was why I'd noticed the change. The distance between them as we stood to chat. The absence of those loving gestures that had seemed to be a part of the make-up of their relationship. And as I'd looked closer, I'd noticed more. A lack of eye contact. Lily always turning away to busy herself when Jon tried to move closer. I was sure this change was coming from her rather than him. I'd seen the quick flashes of pain in his eyes, the way his head lowered and he moved back as if she'd put up a barrier he didn't know how to break through.

I wondered if he had any idea what Lily had been doing to fill the time while he'd been away for work. If *anyone* knew. She had called earlier today to change our plans. I'd originally said I would go to hers first and we'd all drive to the beach together, but then she'd changed her mind. I hadn't really thought about it as I'd got in my car, driving on autopilot to her house, despite her instructions not to, but I hadn't been surprised to see the red Honda on the driveway as I crawled past, feeling betrayed and angry. I'd known from the tone of her voice that she was hiding something. And now she was pregnant. And if I had to guess at why she was so distraught, it was pretty simple to come up with a list of reasons.

Jon was a decent man, hard-working, kind and a bloody good father, but clearly that wasn't enough for Lily. I knew she carried resentment over having to put her career aside for the sake of the children. I'd thought Jon was beyond reasonable during the discussions they'd had about what to do when William reacted so extremely to starting at school. He'd never told Lily she couldn't retrain or go back to work, never made a single demand of her, and Lily would be lying if she tried to backtrack now and say that she'd not been completely relieved when Jon had put the offer for her to be a stay-at-home mum on the table. They had a mortgage to pay, bills to worry about, and he'd been prepared to shoulder that burden alone for the sake of his family.

I hadn't forgotten the day Lily had told me she was going to focus on the children and wouldn't be going back to work. She'd been smiley and full of energy, happier than I'd seen her in a long time, all the worry over her future lifted, simply because Jon had come up with an idea that made perfect sense. But as the children got older and she began to realise what she'd sacrificed for them, she'd grown dissatisfied with what she had. She'd started comparing our lives, voicing complaints over the stark differences between hers and mine. She wanted it all, and that was something I was beginning to understand myself – the desire to have more balance between home and work – but she had let herself forget the things she *did* have, the many reasons in her life to be grateful. And now it seemed that the dissatisfaction had grown too large; she'd made a choice to spice up her life and look elsewhere, and she'd messed up and got herself pregnant. No wonder she was worried. How could she dare to have this baby and present him or her to Jon as his own, make him raise another man's child?

Or was it worse than that? I thought suddenly. Was she considering leaving Jon and starting a life with this new man? I couldn't believe her capable of it, and worse than that, I couldn't understand why, after all we'd been through, she wouldn't confide in me. I would have been disappointed, disapproving even, but I was her best friend and this was the kind of thing I expected her to share. Her hiding it from me, and doing a bad job of it to boot, had formed a crack in our friendship I didn't know if we could ever repair.

I watched her now, wading out to her knees and standing in the calm water looking out to the horizon. The thought that she might get rid of her baby when I was so desperate for one of my own was sickening to me. I stared at her and realised I was shaking. How dare she? How could she even conceive of just terminating the life inside her when there were so many women who would have given *anything* to have what she had?

I grasped a handful of sand, squeezing it hard in my fist as I watched her paddling in the shallow sea, consumed with her own thoughts, her own selfish desires. I wondered if she was thinking of *him* and felt another rush of anger. She didn't offer to play with Maisy, didn't bother to answer as William called to her to look at his sandcastle. It wasn't fair that I had to go to such lengths to conceive a child and Lily could just fall pregnant without even trying. Without understanding what a privilege that was. She'd been given so much, had so much to be thankful for, but she didn't see it. And sometimes I wondered if, perhaps, she didn't deserve it.

CHAPTER FIFTEEN

I crossed my legs, then uncrossed them again, picking up a magazine from a stack on the low table and flicking through it without seeing the words. A door opened nearby and I glanced up, wondering if it was time, watching as a woman walked past me and out the door without stopping at the receptionist's desk. I tossed the magazine down and folded my hands together, wishing I had someone with me, but then, doing this alone was becoming a badge of honour for me, so perhaps this was more fitting. I couldn't have asked Lily. Not anymore.

The receptionist walked round the desk, disappearing into the room the woman had emerged from, and a moment later she came out, smiling warmly at me. 'Miss Adams, if you'd like to go through?'

'Oh, yes, thank you.' I stood, feeling the thrum of my heartbeat in my pulse points, vibrating in my throat, as I cast a final look around the smartly decorated reception area with its magnolia walls and cherrywood furnishings. My heels clicked on the hardwood floor as I made my way to the doctor's room, and I suddenly wondered if I should have worn something different. I'd dressed for a business meeting – a grey cashmere trouser suit and silk camisole, kitten heels and full make-up – hoping to make a good impression and come across as a woman who knew what she wanted and was ready for the challenges ahead, but now I wondered if I should have opted for something more maternal-looking, something that would enable the doctor to picture me in the role I wanted to step into – jeans, perhaps, or one of those floaty dresses Lily always liked to wear. But it was too late to worry about that now.

I thanked the receptionist as she held the door open for me, and stepped into the room. A man with dark hair blending to grey at the temples was sitting at a desk, frowning as he stared at the computer screen in front of him. He looked up as he heard me come in and offered a professional smile, standing to shake my hand and gesturing for me to take a seat. On closer inspection, I decided he was much older than I'd initially guessed, perhaps close to sixty, though he wore it well. 'Well, Miss Adams—'

'Call me Hannah,' I said, adjusting myself on the seat, keeping my back straight and my body language confident, though I didn't feel confident right now. I was used to heading into difficult meetings. I frequently had to stand up and present my ideas in front of a room of twenty strangers, or convince department heads and buyers to choose my designs over someone else's. I knew high pressure. I *lived* it. And yet I couldn't recall a time I had ever been as nervous as this.

Perhaps it was because after years of thinking I didn't want a child, I had realised now that the opposite was true. I wanted it more and more with each passing day, to the point that it was fast becoming an obsession. It was the first thing I thought of when I opened my eyes in the morning. I gravitated towards every baby that passed on the street. At the weekends I watched films about parenting, documentaries on pregnancy health. Even my dreams revolved around babies – carrying a child in my arms, the hugs, the warmth, the love I already felt for a child that did not yet exist, spilling out at every opportunity.

Since she'd confessed her secret to me, I hadn't stopped thinking about Lily, her baby, the gift she'd been given that she didn't even appreciate. I hoped she would change her tune and see her unplanned pregnancy as a pleasant surprise as opposed to a problem to be solved.

'So, Hannah.' The doctor smiled. I tried to remember his name and drew a blank, which was completely out of character for me. 'How can I help you today?'

I smiled warmly. 'I'm interested in finding a sperm donor. I want to have a baby.'

'I see. And may I ask why you've landed on this option?'

I shrugged. 'It just makes sense to me. I don't have a man in my life and don't want one.'

He rubbed his chin with his fingers, fixing me with an intense stare that made me want to look away. There was something predatory about him, and I recognised the condescending tone of his voice, the expression on his face, which screamed to me that he thought he could dominate my choices. I'd seen it a thousand times before in my professional life, and I wasn't cowed by him, any more than I had been by the chauvinistic men I'd left behind as I climbed a ladder they couldn't begin to reach. 'You don't want to wait and see what the future brings? If you don't mind my saying, you're a pretty girl, I'm sure you could find a husband if you wanted.'

I raised an eyebrow. 'Actually, I *do* mind you saying. I've stated quite clearly that a husband is not something I'm looking for. I do, however, want a child. I'm perfectly capable of providing for one without a man, and I would appreciate it if you could give me the information I need to get started, Dr Larkin,' I said, remembering his name at last.

He looked taken aback, but he gave a short nod, reaching behind him for a leaflet and opening it for me to look at. 'Okay, Miss Adams. You've made your point, and I can see you're committed to this idea. Let me walk you through the process, shall I?'

I nodded, feeling my confidence return, my first challenge on the road to motherhood already faced and overcome. I'd not waited two weeks for an appointment and come all this way to be talked out of it. I knew what I wanted, and I couldn't wait to get started with the next step.

CHAPTER SIXTEEN

Now

The knock at the door made me leap from the chair by the window, my heart skipping a beat as I glanced from the locked hotel-room door to the sleeping baby lying on the middle of the mattress. I dug my fingernails into my palm, my entire body shaking as I fought off the urge to vomit. Who could it be? How could we have been found so quickly?

I glanced at Ella again, then padded barefoot towards the door, trying to keep my footsteps light, my movements silent. I leaned close to the peephole to see who was waiting on the other side and let out a burst of laughter when I saw the smartly dressed bellboy holding a tin of formula in his arm. Sucking in a shaky breath, I opened the door, smiling apologetically, though I could still feel the tremble in my top lip.

'I'm so sorry to keep you standing here all this time – I was just settling the baby. I really appreciate this,' I said, taking the tin from his proffered hands and holding it tightly, glad that I'd be able to keep Ella nourished – assuming she would take it.

'Not a problem, madam. I didn't want to knock, as I can see you have the Do Not Disturb up, but Marissa said you wouldn't mind.'

'Marissa?'

'She checked you in.'

'Ah, of course.' I nodded, feeling stupid.

'Is there anything else I can get for you this evening?'

I shook my head and thanked him again, pushing the door closed and leaning back against it with a shaky sigh. I don't know what I'd expected – a police raid, Lily and Jon raging and ready to confront me and take Ella back… I couldn't say, but the terror that filtered through my nervous system now was undeniable. I'd spent the past hour staring out of the window into the growing darkness of the world outside, feeling an increasing sense of panic with every minute that passed. As I'd watched Ella drift back to sleep, I had felt anything but relieved. What I'd done, the stupid, irresponsible choice I'd made in the heat of the moment on a beautiful summer's afternoon, had slowly begun to dawn on me, and as I'd laid her down trying not to wake her, my skin had felt as if it was crawling with a sense of dread that seemed to be spiralling out of control.

I'd stolen a baby. Not just a baby. Ella. *Lily's* baby. My best friend in the world since I was eighteen years old. I tried to imagine what she might have felt as she came to meet me after going on the roller coaster and found us gone. How would she have reacted? Would she have turned to Jon, confessed even, or would she have called Ella's real dad to beg for his help? Would she even have cared? I shook my head. Of course she would have. Even Lily wasn't as selfish as that. She would have been shocked, confused, devastated. And now, as the reality of her situation began to sink in, her shock would transform, morphing into something darker, something primal and dangerous. What mother could feel anything but hate and fury towards the person who had broken her trust and taken her child when her back was turned?

With trembling fingers, I placed the formula down on the dressing table and covered my face with my hands, the urge to scream building inside me. I shoved it down, refusing to let it come. I felt lost, afraid, and I had no idea what to do next. I knew what I *should* do – the only right choice I could make in this situation. I should take her back, without hesitation or preamble. As much as I wished it, *longed* for it, Ella wasn't mine and I had no right to keep her. But taking her back now would open up a whole new nightmare for me.

I could picture the scene playing out before me in vivid colours and stereo sound. They would snatch her from my arms, treat me like a criminal, a monster. The house would be full of police coming and going, looking at me like a piece of dirt on the bottom of their shoe. I would hear the whispers as the neighbours crowded outside, watching, condemning me without ever pausing to question my motives. *Kidnapper. Child abductor. Her best friend*, they would mutter. *How could she do it?*

I'd be arrested, of course, taken to a cell and left to cower in a corner. And then what? Prison, no doubt. How long did you get for taking a baby? Five years? Ten? By the time I got out, any minuscule chance I might have had to have a baby of my own would be lost. My career would be long gone, my reputation ruined, and I would be left with nothing. No home. No money. No friends, and worst of all, no family. The baby that had filled my dreams, dictated my every action, every choice for months now would be lost to another life, and perhaps the impact of that would be too much for me to bear. The thought terrified me to my core.

I stared at Ella, wishing things had been different. That *I* could have been the one who fell pregnant with her rather than Lily. I would never have considered throwing her life away, never. I would have held on to her and done everything in my power to keep her safe, whatever it took. I felt a tear slip from the corner of my eye as my resolve hardened. I couldn't take her back. Not now. I had come too far to change my mind. There was only one choice left for us. We had to keep going. The alternative was just too frightening to consider.

CHAPTER SEVENTEEN

Lily

Then

I watched from the doorway of the room as Jon climbed into bed, leaning heavily against the pillows. William had spilled a cup of juice all over the duvet before I'd even fully woken up this morning, and though I had stripped the bed and hung the quilt to dry, I'd forgotten to turn the washing machine on. Now the quilt and pillows were covered in our one and only spare set of bedding, an ugly brown and yellow striped polyester blend gifted to us by a great-aunt of Jon's on our wedding day. I didn't know why we kept it, why we didn't make the effort to replace it with something more attractive, but the years had passed and every few weeks we ended up having to sleep between these awful sheets again. I looked at them now and resolved to do something about it. It was a tiny problem, considering the rest of the worries burdening my mind lately, but perhaps because this was something I could actually fix, I honed in on it, unable to let it go. If it meant avoiding all my other problems for a little while longer, that couldn't be a bad thing.

I watched as Jon shifted around, kicking at the covers. He seemed smaller somehow, his body shrinking into the mattress, his chest rising and falling heavily beneath the black cotton T-shirt he'd taken to wearing to bed. Neither of us slept naked anymore, though we'd never had a conversation about it. It was just something that had evolved over the last few weeks and months, so that now it felt like our new normal. It had been a long, exhausting struggle with Jon away and me having to do all the household tasks, the childcare, the night-time parenting and the early mornings without a break, but he'd finally arrived back from his work trip, and I knew my time was up. I couldn't keep this from him any longer.

He raised himself up onto his elbows, looking at me with a half-smile. 'You just going to stay there?' He grinned. 'Not that you don't look lovely propping up the doorway, but my bed's been empty for far too long and it would be lovely to have a beautiful woman in it for a change.' He winked.

I grunted, feeling irritated. I hated when he acted like this, flirting like we were twenty and free, like we didn't have the weight of the world on our shoulders. He knew as well as I did that the most action that bed would see tonight was a bit of gentle spooning at best.

'What's wrong?' he asked, his brow creasing as he finally paused to look at me properly.

'I'm pregnant.'

'You're kidding?' he exclaimed, his eyes widening as he took in the shocking revelation.

I shook my head. 'I wish I was.' I waited for him to say something, feeling the roller coaster of emotions play out inside me, though I stood frozen, unmoving, waiting. A part of me wanted him to tell me we could make it work. That somehow, despite the odds, we could have this baby and play happy families and pretend everything was as it should be. But the other side, the logical part of my mind, knew that it could never work that way. It didn't matter what I wanted. Only that bringing another person into the mess that was our lives right now wasn't fair to the child.

'Oh, babe,' he said, leaning forward. 'Come here.' He held out his arms. I hesitated for a moment, not wanting to, yet knowing it would only make everything worse if I refused. I walked towards him, sitting down on his side of the mattress, letting him draw me into a hug, the way he used to, though my own body was stiff and unresponsive. His hands wrapped around me, cradling my head, and I felt his breath in my hair. 'This is the best news,' he murmured.

I pulled back. 'What? How can it be?' I asked, stunned at his reaction.

'We always wanted more. I didn't think we would get the chance to do it again, but this is incredible.' He pushed back a strand of hair that had fallen into my eyes, tucking it behind my ear with a gentle finger, his expression full of hope, his eyes shining as if he might be about to cry, though I hoped he wouldn't. 'You always said you would like to have another one.'

I shook my head. 'I said I *might* like to. But I can't do this now. *We* can't do this.' I wrapped my arms around my abdomen as if I could muffle the words that I didn't want to say. 'Jon, I can't keep this baby, I just can't. It's the wrong time – we're barely surviving as it is. I'm stretched to my limit, and so are you. William's still as intense as he was at two years old, and I feel like Maisy is slipping away from us as each day passes. Sometimes she feels like a stranger to me,' I admitted. 'And we're... you're—' I broke off, not willing to lead him into a conversation neither of us wanted to broach, the constant elephant in the room we both refused to acknowledge. I sighed, pulling my emotions back in check, and looked up at him, seeing the familiar soft eyes that had been a part of my world for so long. 'How could we manage? How would I cope?'

He smiled, his hand cupping my cheek. 'You just will. You always do. You're strong, Lils, you always have been, and you have to do this. You will regret it for the rest of your life if you don't. Babe, we might not get another chance. Take it. We'll find a way to make it work.'

I realised that this was what I'd dreamed he would say since the moment I'd found out I was pregnant. That he would give me an option I could live with, brush away all the complications, all the reasons it couldn't work, and somehow make everything okay. It was so like him to avoid the big issues and romanticise the whole thing. I should have said no. He was wrong when he said I was strong. If I was, I would have made the logical choice. I would have ended the pregnancy without hesitation, made sure I protected this child from the pain he or she might have to go through in the future. But Jon had given me permission to grasp hold of what I wanted more than I had dared to admit, even to myself, and I couldn't resist. I let myself be swept into his warm arms again, and for the first time since taking that test, I allowed myself to feel hope for the child I was carrying.

CHAPTER EIGHTEEN

Hannah

I stared between my thighs into the bowl of the toilet, feeling my hopes drain away at the unmistakable splash of claret staining the water. My period had arrived. No baby was coming this cycle.

I'd been so sure the donor sperm insemination would work my first try. I'd had every test going, the STDs, the genetic disorders, my medical information carefully compared and analysed with that of the donor I'd chosen from the sperm bank. I'd spent hours scrolling through baby pictures, little boys who had grown up to be the men offering the gift of life with their own fertility. I'd hovered over chubby toddlers with big brown eyes, newborns with pursed lips and tufty blonde hair, wondering if someday soon I might hold a child who looked like they did, cradle him or her in my arms and feel like I truly did have it all.

In the end, I'd settled on a donor whose picture I kept coming back to. There were no photographs of the donors as adults, but his baby photos felt familiar to me somehow, as if I'd been looking for him from the start. He had soft light brown hair and huge blue eyes, and after placing my order, shocked that one straw – one single opportunity to get it right – combined with the compulsory pregnancy slot at the clinic was going to wipe out close to a grand from my savings account, I'd sat back, giddy with excitement about what would come next. I'd felt like a child on Christmas Eve as I'd waited impatiently for the clinic in Bournemouth to contact me to let me know that the delivery had arrived. It was the best gift I'd ever bought for myself.

I *had* hoped to inseminate myself in the privacy of my own home – it seemed far too personal a thing to do anywhere else, or invite strangers to witness – but the law stated that sperm could only be sent to a registered clinic and that the insemination must be assisted, so I'd grudgingly agreed to the terms. I wasn't about to go into battle over a small irritation. I had to save my energy for bigger things. Allowing the team of nurses to take over, I'd closed my eyes, thinking how strange it was that the conception of my baby could happen in such a cold, unromantic environment. Perhaps it was the weight of what I was going through, the feelings I was unable to pour out to anyone, but I'd found the experience far more emotional than I'd anticipated.

I'd come home from the clinic that day feeling changed, certain that it had worked. I knew I was ovulating. They'd told me my womb lining was thick, which I knew now was what they wanted at the time of insemination. I was a strong, healthy woman of thirty-four years old. Why shouldn't it succeed?

I'd lain on my bed with my feet climbing the wall, the way Lily and I had done as teens as we'd listened to Eminem albums and talked about every little thing under the sun – her relationship with Jon, my dating life, our hopes and dreams – and as I'd rested quietly, I tried to imagine the life igniting inside me. In the days that followed, I began to feel a tenderness in my breasts. I felt queasy in the mornings. I craved oranges and fried eggs, and I smiled at each change, each sign that things were happening to my body. Now, staring down at that treacherous splash of blood, I felt like an idiot. It had clearly all been in my head. There was no baby, and there never had been.

I washed my hands, staring at my reflection in the mirror, seeing the disappointment in my eyes, the anger at myself that I couldn't get this right. Part of me wanted to do something crazy. Go online and arrange a date for every night around the time I'd next be ovulating. I could do it. Have a one-night stand and then another, increase my chances. Plenty of women found themselves pregnant after a night of reckless fun. But there were so many risks to doing it that way. I might catch something; the man might be a serial killer or have a genetic condition that was triggered by something in my own genes.

If I were in a long-term relationship, perhaps things would be different. We might be planning for it, and I wouldn't second-guess everything that could go wrong. I might let go and trust in nature to get it right. But doing this alone, knowing the challenges I would face as a single working mother, I didn't want to risk adding any extra complications into the mix. I sighed, turning away from the mirror, knowing I could never go through with anything like that. Though I'd never been in the market for a serious relationship, I wasn't comfortable with one-night stands either. I always needed several dates – time to get to know a man – before I would consider letting him into my bed. The thought of a stranger pawing me, seeing me naked and vulnerable, made me feel sick, and using them for their sperm wasn't fair to them either. It would never work.

It would have been so much easier if I could have just found a boyfriend and done things the normal route, but as much as I hated to admit it to myself, the idea that a man might develop strong enough feelings for me to want to hang around long term was something I found laughable. My own parents hadn't known how to love me, not properly, and though I was intelligent enough to realise that the issue was more theirs than mine, it didn't stop the endless insecurities from surfacing any time I began to feel myself falling for a guy. I had wasted enough of my life trying to garner my parents' attention, all to no avail. I wasn't about to waste any more time chasing after a man, letting myself be sucked into a relationship with someone who would eventually walk away, leaving me hurt and broken. It was better that I stayed single, in control of my emotions, so that I couldn't be damaged by any more rejection.

Opening the bathroom door, I walked into my bedroom and sat down on the edge of the mattress, and my thoughts turned to Lily. I felt bad for how things had gone between us the last time we spoke. I was still frustrated and angry with her for not telling me the whole truth, but I knew my own feelings had clouded my response when she'd admitted her pregnancy. It had set off a succession of emotions, and I hadn't been able to hide my shock when she'd said she might not keep the baby. I hadn't been fair to her. She had no idea what I was going through. I'd judged her too, not been the friend she needed or expected, but it was so hard when she only offered half the story. We'd been so close for so long. It hurt that she wouldn't share this with me.

If she would let me, I could help. Be there for her, support her in raising this baby. I wanted to. I knew I hadn't been all that hands-on when it came to the first two – I had felt out of my depth with their tiny fragile bodies, not wanting to make a mistake or do anything that might hurt them. Even changing nappies had been something I'd held back from offering to help with, watching with a sense of barely concealed panic as Lily deftly unbuttoned tiny Babygros, one hand securing the kicking feet as she whipped away the dirty nappy and replaced it with a clean, fresh one. She had always seemed unfazed by the many tasks that came with taking care of her children, and I'd been in awe of how naturally it seemed to come to her. But now, I felt ready to try too. I could help her with the baby if only she would consider it. I could take him or her out for walks, give Lily a break; I'd even stay overnight if she wanted me to. It would keep me from going mad as I tried for one of my own, give me something to focus on other than my own broodiness. Because right now, I was on the verge of obsession with my need to conceive and I knew a distraction would be healthy. And if next month I found myself pregnant, then it would be all the better – we could go through it together. Raise our children side by side helping each other along. It could be so perfect.

The thought of having a baby to hold and take care of, even if it wasn't my own, was enough to make my heart sing, warmth spreading through my veins. I needed this. But it could only work if Lily was willing to keep the baby, and having seen the trepidation on her face, knowing how hard it would have been for her to admit her thoughts about ending the pregnancy, I knew how serious she must have been. What if I couldn't convince her to let me help? If she was determined to pretend it hadn't happened and go ahead with a termination?

My head snapped up, and I drew in a sharp breath as an idea sparked in my mind.

Lily was carrying a baby she didn't want. And I, despite my best efforts and a thousand pounds literally flushed down the toilet, was still not pregnant. Would she even consider it? If it transpired that she was set in her decision to turn her back on this baby, might she consider an alternative? Could I bring myself to ask her?

I stood up, pacing as I tried to figure out the mess of ideas spiralling in my head. It wouldn't be like I'd asked her to be my surrogate – there was no decision to make about the hardship she'd have to go through: carrying a baby, dealing with the morning sickness and the hormonal roller coaster, experiencing labour again. She'd already taken the plunge, her body changing and adapting every day. And knowing Lily as I did, I was sure that she'd had sleepless nights over the idea of a termination. She would hate the thought, and the guilt would stay with her long after the procedure.

Would she have this baby for me? We were like sisters… closer than blood, and this could make sense for both of us. I had seen the cracks in her marriage with Jon, the tension between them in recent months. This baby could push them over the edge, tear them apart for good, especially if my suspicions about Lily and the other man were right. My taking the baby would give them the time and space they needed to get back on track. They needed to focus their energy on that.

If I told her the truth about what I'd been doing, what I'd been going through, I was certain she would see how much it would mean to me. And perhaps if I opened up, shared the truth, she might in turn tell me her secrets, and I could help her figure out what to do, how to save her marriage, if it could indeed be saved.

I clasped my hands together, excitement and hope bubbling inside me, and turned, rushing to the front door and grabbing my car keys on the way. This idea could be the catalyst for a new start, for all of us.

'Hey,' Lily said, offering a weak smile as she opened the front door, giving me a brief hug. She looked pale, her cheeks hollow, her eyes red and swollen, and I wondered if she'd been hit with morning sickness already. I remembered just how much she'd struggled with it in her previous pregnancies.

'Hi,' I replied, sensing an awkward vibe between us, left over from the sour conversation at the beach. I hoped we could clear the air and move forward so I could ask her the question that was bursting to escape my lips. 'How are you feeling?' I asked, reaching forward to touch her arm, waiting for her to look me in the eye.

'I'm good… I'm okay,' she said, dipping her head and turning away. 'I didn't know if I'd see you this week.'

'Where's Jon?'

'Oh, he's upstairs sleeping. He flew back from Patagonia yesterday and he's exhausted.'

I frowned, feeling something off in the way she spoke. Her words weren't anything unusual, but the way she said them, her eyes flicking away, her hands fidgeting in front of her, made me feel uneasy – as if she were lying to me.

'You want a cuppa?' she asked.

'Yes please. I'll make them, shall I?'

She shrugged and followed me into the kitchen, and I looked around for the kids. The house was unusually silent, and I turned to her with a raised eyebrow. She answered automatically. 'Jon's parents' are down – they're going up to London tomorrow to meet some friends but decided to stay here overnight so they could spend some time with the kids. They've taken them out to a farm to feed the lambs. William wasn't sure about going without me, but I think the lure of unlimited ice cream and the chance to talk to Grandpa about wildlife swayed him. So,' she said, smiling, 'blissful quiet until dinner time.'

'Must make a nice change?'

'You have no idea,' she replied, sitting down on a bar stool at the counter as I filled the kettle and found a box of herbal tea. 'I'll have a coffee,' she said, making a face at the box in my hand. 'Can't stand that stuff.'

'Is that okay? For the baby, I mean?' I frowned, thinking of the tiny life growing inside her. I'd been putting up with a caffeine detox for two months now, and I wasn't even pregnant yet.

'It's fine. One or two a day won't make a difference, and you have to take your pleasures where you can in this life. It's too short to spend it drinking things that taste like warmed-up medicine.'

I nodded, scooping half a teaspoon of instant into her cup, mixing it with plenty of water and more milk than usual. She took it with a grimace I pretended not to see and set it down, giving me the feeling she was planning to wait until I left so she could make a proper one to enjoy.

'So, how are you?' she asked as I bobbed a fennel tea bag in my steaming cup of water. 'Haven't seen much of you the last few weeks,' she added pointedly.

'I've been really busy,' I replied.

'New work project?'

'Something like that. Look, Lil, I wanted to talk to you about something. That day at the beach, I was taken aback by your news. I know I wasn't fair to you and you needed more from me, and I'm sorry for that.' I shrugged, feeling uncomfortable. 'I shouldn't have been so harsh.'

'It's okay.' She smiled. 'I get it. It was a shock to me too, finding out I was pregnant when I thought I'd been so careful. A baby is such a life-changing commitment, even when you already have children. I won't lie, the idea of going through it all again is pretty overwhelming.'

I noticed she didn't bring up the awkward exchange we'd had when I'd asked point blank if the baby was Jon's. She seemed relaxed now, calmer than the last time we spoke, and I dipped my head, deciding not to probe her about the man in the red Honda just yet. I didn't want to get off the topic of the baby, not when she was opening up to me like this, sharing her real feelings.

'I've been thinking about that a lot lately, how much you already have on your plate, how little sleep you get. What with home-educating both of them, William's need to be by your side as often as possible and Jon away so often, I know it isn't easy for you.'

She shrugged, brushing off my words and picking up her cup. I watched as she took a sip then seemed to remember why she'd pushed it away. She swallowed and I put my own cup down, afraid that I might spill it. My hands were shaking, my heart thudding erratically, and I felt suddenly terrified. I didn't know if I wanted to convince her to let me help with the baby, or if I was hoping she'd say her mind was made up so I could ask her to consider having this baby for me. Now that I was here, standing in front of her, it felt so much more real, more difficult, the words sticking in my throat. You couldn't just ask someone to give you a baby. It was ridiculous. But to let her get rid of it without even offering? I didn't think I could live with that.

I opened my mouth to speak, but she beat me to it. 'It's not easy, you're right. But,' she said, her eyes meeting mine, 'I've made up my mind to keep the baby.'

'What?' I stepped back as if I'd been punched in the guts, feeling the air deflate from my lungs. The weight of my own disappointment shocked me, and I realised I'd been hoping she'd make another choice, one that would leave a door open for me to present an alternative solution. 'Does Jon know?' I asked quietly, picking up my tea, clasping the mug tight between my shaking palms.

She nodded. 'I know it's a surprise after the way I acted at the beach. I was in a bit of a state that day, and if I'm honest, I should never have told you before I'd spoken to Jon. It wasn't fair of me. He really made me see things clearly. He convinced me that I can do this, that I shouldn't end the pregnancy. He made me see sense. I know it's not going to be easy. It isn't at the best of times, and God knows we're pretty damn far from good times right now, but if you want something enough, you find a way to make it work. It will be hard, but we can do it. This baby might be the one thing that keeps me sane,' she added softly.

I stared at her, holding back the crushing disappointment that had descended over me in one fell swoop, my hopes, my grand plan lost to the wind. 'I'm happy for you,' I managed. 'And I'll do anything I can to help. I'd like to. It's about time I learned how to change a nappy.'

Lily laughed, clearly taking my offer as a light-hearted remark, not seeing how much I really meant it. How desperately I needed it. I closed my eyes, determined not to cry, and took a sip of my drink, trying not to think about what might have been. Her words replayed in my mind as I took a steadying breath. What had she meant when she said they were damn far from good times? From where I was standing, her life looked pretty much perfect. But then, there was the red Honda man. And her strange coolness with her husband.

'Lil, what's happening between you and Jon?' I asked, trying to ignore the strain in my voice as I looked her in the eye. 'Why are you in such a rocky place?'

I stared at her, willing her to tell me the truth, so that at least one good thing could come out of our conversation. I felt so cut off from her world; there was so much between us, blocking the closeness we'd once shared. If only she would open up to me now, we could get back to how we'd once been. I could cope with my disappointment if I knew I had her to confide in, but until she stopped keeping secrets, I didn't know how we could bridge that gap. This was the first time she'd let slip that they were even having problems, though she'd have to be mad to think they had gone unnoticed – to believe I'd bought her flimsy lie that the man I'd seen had been a tutor for the children.

She waved a hand dismissively, hopping off the bar stool and walking round to the sink, filling the washing-up bowl with hot soapy water. I waited silently as she stacked the few items, a couple of plates and cups that could easily have waited beside the sink. Her voice was washed out by the sound of rushing water. 'We've been together twenty years – it's just normal ups and downs. These things come and go. We'll be back on track before you know it,' she said evasively.

I waited in case she had more to say, but she offered nothing else.

'Lil, if you ever want to talk to me, I'm here. I want to help if I can. Even if it's petty disagreements. You always used to vent to me and you said it helped.'

She looked down at the bowl, her shoulders slumped. 'Thanks, Hannah,' she said softly.

I watched her pick up a glass, dipping it beneath the surface of the water, and sighed, feeling sad and deflated, wondering when she'd begun to pull away from me, whether I'd missed something I could have fixed. I was losing her, and I didn't know how to rebuild the friendship that had broken while my back was turned.

CHAPTER NINETEEN

Lily

The day it all began

It had been the most perfect day, I thought, smiling to myself as I watched the serene faces of my two children, fast asleep across the floor cushions on the patio. The birds were coming in to roost, their chirruping and flapping providing a soothing background music as they jostled for position in the old oak tree at the end of the garden, the sun sinking low in the sky behind it. I unfolded the light fleecy throw in my hands, covering William and Maisy with it and stepping back quietly, moving to the fold-out table on the lawn to tidy away the remains of the buffet.

It really had been such a special occasion; I'd looked forward to it for months, and it hadn't disappointed. It was incredible to think that Jon and I had been a couple for twenty years as of today. I could still remember the first time he'd kissed me, the way our mouths had just seemed to fit. I'd expected it to be wet or embarrassing somehow, but it hadn't been. At fifteen, Jon had been my first kiss, and I his, but I'd known even then that his would be the only lips I'd ever want to kiss. We'd met in school – he'd moved to the coast from a town just outside London, and when he'd turned up late for the first class of the new term, he'd been given the seat beside me. I'd been annoyed, to begin with. I had been saving it for my friend Shauna, and almost refused to let him have it, but I hadn't wanted to be mean to a new boy, knowing how hard his first day would be. As it turned out, Shauna was off with the flu and never arrived, and by the end of that first class, any irritation at being seated next to a stranger had long gone.

He'd walked with me to our next class, and neither one of us had questioned that we would sit together. It had just happened. Within days, we became inseparable. He was charming, funny and confident, without being mean like so many of the other boys in my year. He had a way of looking at me that made my stomach flip and my face flush red, and right from that very first meeting, I'd known I didn't want him just for a friend. I'd never had more than a passing interest in a boy before him, but I knew this thing I felt for Jon was different. He made me feel seen, in a way I didn't think I'd ever experienced before, like he could look right into my heart and understand me on a whole new level. He got my jokes, laughing when everyone else shook their heads in despair. He read the same books as me, and he understood my passion for the sea. He loved to sail, though he was a self-confessed beginner, but his grandparents had taught him the basics as a boy and he'd spent his summer holidays visiting them in Bude and spending every waking hour either on the ocean or in it. He loved to swim, to surf, to always be on the move, but though he never seemed to stop, he did it all with a sense of calm control that made me feel safe.

I had taken him out with my mum and dad on our Bavaria Cruiser, a boat my family had sacrificed foreign holidays and luxuries to be able to afford in order to give us the freedom of weekends out at sea. The boat was my favourite place to be in the world, and to share it with Jon was letting him into my heart in the best way I could think of. We'd jumped off the side into the freezing water, splashing and racing through the choppy waves while Mum buttered bread and slapped together ham and mustard sandwiches, which we ate shivering under a rough towel, salt water still dripping from the ends of our hair onto our lips. We sunbathed on the deck, though Jon never made it five minutes without hopping up to assist my dad with a rope, an adjustment, loving the many little jobs that needed to be done throughout the day. My parents had liked him instantly, just as I had.

When I'd invited him to my house to watch a movie three weeks into the start of that magical school term, knowing I would have the place to myself all afternoon, I'd hoped he might tell me he could feel this thing between us too, but he hadn't needed words. The kiss had said it all. And we'd been together ever since.

It hadn't always been perfect, of course. There had been times where he'd pulled back, or I had, temptations and rows and challenges, periods when things felt too stressful to stay, but we always did, and despite the ups and downs, I'd never doubted that Jon would be by my side until we were old and grey. I loved the image I carried in my mind of us surrounded by our children and grandchildren, telling tales and sharing the memories we'd created over our lifetime together. Celebrating the twenty-year anniversary of becoming boyfriend and girlfriend had been something I was immensely proud of, and now, clearing up the remains of the buffet after the rest of our family and friends had left the garden party, I was exhausted but glowing with pleasure. I was so pleased everyone had been able to make it, my family travelling from Cumbria, Jon's from Cornwall. I'd wondered if we might have a hard time getting everyone here, but my dad had hired a minibus to transport my elderly relatives and most of Jon's had got the train, taking up a whole carriage and arriving tipsy and ready for a celebration. Everything had worked out like a dream.

Jon was leaning back on a lounger on the lawn, soaking up the final rays of the warm evening sun, and I dropped the tea towel I'd been using to mop up a spilled glass of water and padded barefoot across the soft cushiony grass, sinking down onto the lounger beside him, my leg sliding over his.

'What a gorgeous afternoon that was,' I said, closing my eyes and reaching for his hand, our fingers knotting together. 'I can't believe how great the kids were. William was in his element. Who knew he was a born host?'

'I know. His confidence seems to shine under his own roof. If only he was so brave elsewhere.'

I shrugged, opening my eyes and turning my face towards him on the sun-warmed cushion. 'He'll get there. Besides, I'm enjoying teaching him myself. He picks things up so quickly, it's actually really rewarding.' I smiled, listening to the guinea pigs squeaking in the run, bundling together to nibble excitedly at the plate of leftover salad I'd deposited in their bowl. 'Can you believe it's been twenty years since the day we decided to become a couple? We were barely more than children then. It's flown by, hasn't it?'

He nodded. 'Too fast. I wish we could do it all over again.' His hand tightened around mine, our eyes meeting.

'I don't. I'm looking forward to the next twenty. I think you'll go bald, you know,' I said in a teasing voice. 'And apparently bald men are very virile.' I laughed, expecting him to join in, but he didn't, and I suddenly worried I'd hurt his feelings. 'You know I'm only being silly, right?'

He nodded. 'You know I love you?'

'I love you too,' I replied softly, surprised by how serious he looked. He wasn't the kind of man to be introspective, but then this was a special occasion and there was a lot to be emotional about. He sighed and swung his legs round, sitting up on the edge of the lounger, his eyes meeting mine. I smiled, wondering if he was about to pull out some vows – promises and hopes for the next stage of our lives together. He looked down at his lap, and when he looked back up, I saw he was crying. I sat up, shaking my head, and reached for his knee with my free hand.

'Oh, babe!' I laughed, delighted to see this sensitive side to him. It had been such a happy day, it was hard not to feel emotional at how lucky we had been, how wonderful our lives were. We had a strong marriage, two beautiful, fascinating children, a small but comfortable home by the beach and wonderful friends and family who had spent the day retelling old stories about the times we'd shared together. I'd laughed until my sides hurt and I could hardly breathe, tears streaming down my cheeks, William rushing to my side to offer me a glass of water, fearful that I was choking when Jon's Uncle Basil had regaled everyone with the story of the first time he'd met me, in a country pub garden for Jon's mum's birthday.

I'd thought Basil would be scary back then, this older man with the thick steel-grey moustache and the tweed jacket. He'd had the deep, authoritative voice and look of a teacher – the kind that loved to shout an inch from your face. I'd reluctantly gone to introduce myself, having greeted everyone else at the table, but in my rush to get it over with, I'd slipped on the wet grass and gone over head first into the mud, grasping wildly as I fell and taking Basil down with me. The two of us had been covered from head to toe, our hair sticking out at wild angles, our faces crusted and filthy. I could remember the rumbling laugh that had emerged from deep within his belly, the roars of everyone else at the table as we tried and failed to get up from the slippery ground. Jon, laughing as much as we were, had come to try and help us up, only to fall and land on top of us in a heap. As it turned out, Uncle Basil was nothing to be afraid of.

I smiled, thinking of it now. It was hardly a surprise that Jon was looking the way he did: tired, tearful, intense. I felt overwhelmed and tired too, but in the best possible way. I squeezed his knee, smiling. 'Hey, you big softie. If you're like this now, just imagine what you're going to be like on the fifteen-year wedding anniversary next month.'

He met my eyes silently, and in the space of half a second, I knew something was terribly wrong. I could see a depth of pain in his eyes that made my heart hurt, the breath leaving me as his face seemed to crumple, his head turning away from me.

'Jon,' I whispered, leaning closer, cupping his cheeks in my hands, forcing him to look at me. 'What's wrong?' My words were strangled, choked, an icy fear spreading through me. Was he about to leave me? Was that what this was about? Surely not. Nobody could be so cruel as to wait for an occasion such as this to break that kind of news, and besides, we were Lily and Jon. We were never going to go our separate ways – it just wouldn't make sense.

'I'm so sorry, Lils. I didn't want to have to do this to you today. If I could keep it to myself any longer, believe me, I would, but it's become too difficult… I didn't want to tell you, not ever, I just couldn't bear to hurt you…'

'Jon?' I whispered.

'I'm so sorry,' he said again as tears rolled freely down his face.

I realised I was crying too, shocked at seeing him like this, wanting to comfort him, yet terrified that he was about to break my trust. My *heart*.

He wiped roughly at his face and took a deep, shuddering breath. 'There's no easy way to say it. I have cancer… it's called Hodgkin lymphoma. I found out two weeks ago and I thought I could manage this alone – keep you from finding out, but the treatment starts on Monday and I… I can't stand the thought of doing this alone. I need you to be there for me, Lils, to have someone to talk to when I come home from hospital. I wish I was strong enough to protect you from this, but I'm not.' He gripped my hand against his cheek, his eyes full of a fear I hadn't known he'd been hiding. 'I had to tell you. I just couldn't keep up the pretence any longer, because honestly, my brain is spinning with a thousand thoughts and questions, and if I don't share them with someone, I think the anxiety is going to make me lose my mind.'

I sat frozen, eyes wide, trying to absorb the words as they echoed around my brain, unable to make sense of any of it. I shook my head. 'You can't have cancer… you *can't*, Jon. You don't smoke. You barely drink. You go to the gym and you're not even forty, for Christ's sake!'

He looked at me sadly, his mouth twisting, and I knew just how ridiculous I sounded, grasping at straws as if I could find a loophole he hadn't considered. I bit down on my lip, feeling the panic rise in me, the desperate need to make him wrong somehow, because this couldn't be happening. Not to my husband, not Jon.

'How long have you known something was wrong?' I asked suddenly.

He looked down, and I saw the unmistakable flash of guilt in his expression.

'Jon!' I said, my voice sharp and accusing. 'You must have been worried? Had symptoms? How long have you been hiding this from me?'

He sighed. 'Six months. Maybe seven. It started with a pain in my stomach that wouldn't go away. I was more tired than usual. I had these shaking fevers in the middle of the night. I thought I might have picked up a virus, but something stopped me from going to the doctor. I think maybe deep down I knew it was something more serious.'

'You never said a word!'

'I hoped it would go away by itself. I tried to exercise more, eat better, get more sleep, but it didn't help. Nothing made a difference. I booked the doctor's appointment a month ago, and then I was referred for tests; it all happened so quickly. I wanted to tell you, but like I said, I couldn't stand the thought of hurting you, scaring you when I still hoped it would be something and nothing. I would have caused you pain for no reason. I couldn't bring myself to do that, Lils.'

'So, you just went through this alone? You got told you had cancer without any support?' The thought made a fresh wave of tears come to my eyes, and I pulled him close, pressing my face to his neck, a sob breaking free. 'Oh God, Jon!' I felt him hold me tighter, his strong hands rubbing my back, trying to soothe me. I pulled back. 'You should have told me... you should never have tried to manage this alone. I'm your wife! Of course I'm going to be there with you every step of the way! Promise me you won't keep any more secrets from me.'

'Hopefully I won't have any more to keep,' he said, his face grim. 'Look, Lils, I know it's a lot to ask, but can we keep this between us? It's hard enough managing as it is – I couldn't stand having to talk about it with everyone else, feel their sympathy, their pitying stares every time we meet. I had to tell you, but I don't want anyone else to know. I need to have some sense of normal to come back to when I'm not fighting this.'

'What about Hannah?' I asked, thinking instantly of the person who could help support *me*.

He shook his head. 'No. I'm sorry. I don't want you to have to lie to your best friend, but this has got to stay between us. I don't want to tell anyone. Not my parents, not the kids, not Hannah. It's too much to have to deal with their emotions on top of what we're going to have to cope with in the next few months.'

I pressed my lips together, understanding his point but wishing he hadn't asked it of me. I knew how hard this would be to hide from Hannah, how much I would need her support and strength as I gave every last scrap of mine to Jon, but if it was what he wanted, how could I refuse?

'Won't it be difficult to hide something this big?' I asked, hoping he'd realise how huge a challenge it would be. 'It's going to have an impact on our whole lives.'

He nodded. 'I know. Which is why I've already switched up my schedule at work, delegated the tasks I can trust other people with. I've looked into chemotherapy and it's going to be fairly easy to manage. It might have side effects that knock me out for a day or two each time, but nothing too awful, and in a few months I should be getting better.'

'You… you won't… die?' I asked, frightened to hear the answer but needing to know all the same. 'The doctors think you're going to beat this?'

He glanced down at his lap and I felt a jolt of fear travel through my body, clenching my stomach in a hard knot. 'Hodgkin lymphoma can be aggressive, but the doctors have said that it's one of the most highly treatable cancers out there. Nobody wants to be told they have cancer, in any form, but if I had to have it, this seems to be a good one to get. They told me I was more susceptible to it because I've had glandular fever.'

'Really?' I remembered it well – the month when he'd been laid up in bed and I'd been hardly allowed to visit and unable to kiss him the whole time. We'd been seventeen and it had felt like a lifetime. Everyone had said it was incredible I hadn't caught it too, that Jon would have been contagious for weeks leading up to him falling ill.

The memory of that first kiss after he got better had stayed with me all these years, the absolute relief that I had him back, the determination never to be parted again. It had made us want each other even more, and it hadn't been long after his recovery that he'd got down on one knee and asked me to be his wife. I'd always known that his illness had been a pivotal stepping stone in our relationship, the catalyst to us taking that next step and committing to each other completely. To think now that it could have weakened him without our ever knowing, bringing this awful thing into our lives, was shocking.

He squeezed my hand. 'They think it played a significant role, but honestly, it doesn't matter what caused it. All that matters is that I'm going to do everything in my power to get better.

And now that I don't have to hide it from you, I can put all my energy into my recovery.' He smiled. 'I promised I would grow old with you, didn't I?'

'Yes.' I nodded tearfully. 'You did.'

He leaned forward, kissing me full on the lips, and I could sense the relief in him at having finally unburdened himself of his heartbreaking secret.

'Well,' he said, leaning back and fixing me with a reassuring look. 'You know I hate to break a promise.'

He smiled, the confident, sexy smile I'd loved since I was fifteen years old, then pulled me into his arms. I looked over his shoulder to where William and Maisy slept peacefully beneath the stars and hoped he wouldn't have to.

CHAPTER TWENTY

Hannah

Then

I stared at the photo on the screen of my phone as the message from Jon popped up. He'd taken it the day before when I'd gone round to their house for lunch, Lily waddling round like a duck, her pregnant belly a constant reminder of how empty my own womb was. He'd caught the two of us side by side in the kitchen, about to wash up, and the message he'd sent alongside read: *Thanks for a lovely afternoon. We should do it again sometime.*

I twisted my mouth, wondering why he bothered to try and plaster over the cracks. In the past few months, as Lily's body had bloomed, the distance between the three of us had only grown more pronounced. I didn't want to let go of the hope that it might turn around at some point, but it was fast slipping away. Lily had taken Jon with her to the twelve-week scan, and then the twenty, and as far as I could tell, she'd managed to convince him that the child she carried was his. I wanted to speak to him alone, confront him with the truth, but I didn't know how, and though Jon and I got on well enough, we weren't close the way Lily and I were. And in any case, it wasn't my place to tell him.

I wished I could move past my suspicions, and maybe I would have let them slip to the back of my mind, but I knew that Lily's relationship with the man I'd seen was far from over. I'd seen him leaving hers on my way home from the office late one evening – long past the children's bedtime, with no sign of Jon's car anywhere. On the spur of the moment, I'd picked up some of her favourite foods from the supermarket, intending to drop them in, maybe have a catch-up and watch a movie together, but those plans had gone out the window the moment I pulled up outside. I'd watched from my car as once again they'd talked on the doorstep before sharing a long, emotional embrace. Lily had been crying when she pulled back, and he'd touched her cheek briefly before reluctantly getting in the now familiar red Honda. I had texted her that night with shaking fingers, furious that she could still be playing such a risky game, inviting her and Jon for brunch the following morning, trying to deduce if Jon was around, working late perhaps. When a text had pinged back saying that he was away for work and she couldn't make it either, I'd felt sick, sure that she had gone behind his back in his absence. The ultimate confirmation though had come when we'd been in the supermarket.

Lily had left the kids with Jon, and she and I had popped in to get some groceries for a picnic on the beach. I'd seen him first, the man in the suit, and recognised him instantly. I had stood frozen, feeling sure that I was about to witness an uncomfortable scene. I pretended to inspect peaches, casting surreptitious glances to the side as he approached, seeing the moment Lily recognised him. I don't know what I'd expected them to do, but I'd been surprised when she had smiled at him warmly yet briefly. He'd returned the smile, given a short nod of acknowledgement and then turned back down the aisle. Lily had bent over to pick up some loose bananas on the bottom shelf without watching him go, and I'd felt sure she was trying to make sure I didn't notice their interaction. Why would she do that if the man was a tutor to the children? Surely she'd say hello – introduce us. She'd been crying in his arms three nights before, and yet here she was acting like he was a stranger. It felt wrong, deceitful, and it only fed my suspicions further.

I sighed and glanced at the clock on the waiting room wall, the same magnolia paintwork and cherrywood furnishings that had surrounded me as I waited nervously for my first appointment all those months before. I'd considered changing to a different doctor after this one had been so patronising during my consultation, but Dr Larkin had changed his tune since I'd put him in his place, and I was determined to stand my ground and get the treatment I wanted rather than running away from him out of a sense of embarrassment. He knew now that he couldn't dominate me, nor make my choices for me, and since that first slip-up, he'd refrained from offering unsolicited personal advice.

I looked at the photograph again, running my finger along the curve of Lily's bump. She always carried so low and heavy, her body changing beyond recognition as the months slipped by. I knew she was uncomfortable, not sleeping well, struggling to eat without heartburn and nausea, even all these months in, but I couldn't feel sorry for her. I was too envious of what she had, her pregnancy a constant reminder of my failure. After months of trying, thousands of pounds down the toilet, heartbreak and disappointment and more tests, scans and doctor's appointments than I could keep track of, I was no closer to being a mother than I'd been at the start. Just being around Lily hurt more than I could even begin to describe, and lately I'd found more and more that I couldn't summon the strength to make myself call her, our meet-ups becoming increasingly infrequent.

'Miss Adams?'

I glanced up, seeing the receptionist, Joan, watching me from her desk. 'Dr Larkin will see you now,' she said, offering a smile.

I nodded, slipping my hand into the strap of my handbag and standing, dreading the chat I was about to have. In the past six months I'd had five failed inseminations – five wasted straws of donor sperm – and I was afraid that there would come a point when the doctor told me we would have to stop trying. That I was putting my body under too much pressure. I'd heard of other women being encouraged to take a break, come back in a year, focus on self-care and other things for a while. If that happened, I had no idea what I would do. I pushed open the door, walking into the now familiar office.

'Hannah, take a seat,' Dr Larkin said, his face breaking into a warm smile.

I slid into the chair opposite him and tucked my hands between my knees to stop myself from fidgeting.

'I've just been looking at your blood test results from last week.'

'Oh.' I glanced down at my lap, unable to bring myself to ask for the results. At the beginning of the process, I'd had a test to determine how many eggs I had left in order to assess my fertility and chances of conceiving. At the time, the numbers had meant very little to me, my head already stuffed full of countless other test results and important pieces of information I needed to retain, but when I'd been reminded of the test last month, Dr Larkin had reiterated that I was on the lower end of the scale for what he'd consider fertile. I could still recall the way my body had stiffened when he said he wanted to repeat the AMH test to see if there had been any change. 'At your age, Hannah, it's possible for fertility to decline quickly. Since you've had five unsuccessful inseminations, it's important to see where we stand.'

I'd agreed readily at the time, wanting to do everything in my power to figure out the problem and find a solution, but now, I realised, I wasn't prepared to hear the answer. I'd deliberately blocked it from my mind since leaving the clinic with a bruise on my inner elbow and a sick feeling in the pit of my stomach, and refused to even google the consequences of a lower egg count in the days since, not wanting to destroy the last scrap of hope

I was clinging to. Now, though, I could see from the way Dr Larkin's defined dark brow knitted over his blue eyes, his fingers steepling beneath his chin, that I was about to hear something I'd rather not.

'It's not terrible news, Hannah, but it's not exactly what I would have hoped for. In an ideal world, you would have remained at a similar count as we saw in the previous test, but I can see from your results that in the six months since your first consultation, your egg count has reduced. Now it's certainly nothing to panic about – in my professional opinion, you still have time, and pregnancy is far from impossible for you. However, I believe you should use that time wisely and maximise your chances of conceiving, and with that in mind, I would recommend IVF.'

'IVF?' I repeated, trying to absorb his words. It sounded like bad news, but he was acting like there was still a chance, and if he wasn't prepared to give up, neither was I. I tried to remember if I knew anything about *in vitro* fertilisation. IVF was a term that everyone seemed to know, but I couldn't admit to having much insight about what was actually involved. One thing I did remember was that it was expensive, unless you could get it on the NHS. I asked if this was possible, and he shook his head.

'Not for a single woman unfortunately. And to be honest, the wait would be long and time isn't on your side. I'm afraid your only option is to continue with private treatment – that is, if you have the finances to do so. We can start this cycle if you choose to go ahead.'

I nodded, silently tallying up the amount I'd already spent. Every test, every appointment cost a fortune, and though I had savings, they were fast disappearing. IVF was only going to chip away at them more, but could you put a price on your dream? I didn't think so.

'Will I have to have hormone injections?'

He nodded. 'I'll give you all the information to take home with you, give you a chance to think about it. I know it's a big decision, Hannah.'

I took the stack of leaflets he passed me but shook my head. 'No,' I replied, my voice confident and strong. 'There's no decision to make. If this is what I have to do, I will.'

I'd been feeling deflated, powerless against the tide of unrelenting failure that had continued to knock me down since the beginning of this journey. But now, I felt like I might burst with the new-found surge of hope that had been offered to me. At last I had something I could do, a way to support my body and make the leap to where I wanted to be. I had no doubt that the next few months were going to be difficult, but I was committed to this. I would do it, whatever the cost. I would get my baby.

CHAPTER TWENTY-ONE

Lily

The floorboards creaked beneath my bare feet as I snuck quietly out of William's bed, tiptoeing across the carpet. I froze halfway to the door, waiting to see if the sound had roused him from his sleep, and breathed a sigh of relief when he didn't stir. He'd been especially clingy over the past month, since Jon and I had sat him and Maisy down to explain that another baby would be joining our family. He hadn't said much, but I could tell that he was worried. He had never liked anything that rocked his routine, and this would be a big change for all of us.

This time last year, I'd finally got to the stage where I could read him a bedtime story then leave him to drift off alone, but now we were right back to square one, and I was finding it increasingly difficult to lie with him until he fell asleep. His single bed was no support for my growing belly, and each time he went quiet and I began to think he had finally given in to the pull of sleep, he would break the silence with another question, wearing my patience down in incremental chips. I sighed now, looking at my watch, hoping I hadn't missed my chance to read to Maisy, then padded along the hall, dipping my head around her door, my heart soaring to see her lying awake on her bed, talking in character as she held two of her soft toys above her in a role play. She stopped as I stepped into the room and I instantly felt as though I was interrupting.

'Hey, sweetheart. Sorry I took so long. Your brother was a chatterbox tonight.'

She looked down at the toys in her hands, distracted. 'It's okay,' she replied. I couldn't tell if she meant it, or if she was quietly disappointed. I always found her so hard to read and was wary of jumping to conclusions.

'Shall I read you a story now? It's late, but there's still time. I could get in bed with you and we can have a cuddle?'

She shook her head. 'Daddy already read me one.'

'You could have two? A treat?'

'Thanks, Mummy, but it's okay. I'm too tired.'

I nodded, unsure what to do. I wanted to stay, to talk to her, hear her thoughts, or even just hold her close. I'd been trying so much harder to strengthen our bond since finding out I was having another baby, determined not to let it slide now. I refused to let my daughter feel as if I was replacing her. They'd told us at the scan that it was a girl. I had nodded wordlessly, unsure what to say, how to find a response. I didn't know what I felt, let alone how to process what was happening. Most of the time I tried to keep focused on the present moment; it was the only way to keep sane. And some nights, I had felt the walls beginning to break down between Maisy and me. I had tried coming in to spend time with her before going to see to William, but it never worked. His need to have me to himself pushed Maisy out, and I knew she wasn't prepared to have to fight for my attention. And why should she? She deserved my full focus, and I'd done my best to carve out time for the two of us to be alone each night. But I could feel her dismissal tonight, and I didn't want to push my company on her if she didn't want it. I had to respect her boundaries and back off when she needed her own space.

'Okay then, sweetheart.' I adjusted her covers and stroked her hair back from her forehead, giving her a kiss. 'Maybe tomorrow then. I'll let you get some sleep.'

'Night, Mummy,' she replied.

I switched off her lamp and headed out onto the landing, feeling strangely hollow, despite the gentle rolls and kicks of the baby growing inside me. Wrapping my hands around my bump, I closed my eyes and leaned my head back against Maisy's closed door. I was exhausted. Overwhelmed both physically and emotionally. There was no question in my mind that this had been the hardest of all my pregnancies, the aches and pains far worse than any I'd experienced before. I had been diagnosed with pelvic girdle pain, which made it difficult to walk without wanting to bite down on something hard, shooting cramps travelling down from my lower back into my thighs, the spasms continuing night and day. I'd had sickness on and off for months now, and I had no idea how I was going to meet the needs of three children when this one made her arrival.

The idea that I might have to do it alone was one I'd refused to think about ever since Jon's revelation about his cancer, but it was getting harder to ignore that crippling fear, despite my best efforts. He'd promised it would be a matter of months before he was back on his feet, but every time I asked him if he was nearing the end of his treatment, he gave me some non-committal reply that filled me with dread. It had been seven months since we'd held each other in the garden, his promises that he would get better falling soft against my ear, and the longer it went on, the more afraid I became.

The trips to the hospital hadn't reduced. He had bottles and bottles of pills he swallowed multiple times a day. He never wanted to talk about what had happened at his appointments, how the chemo had gone or if the doctors had done more tests, telling me that all he wanted was a sense of normality: to watch a movie on the sofa together, walk to the beach or chat about the children.

We'd sold our first boat just after William was born, intending to buy something a little bigger, but we'd never replaced it, and now, I craved the sea with every waking breath, longing to get out alone on the open ocean, to clear my head, if only for a few hours. Jon insisted we'd get another one someday, but someday felt an eternity away and I resented that he was refusing to give me this one line of independence. I felt trapped, suffocated by responsibility and cut off from his pain, as if I didn't deserve to be in his inner circle. Despite his initial claims that he wanted someone to share his fears with as he navigated his way through his recovery, it hadn't panned out that way. Instead, he had formed a protective bubble around the subject and he refused to let me close enough to pop it. It made me feel isolated and lonely, even when he was right beside me.

Recently I'd found myself waking in a cold sweat, reaching for him in the darkness. He slept so deeply some nights, and others not at all. So many nights he'd woken to find me shaking him, having been unable to find a pulse, my panic that he'd slipped away from me while I dared to close my eyes radiating through me, making me sob with relief as he held me close, whispering reassurances.

That day in the garden, he had told me that he would get better, that the medical team supporting him through his treatment had given him every reason to be hopeful, but that didn't stop my mind from jumping to the worst possible conclusion. When I woke him, desperate for answers, he would chuckle into my hair, telling me to calm down, he was getting fitter by the day, it would all be all right. There were thousands of types of cancer and Hodgkin lymphoma was one with a high recovery rate. He reminded me of this time and time again, but if I tried to probe deeper, ask more, he would change the subject instantly. And despite his words of comfort, I had begun having a recurring nightmare that I was sleeping next to a corpse, a dream I'd been unable to talk to him about for fear of upsetting him.

I prodded my belly, giving a small smile as I felt the responsive press of a tiny foot in reply, and went to my bedroom, intending to get undressed and run a bath to soothe my aching muscles. I stopped with a jolt as I saw my husband already fast asleep in the bed, though it wasn't yet 9 p.m. Watching him from the doorway, I forced myself not to look away. To acknowledge the changes in him. They were subtle, but knowing him as I did, they were impossible to mistake. The newly shaved head that anyone might guess was down to fighting off balding rather than the poison of the chemotherapy. The way his once full cheeks now sank into the hollows of his skull. The weight loss that made him look so much smaller than the strong, powerful man I'd married. Jon had always been a tank, and though he still had the broad shoulders of the man I recognised, his frame looked stripped bare.

I wished I could talk to Hannah about what was happening to him, the struggles he refused to accept any support with. He insisted he was doing well, that the treatment would get him back on his feet in no time and there was no need to cause anyone else distress by sharing his news now, all these months on. He considered it a private matter, and knowing how much my silence meant to him, discussing it would have felt like a betrayal. I didn't think it fair to complain that *I* needed someone to talk to, a shoulder to cry on and express my fears to – not when he was still managing to work, albeit on a reduced schedule, and travelling back and forth to hospital so often.

Since he wouldn't allow me to tell our friends or family, the only remaining choice had been for him to make those trips alone, which I hated and frequently complained about. I couldn't stand the thought of him going through all that without someone there to comfort him. We'd been together for twenty years; he'd been by my side at the birth of our children, nursed me through several bouts of flu and countless stomach bugs. I'd waited on him hand and foot the summer he broke his leg slipping on the deck of my parents' boat, and applied cream to his blisters when he came back from trekking some far-off jungle or mountain. We'd always been a team, *always*, but now it felt like there was a chasm opening up between us. I knew he was trying to keep me at a distance to protect me, and that made me angry. I deserved better. I didn't *want* to be shut out from his pain and struggles – that wasn't what it meant to be married. I wanted to be allowed to be there for him as I always had before, and the more he pushed me away, the more I felt a sense of resentment and abandonment growing inside me.

He hadn't shared any details, but I wasn't an idiot. I knew he must be suffering horribly. Each time he went for treatment, he would spend a night at a hotel afterwards so as not to let the kids see him feeling the side effects. I felt constantly torn between my desire to continue to do what he wanted and my own wishes.

I turned from the bedroom door, going to run the bath, needing a bit of time to just wallow in the warm water before I had to get up and do it all again tomorrow. I stripped off my jeans, pulling my phone from my pocket, swallowing back the wash of hurt when I saw that there was still no reply from Hannah to the message I'd sent three days before. I hadn't seen her in two weeks, and I missed her. I felt like everything was off balance without our friendship to keep me steady, and part of me was angry that she'd chosen now of all times to pull back from me. I needed her more than ever, but she had no idea what was happening to me, to Jon, and as much as I longed to, I couldn't tell her. Like everything else in my life, the friendship I'd always held so dear was slipping away from me, and I was powerless to pull her back.

I stared at the water rising up the edge of the bath, my vision blurring as I watched the ripples on the surface, and thought how ironic it was that I had a husband, two beautiful children and another on the way, and yet right now, I was more lonely than I'd ever been in my life.

CHAPTER TWENTY-TWO

Hannah

'I can't believe she's already outgrown these,' Lily exclaimed, holding up a minuscule cotton Babygro and shaking her head. We were sitting on her bedroom floor, the carpet tickling the backs of my legs as we sorted through the stack of newborn clothes, Lily keen to take advantage of the rare child-free time while Jon was out taking all three of them to the beach. Each item, every tiny sock or doll-sized vest, looked precious to me, and I stared in disbelief as Lily shoved them one by one into a bin bag, no trace of emotion on her face.

It had been two months since she'd given birth to her beautiful daughter Ella, and though I'd found it almost impossible to be around her during those last few months of her pregnancy, her blooming body reminding me of everything I was struggling for, now things were different. There was still a wall between the two of us, the undeniable knowledge that we often skirted around issues, guiding one another onto softer, more palatable subjects. I sometimes found it difficult to believe that I'd been through so much this year and Lily, the woman I loved like a sister, hadn't been by my side to support me. I could never have guessed there would come a time when we felt like strangers, and the longer it went on, the more I lost hope that we could get back what we'd had before. I had been conveniently busy during her final trimester, making excuses not to visit as often as I dared, but now Ella was here, the draw was irresistible.

I was pulled to her like a magnet to steel, needing to see her, hold her, carry her compact little body in my arms. I didn't want to put her down, and Lily seemed not to mind, content to take her from me for feeds before handing her back, sleepy and milk-drunk. I felt a visceral need to be with her, and sometimes I worried that my desire for a baby was making me act in a way that could be considered unhealthy.

Jon, seeing my powerful attachment to Ella, found it amusing that she had captured my heart so fully, and made constant jokes about me getting broody and how it would be my turn next. I knew he didn't really mean it. He and Lily were both so wrapped up in their own lives that they hadn't seemed to notice how much mine had changed – my long evenings out with colleagues replaced by early nights in front of the television, my once full weekends now used to catch up on sleep and squeeze in the work I'd failed to do when I'd been too nauseous during the week. The IVF had wiped out my energy, bringing with it a whole host of symptoms that made any thought of a social life impossible. Even coming here was a struggle some days, the call of my bed hard to ignore, but it was worth it to see Ella. I knew Jon was only teasing; he could never have guessed how much truth there was to his words, how deep his light-hearted banter cut, each remark a dagger to my heart, but even that couldn't stop me from coming back.

I wished I could confide in Lily, tell her all I'd been going through, though I knew she'd be shocked if I did. I'd held back, unwilling to share my secrets after she'd turned away from so many opportunities to tell me her own. She refused to be drawn into anything like the kind of deep talks we'd once shared. I wondered if maybe my telling her about the IVF might be the key to breaking down her walls – one of us had to be the first to be brave. Be vulnerable. But as the months had passed and small talk became a habit between us, I stopped looking for ways to broach the subject of my desire to have a baby. The pain of living through one failed attempt after another was too raw, too difficult for me to voice out loud, and Lily was still as distracted as ever.

I hadn't seen the man in the red Honda again, but I knew that didn't mean anything. Jon had been around more, working abroad less often, and his presence made the strain between the two of them impossible to ignore. They both looked worn down and jaded, and Jon had lost weight. He was always making green smoothies and skipping dinner, going for swims in the sea and talking about its healing properties. I hoped he didn't feel he had to do it to win Lily's attention back. He shouldn't have to go to such extremes, and personally, I thought he'd looked better before the so-called health kick. What was wrong with a dad bod when you were in your mid-thirties anyway? I thought the whole point of marriage was unconditional love, not having to become someone you weren't to keep your partner from straying. I often wondered how much Jon knew, if he had any idea what Lily had been up to in his absence.

Lily picked up a tiny sleep suit, stretching it out across her lap. She took a breath, and for just the briefest moment, she looked almost sad. It humanised her and I was glad to see the flicker of emotion. It was nice to know that these things did actually have some impact on her. She glanced up, finding me watching, and shrugged. 'I guess I won't need this anymore. It's mind-blowing how fast it all goes. Really makes you see how little time we get.'

I nodded. 'It passes in the blink of an eye.'

She sighed, and then seemed to pull herself together, crumpling the little sleep suit into a ball and adding it to the bin bag, then tying the top in a knot. 'I'll take them to the charity shop tomorrow. At least it makes room for all her new clothes. Maisy's not impressed. I've told her she'll have to share her room once Ella's old enough to leave ours.'

'That's going to be hard on her. I know how much she loves her privacy.'

'She does, but we can't afford to move, and besides, maybe it will do Maisy good to have some company.'

'Other than Mr Cranky the cat?' I teased, seeing the instant grimace on Lily's face at the mention of Fluffy.

'Yeah, that plan certainly didn't go as we'd hoped. I knew we should have just stuck with the guinea pigs, but Jon said he wanted something she could chat to at night, confide in, and a dog was out of the question. I'm still hoping Fluffy will simmer down and we'll see a less feral side to him.' She picked up the black bag, bundling it on her crossed legs. 'But to have a sister is a special thing,' she continued, her voice thoughtful. 'Maisy might not see it now, but in time, they'll be close. And sharing a room will be a way to fast-track that bond.'

I nodded, hoping Maisy wouldn't retreat into herself even further at the intrusion of a new little person invading her space. I had a feeling it might not go as smoothly as Lily would like. I cocked my ear, hoping to hear Jon returning from the beach with the three of them, desperate to see Ella and get a cuddle with her, but there was no sound from downstairs, and I knew that if I didn't leave now, I wouldn't be prepared for my meeting on Monday.

I'd fallen behind with my work in recent months, and now I felt like I was constantly playing catch-up, having to cram in paperwork and plan presentations at weekends and late into the evenings. I was grateful for the distraction, but I was reaching the point of burnout, and I knew that sooner or later, something would have to give. I stood up, holding my hand out for the bag. 'Here, I'll take those to the charity shop for you. It's on my way and you've got enough on your plate.'

'You don't mind?'

'Course not.' I smiled, and for a second, she smiled back and I felt a glimmer of that old connection between us. I opened my mouth to speak, but she glanced away, handing me the bag and clambering to her feet.

'I'll see you out,' she said, following me to the bedroom door. 'I still can't believe you have to work on a Sunday. That can't be fair.'

We walked down the stairs and I paused by the front door. 'It's my own fault for letting things pile up. And I've taken on a new contract that I couldn't miss out on, when I probably should have passed on it.'

'You should learn to say no sometimes.'

'You're right.' I nodded. The truth was, I knew my absences at work had been noticed. The IVF had caused more side effects than I'd anticipated, not to mention all the back and forth to the clinic every month. I'd had crippling sickness and nausea, which stung considering how desperate I was to go through *real* morning sickness. All the fun with none of the benefits, it seemed. My designs had been lacking their usual flair, my creative spark having fizzled under the pressure, the hormones and mood swings making everything that much more difficult. And the exhaustion was sometimes so extreme I could barely get out of bed. I knew that this afternoon I would have to battle against my desire to head to the bedroom for a long nap when I should be working. I was so damn tired all the time, and no matter how hard I tried to juggle everything, I always seemed to drop a ball one way or another.

I'd had to take out a loan to have a second round of IVF when the first hadn't worked, and I was constantly fretting about the possibility of pushing my luck too far at work and losing the income I *did* have. I was starting to worry about money in a way I'd never had to, my savings no longer the buffer I'd been so confident about. Every last penny and more had gone into this dream, and now I knew I would bankrupt myself before stopping. I'd come too far to quit now. But losing my job, or having my responsibilities at work cut, would drive a knife right into those dreams, and I couldn't let that happen, so when Eloise had asked me to take on the extra workload, I'd said yes instantly, even knowing I was barely coping with the strain as it was. I couldn't let myself become replaceable.

I gave Lily a brief hug and headed to my car, throwing the bag of baby clothes on the passenger seat.

The drive home was short, and when I pulled up outside my flat, I switched off the engine and stared at the bag, trying not to feel guilty that I'd deliberately avoided the route that passed the charity shop. I picked it up and carried it inside, heading straight to the sofa without even bothering to take off my shoes.

I tipped the clothes onto the cushions and was rewarded instantly with the heady aroma of newborn skin, that fresh, powdery, milky smell that made me feel calm and happy in a way nothing else could. I sat amongst the mound of white and yellow and pink and green, sifting my hands through it, picking out tiny booties, little hats, soft brushed-cotton vests and dresses, bringing them to my face and holding them reverently against my cheek. I could feel the ball of emotion lodged in my throat. The fear, the longing, the need pulsing and squirming inside me. It was all I wanted. A baby of my own. When I'd started this journey, it had almost been a whim, but not now. Now I would be prepared to give up everything if I could have this one gift. One child. It was worth any price.

I held a little vest against my face and felt the tears I'd fought so hard all morning begin to fall. There was a chance I might not be able to make this happen. That the money would run out and my body would continue to fail me. I'd never backed down from a challenge before, but there was only so far hoping and wishing and working hard could get you.

The rest was out of my control, and I didn't know if I could accept that.

CHAPTER TWENTY-THREE

Lily

Now

I probably shouldn't have been driving. My body felt shaky and depleted from hours of surging adrenaline, and I could feel my heart palpitating uncomfortably against my ribs, the sensation making me all the more anxious. I squinted against the glare of the lowering sun as it hit the rear-view mirror, making black spots appear in my vision as I searched for an empty parking space. I hated having to park this tank of a vehicle, always looking out for the biggest space possible to manoeuvre it into. I'd got stuck on more than one occasion halfway through a turn in the road, or a tight parallel park, only to realise I didn't have the space I'd been used to with my old compact Fiesta. Whenever I drove with William, it was worse – trying to move in incremental fragments with him offering his sage advice from the back seat was always guaranteed to raise my blood pressure to dangerous levels.

A delivery van vacated a space on the opposite side of the road and I swung into it, twisting to glance over my shoulder as I reversed. The sight of Ella's car seat made me freeze, my foot slamming hard on the brake, pressing it to the floor, as I felt the panic ignite inside me, picturing my tiny baby daughter as she cried for a mother who couldn't get to her. I felt severed in two, and until she was back in my arms, I knew nothing would make that feeling go away.

What if I never get her back? The thought caused an audible moan to escape my lips, and I squeezed my hands on the steering wheel, digging my nails into the soft rubber. My throat felt thick, my mouth dry, my head spinning with all the awful things that could have happened to my child, and I knew I was on the verge of a panic attack. I closed my eyes, willing myself to calm down. I didn't have time for this, I couldn't fall apart – not now, not when I had to keep going, to do everything in my power to find her.

A sudden sharp beep ripped me away from my thoughts, and I looked up to find that I was only half parked, the front end of my car sticking out into the road, blocking the oncoming traffic. An irate-looking woman stared at me, pressing down on her horn again and gesturing for me to move. As I edged the car backwards, making space for her to pass, I caught a glimpse of three small children in the back, talking animatedly, holding up colourful magazines to show each other. I stared after them with a feeling of empty longing, wondering if that woman might have been calmer, more patient, more understanding if she only realised how lucky she was. How many times had *I* been in that same situation, rushing from one task to the next with William chattering incessantly, winding Maisy up, Ella crying for a feed the second we hit traffic? How many times had I wanted to scream out loud, to just get out of the car and run as fast as I could in the opposite direction? If I'd seen this coming, would I have made the time to appreciate what I had without thinking constantly of the future? Of what I might lose? I couldn't say for sure.

I clambered out onto the pavement and walked down the narrow side street that led to Hannah's flat, noticing the changes that had taken place in my absence. A house that had been repainted from top to bottom, transformed from its original crumbling beige to a pretty teal colour; a little corner shop now standing where an art café had once been. How much time had passed since I'd last visited? For years, we'd had a standing arrangement for me to come to Hannah's for a movie and popcorn every other Saturday when Jon was home to look after the children. It had been a chance for me to have a break and for us to catch up without distractions. A time we'd both looked forward to, and yet I couldn't even remember the last time we'd done it.

I walked towards Hannah's block of flats tucked away at the end of the no-through road, fronted with wrought-iron fencing and a small garden filled with plants. The building was rendered white and looked safe and inviting, and I knew Hannah had been bursting with pride the day she'd exchanged on the two-bedroom flat, picking up the key and inviting me round to the bright clean kitchen to crack open a bottle of champagne. It had been such a big moment for her, being able to put down a deposit and afford a mortgage off her own back and hard work, and though I'd been ecstatic for her, it had been a reminder of how little I'd achieved when it came to my own professional life.

I held up a hand to shield my eyes as I looked up at her window on the second floor. It was open wide and that made no sense to me. Why would she have left it open if she had no intention of coming back? I glanced left and right, hoping not to catch sight of any police, anyone watching surreptitiously from a nearby window, but there was no one around. I was half grateful for the privacy, and half irritated that they weren't waiting here just in case she returned. How could they expect to find Ella without covering all bases?

I marched up to the main door, still gripping my keys tight in my palm. Flicking through the bunch, I found the spare and inserted it into the lock, then glanced over my shoulder one last time before stepping into the cool interior of the hall. I pushed the door closed behind me and jogged up the stairs to Hannah's flat.

I let myself in and stood in the silence of the place, feeling uncomfortable there in a way I never had before. It was a modern open-plan space, with huge sash windows looking down on the shared back garden and a sleek white kitchen leading onto a sunny dining area. Across from that was the sitting area, where Hannah and I had spent countless hours lounging on her wide squashy sofas watching romcoms and laughing like we were still teenagers.

Only nothing here was as I remembered.

It felt cold, empty somehow, and I realised that half of her stuff was missing. I dropped my bag on the floor, walking through the kitchen. The countertops were empty, her state-of-the-art coffee machine absent, her combination smoothie maker and juicer gone. Her antique oak dining table and chairs had disappeared, the space once so inviting and homely now bare and cold. The fridge was still covered in photographs, and I reached out, snapping up a picture of her holding Ella, Maisy leaning over her shoulder with a rare smile on her face. The photo had been taken at the beach only a few weeks before – I could remember Jon promising to forward it to her. I stared at the image of my baby daughter, my skin crawling with need... with fear.

Placing it down on the counter, I turned from the fridge, walking towards the living area. The sofas, old and worn, were still there, but the widescreen television was gone, as was the Blu-ray player, the quirky collection of tables and lamps she'd collected on her travels over the years, and the hand-woven rug she'd never let me walk on wearing my shoes. I looked to the shelving unit behind me and saw that her record collection was missing too. It didn't make sense. It was too neat for a robbery. Nothing was broken, nothing out of place. Just missing.

I walked silently into her bedroom and saw that her bookshelf was still brimming with the trinkets she'd always treasured. Her set of Enid Blyton books passed down to her from her mother, dog-eared and well loved, remained piled on the top shelf, next to the homeware design award she'd received from a prestigious studio in Paris, given to her for a unique and beautiful range of curtains and window dressings. I had gone with her to the ceremony and drunk countless glasses of ice-cold champagne, cheering loudest of all when she went up to collect the sleek golden trophy. The picture of her parents on the deck of their boat, smiling widely as the sun set behind them, was still in its usual place on her dresser.

None of these were things she would have left behind if she'd planned to kidnap Ella. She would have taken them with her. They were worth nothing in financial terms, but they meant the world to Hannah. I frowned, opening drawers and cupboards, finding them still jam-packed with clothes, though I couldn't see as many in her wardrobe. Her designer coats were missing, and most of her handbags too.

I squatted down beside her bed, reaching under it to see if they'd been moved. My hand collided with cool hard plastic and I slid out a purple storage box, yanking off the lid. As I looked down at the contents, my heart seemed to freeze in my chest.

I reached down slowly, my fingers trembling, and plucked an item from the top of the pile. I fell back, slumping against the wall, as I recognised it. The storage box was filled with baby clothes, and in my hand was Ella's old vest. I brought it to my face, breathing in the scent of her, feeling the tears pool in the corners of my eyes. 'Oh, Hannah,' I whispered, gripping the vest tighter. 'What have you done?'

CHAPTER TWENTY-FOUR

Hannah

Then

'Hannah, grab that bag for me, will you?' Lily said, pointing to the changing bag on the floor by the armchair I'd just sat down in. I'd been at the house half an hour, and honestly, I was beginning to feel like hired help. Lily hadn't asked how I was, how work was going, what was new with me, and though I wanted to be patient and understanding, it was hard not to be offended by her lack of interest in anything other than her own problems. I tossed the bag across the living-room carpet towards her and she took it without a word of thanks, pulling out a tiny white nappy and a thin rainbow-coloured mat, placing her two-month-old daughter down onto it.

I stared at the baby with a feeling of longing deep inside me, then turned my face away, picking up my glass of water as Lily unbuttoned her vest. A part of me knew that I was only this irritable and sensitive because of the cocktail of hormones I'd been pumping into my body recently. On top of the necessary daily injections that were required as part of the IVF process, and which sent my body spiralling into a hormonal nightmare, there was also the background fear that it wouldn't work. The first try hadn't. I'd been so elated when I'd heard that four viable embryos had been created from my harvested eggs and the straws I'd paid for from the sperm bank. Four potential babies, four chances when I only needed one to work.

I'd told Eloise I was working from home as often as I could in the weeks leading up to the implantation, and then, when I'd been given the news about the successful embryos, I'd taken the decision to have two weeks' leave. I wanted to relax, sleep, take gentle walks and do everything in my power to increase my chances that one of those precious eggs would successfully implant.

At the start, Dr Larkin had told me that there could be up to fifteen embryos, but I hadn't been disheartened. Four was plenty. I'd spent weeks thinking of babies, sometimes waking with a smile having dreamed of twins or even triplets. The idea that more than one might take hold was overwhelming, but I knew I would be up to the challenge. I wanted it. I would have loved multiples, but I wouldn't have been disappointed with one.

But none... not a single embryo successfully implanted? That was something I hadn't wanted to consider and had not been prepared for, despite the warnings of the nurses, the advice to keep in mind that pregnancy was not guaranteed. I couldn't understand what I was doing wrong, and it made me angry with my body, filled with a boiling vat of self-hatred and loathing that was entirely new to me.

The second attempt had produced just three viable embryos, and again none of them had taken hold. Lily had been eight months pregnant at the time, and seeing her glowing and full with the life she carried had broken my heart. I'd done everything I could. Tried my best to keep rested, to try and think positive, but it hadn't made a difference. Hearing that news for a second time had been even harder. Now there was a pattern forming, and I couldn't ignore it, could no longer manage to hold on to that last shred of hope. I felt numb, though each time I looked at Ella, a cascade of emotion hit me like a landslide.

It would be another week before I found out the result of this third attempt. There was a chance I could be pregnant right now.

Just the thought of it made me wrap my arms protectively around my stomach, closing my eyes as I tried to visualise a spark of life inside me, sending out a silent wish to the universe.

I hadn't got my hopes up, hadn't dared to dream, but that didn't stop me wishing. I didn't want to give in to negative thinking and doubt, but it was becoming harder not to feel deflated... defeated. Time and time again I had been crushed by the weight of my disappointment. I kept going, pushing forward, but the strain of working so hard for a goal that never materialised was exhausting, and right now, being ordered around by Lily, watching her act like she had the weight of the world on her shoulders when she had more than any woman deserved, was making me want to shout and cry and storm out so I didn't have to see how fucking ungrateful she was.

She finished changing Ella's nappy and lifted her up, pressing a quick kiss to her forehead before passing her to me. I took her without hesitation, holding her reverently against my chest. 'Suits you,' Lily said, flashing me a wink. 'You should give it a go someday, Han. You'd be good at being a mummy,' she added, picking up a Duplo train from the carpet and dropping it into the children's toy box.

'Thanks,' I muttered, blinking back the onslaught of hot moisture in my eyes, focusing on Ella's face, my jaw clenched. I stroked a finger through her silky soft hair, wishing Lily would just go away and let me enjoy this moment in peace. Lately, I craved solitude constantly, but when I was home alone, I drove myself crazy with thoughts of my future, spending hours online trying to find some magic way to get pregnant. I'd never expected it would be this hard.

I had struggled to sleep since starting the IVF, and Dr Larkin had joked that it was good practice for night feeds, which had made me break down in noisy uncontrollable sobs, right there in his office. He wasn't the person I'd have wanted to turn to for comfort, but he was the only one who knew what I was doing, the battle I'd been waging against my own body all this time, and I'd been unable to hold back any longer, desperate to just let myself be vulnerable for once and voice the fears I'd kept inside that had tormented my every waking thought for so long. All the emotions I'd been hiding from Lily, Jon, my family, my colleagues had poured out with frightening rawness, and once I'd let it start, I'd been unable to stop it.

Dr Larkin hadn't said much. He hadn't needed to. I wasn't looking for anything from him other than a listening ear, and as I talked and sobbed and exposed my deepest fears to a man I'd once disliked, he'd sat still and let me keep going, without meaningless placating words or any sense of discomfort on his part. As it turned out, he was quite good at listening when the occasion called for it.

Leaving the clinic that day with mascara-stained eyes and a balled-up tissue clutched tightly in my fist, I'd gone home feeling numb and exhausted. The big cry should have helped – made me feel calmer somehow – but it hadn't. Other than seeing a positive pregnancy test at the end of this month, I didn't think anything could take away this dark cloud that had settled over me. Well, perhaps with the exception of a cuddle with Ella.

I smiled down at her, watching her wide eyes as she stared up at the ceiling, her tiny hands in a constant state of motion as she opened and closed them, balled them up and then stretched her fingers out up above her. She was fascinating to watch, so innocent and sweet, every part of this world brand new to her. Lily bustled around the room, talking incessantly but never saying anything worth hearing, her constant small talk irritating me.

I heard running footsteps on the stairs and looked up as Maisy rushed into the room, closely followed by William. 'Mummy, William keeps taking my teddy and he won't leave me alone.'

'I just wanted to look at it! And you need to share,' William replied. 'Mummy, isn't that right? Sharing is important.'

Lily sighed. 'Were you playing with it, Maisy?'

'She wasn't!'

'William, let Maisy tell me,' Lily said, looking at her daughter.

I watched, hopeful that for once she wouldn't side with William. He knew that the more he complained, the more easily he could wear her down. Maisy shrugged, looking down at her pink socks, and I wished I could hug her. 'It's mine,' she said softly. 'And William will break it.'

'No I won't!' he said, clearly offended. 'I promise I won't.'

Lily turned from the two of them, resuming her tidying as she piled loose toys into the chest. 'Then William can have a turn. As long as you're careful with it. In this house, we share,' she said, her voice firm and unapologetic.

I saw Maisy's face crumple, her eyes trained on the carpet as William rushed past her, his feet thundering on the stairs as he headed uninvited back to Maisy's room. I was so angry I could taste it, and I stood up, moving towards the Moses basket and placing Ella down, not wanting her to feel the depth of my rage. I moved automatically to Maisy, wrapping my arm tightly around her shoulders, and when she looked up at me, I could see the sadness etched into her features.

'What kind of lesson is that?' I demanded, turning to Lily.

Lily paused. 'What? Sharing?'

I shook my head. 'No, Lily, this isn't about sharing. It's about control. You know as well as I do that William doesn't give a damn about playing with that teddy. He only wants permission to play with it to prove that he can, and to get one up on his sister. And Maisy, who values her private space and a few special toys above everything, is told that she can't even have that. That she has to hand them over to her brother, who you know as well as I do has broken more of her things than I can count. You aren't respecting her personal space and you're not being fair.'

'It's okay, Auntie Hannah. I'll just go outside in the garden until he's finished.' Maisy offered a small smile and walked out of the room.

Lily watched her go, then turned to face me. 'I'm doing my best, Hannah, and she wasn't even playing with it.' She folded her arms. 'And in future, I'd prefer if you spoke to me about these things in private. Maisy didn't need to hear that.'

I shook my head, holding back the urge to shout, unapologetic that I'd spoken up. Maisy deserved to know that someone had noticed her struggles and was prepared to stand up for her. I couldn't help but think of how *I* would have valued an adult to take my side, be an advocate to me whilst growing up. I knew it would have made a world of difference to have someone show me they cared, even if it wasn't my own mother. Maisy had needed to hear me defend her. I was only sorry I'd been put in a situation where I'd had to do it. Taking a deep breath, I managed to speak at a reasonable volume. 'You don't get it, do you? You really don't see?'

'See what?' she snapped.

'You're oblivious to how much more she needs from you. She's quiet, but that doesn't mean she doesn't need all the same things William does. But you use it as an excuse to ignore her. Even now, I bet you won't go and speak to her.'

'What's brought this on? If you think she's upset, why don't *you* go and speak to her? You'll see that you won't get anything out of her. She's fine, Hannah, honestly, this isn't a big deal. This kind of disagreement happens here daily, and believe me, I don't always take William's side. Look, go and find her and you'll see for yourself – she'll already be playing with something else.'

I shook my head and picked up my bag. 'I have a job, Lily. I don't have time to parent your children for you.'

She opened her mouth, then shut it, biting back whatever comment she'd been intending to throw at me. She rubbed her temples with her fingertips as if all this conversation about parenting was too much for her to deal with. 'I thought you were staying for lunch?'

I shook my head. 'Not today. I have to go.'

She frowned. 'Okay. But call me later. And, Hannah, please don't worry about Maisy. She's stronger than she looks.'

I nodded, my mouth tight as I walked to the door, feeling Lily's eyes on me, not daring to speak again for fear that I might say something I couldn't take back.

CHAPTER TWENTY-FIVE

I walked through the car park towards my office, sighing with relief as I headed through the double doors and into the blissfully cool interior. The summer had been long and hot and I'd been struggling with the heat ever since beginning my hormone injections. I nodded to the receptionist, Luella, seeing she was on the phone, and she flashed me a smile, blowing me a kiss with her free hand. I smiled back, the feeling alien and unexpected, and reached up, touching my fingertips to my mouth, a warm glow spreading through me, a happy secret brightening all the colours around me, my blood fizzing with hope.

The doors for the lift opened as I approached, and I walked straight in, feeling like the world was finally on my side today. I got out on the third floor and walked through the hall into the open-plan office, heading for my desk by the floor-to-ceiling window that looked out over trees and blue sky. I could appreciate the beauty of a summer's day when I could look at it without melting into a puddle.

Dropping my bag on the desk, I sank into my chair. It was still early, and it looked like I was the first one here, which hadn't happened in months. I hoped Eloise would walk through and see me here, raring to go. It would give her a boost of confidence about my dedication to the job.

I rifled through my bag, pulling out the stack of post I hadn't yet had a chance to open and which had been accumulating on the table by my front door all week. I hadn't had the energy to look through it, studiously ignoring it every time I came home, half tempted just to throw the whole lot into the bin, but this morning I felt ready to tackle it head on.

There was a postcard from an old colleague, Craig, who'd recently retired and was now sailing around the Med with his wife, making the most of his free time. It was nice to think of them sipping sangria on the deck beneath a hot afternoon sun, though I found it hard to picture Craig properly relaxing. He'd never been the type to laze about of a weekend, always needing a project, something to keep him occupied.

I put the postcard down, moving on. Next in the pile was a bank statement, then three bills and a reminder about the overdue payment for the second of the two loans I'd taken out. My confidence faltered, my instinct to push them aside – shove them in the shredder even – flaring once again, but the responsible part of me couldn't allow such reckless behaviour. I picked up my letter opener, slicing open the envelopes one by one, forcing myself to look properly at the figures, the ridiculous interest rate I'd agreed to in a moment of desperation, the raw truth of the terrible state I'd got myself into.

Other than my mortgage, I'd never been in debt before. Loans, in my opinion, were for people who put off their responsibilities for a future date, people who hadn't thought of the consequences. And now I was one of them. I bit my lip, trying not to worry about how tight I'd stretched myself. Every penny of my savings was gone, and the loan repayments were sapping my wages every month, making it impossible to rebuild that nest egg. I'd asked the bank if I could remortgage my flat, but the request had been refused, and if I was honest, I'd been an idiot to think they would even consider it with the state of my finances right now.

I'd cancelled everything I could live without – the TV packages, my subscriptions to magazines, my sailing club membership. I'd sold everything of value, collecting the pennies and storing them with care, constantly aware of choosing the frugal option, never buying anything that wasn't completely necessary. Outside of work lunches, I hadn't been to a restaurant in months, let alone bought a coffee, instead packing cheap sandwiches made from own-brand bread and fillings. I made my fennel tea in the kitchen at work rather than going off to Costa with the gang. If I was careful from now on, I would just about dig myself out of this hole without ending up on the streets. But there would be no more chances. No more money for donor sperm or IVF – I had put everything I had into this. The thought should have devastated me, but instead, I smiled secretly to myself, my hands pressing lightly against the silk shirt tucked into the waistband of my pencil skirt. I closed my eyes, imagining the frenzy of activity working away inside my body, silent and secret. This time felt different.

It had been three days since I'd stormed out of Lily's house in a rage after the sharing incident. She'd sent a casual message I'd yet to reply to, not mentioning the fallout but inviting me to go to a theme park with them the week after next so that she could take the big ones on the rides whilst I held Ella. I'd agreed after a quick moment to think. A theme park wasn't the easiest place for me to be when the sight of happy families had the power to set me off in floods of tears, but I would have Ella to keep me focused and she would give me an excuse not to go on the rides – I couldn't possibly do any of those!

I wondered if next time we met, I might have news of my own to share with Lily. Would I tell her right away, or wait until the twelve-week mark? It seemed a long time to hold on to such a big secret, but then I'd had a lot of practice with hiding things this past year. Lily would be speechless, I thought, smiling. I still had four days to go before I could take a pregnancy test, but I had already begun to feel something change inside me. My mouth tasted of metal, my breasts were swollen and tender. I had sensations of pulling and tugging low in my abdomen, as if my body was already beginning to stretch in order to accommodate this new visitor. This morning, I'd had to push the fried egg on my toast aside, the smell of it making me queasy. Every new symptom gave me a burst of pleasure, and for the first time in as long as I could remember, I felt confident. Sure of myself.

A flurry of activity at the door caught my attention, and I shoved the bills back in my bag and looked up smiling as a handful of my colleagues came in chattering loudly. Ryan stopped at the front of the group, clapping his hands together in front of his chest and giving a squeal of delight. 'Hannah! You're back,' he exclaimed, making a beeline for my desk. 'We've missed you so damn much. Where have you been?'

I smiled, noticing that his hair was dyed in wide stripes of orange and purple this week, spiked up with copious amounts of gel. He perched on the edge of my desk, and I shrugged. 'Just getting stuff done at home. You know how everything seems to pile up and you never have time to do it.'

His brow arched. 'You could have hired someone to do the boring shit and taken yourself off to the Maldives for a nice break. I would have.'

I grinned. 'You're probably right. Next time.'

Ashley, a blonde-haired blue-eyed designer who still looked nineteen despite being well into her forties, appeared by Ryan's side. 'Hey, gorgeous,' she said, smiling at me warmly. 'Good to have you back in the crazy house. We missed you.' She held out a box, opening the lid for me to peer inside. 'Blue cheese breakfast muffin? The café over the road has started doing them, and I can't get enough!'

Ryan laughed. 'She's not even kidding, I've seen her eat three this morning already! You wouldn't believe the amount of food this woman can put away.'

Ashley shoved him playfully with her shoulder and held the open box towards me. I shook my head, feeling smug. I couldn't eat blue cheese, not if I was pregnant. It was on the list of banned foods that might be harmful to the baby. 'I already ate, but thanks for the offer. They sound… interesting.'

'If you change your mind, come and find me.'

'You'll need to be quick, mind, or she'll have devoured the lot,' Ryan added, flicking his hair and flashing me a wink as he strode towards his own desk.

I turned to my computer with a grin, feeling like the old Hannah. I hadn't realised quite how much I'd missed since starting out on this quest for a baby, but it felt great to be present, able to smile and listen to everyone talk and not have my mind on some far-off place in the future. Although chatting with my colleagues and actually doing some work were two very different things.

I fired up my computer, my hand fluttering to my belly once again. I wanted to take a test now. There was one in my bag, but I refused to give in to the pull of it. It would only be a disappointment to see that negative result, a consequence of not waiting the full two weeks. I had to be patient. I couldn't pinpoint why, but I was convinced I was carrying a girl. I could almost sense it. I would have been over the moon with either, delighted to have any baby my body was prepared to carry, but having bonded so tightly with little Ella in her short life, I had to admit, I loved the idea of a daughter of my own.

'Hannah?'

My head snapped up, my fingers hovering over the keyboard in an automatic pretence, wanting to be seen to be working. 'Eloise, hi,' I said, seeing her standing by the door to her office.

'A word?' she asked, not waiting for an answer as she turned, disappearing through the doorway.

I pressed my lips together, trying not to let my nerves take over. Breathing in deeply, I stood, walking purposefully towards her office, my head held high. Ryan and Ashley offered sympathetic smiles as I passed them, and I wondered suddenly if there had been gossip about me during my absence. I hoped not. I would have liked to think we respected each other too much for that.

I stepped through Eloise's door, closing it behind me, and took a seat without waiting to be asked. She tossed a pile of papers into a drawer and fixed me with a piercing look. 'Hannah, it's good to have you back. Did you go anywhere nice?'

'No.' I shook my head. 'Just a couple of weeks of relaxing and getting stuff done at home. We travel such a lot for work, I didn't fancy navigating flights and airports during my free time,' I said, improvising.

She nodded. 'And how are you? I mean really?'

I shrugged. 'I'm fine. Raring to go.'

'Right. It's just that before you booked this leave, I noticed that you'd been working from home more often than not. And you passed on the Rome trip and the Madrid meeting to your colleagues, which is most unlike you. Are you becoming less enamoured with the job?' She raised a questioning eyebrow, leaning back in her brown leather office chair.

'Absolutely not. Not at all. I didn't want to say anything, but there was a bereavement – an old family friend – and I was feeling a bit emotional and burned out. I know it's out of character, but I just needed to work somewhere quiet, to concentrate without any distractions, you know? But I'm feeling fine now. And I apologise if I caused you any inconvenience,' I added, though I felt irked that after working myself to the bone for so long, I was being penalised for a few weeks of slacking off. I had stayed late every week since I got the job, and had never once uttered a word of complaint. But I didn't say any of that now. I couldn't afford to.

Eloise nodded. 'I wish you'd told me. I could have helped you reorganise your schedule. I'm very sorry for your loss.' She clicked her pen against her teeth. 'But you're back now. And I take it you'll be in the office and returning to your normal routines from here on in?' Her face was warm and smiling, but there was a warning behind her words. I was skating on thin ice. This was a career I was privileged to have, and she wanted to remind me of that.

'Yes,' I said quietly. 'I'm glad to be back.'

'Good.'

I stood, sensing her dismissal, and she picked up her phone, already dialling with lightning-fast fingers. I walked back to my desk, determined not to lose the job I'd worked so hard for. I would need it to support my baby when she arrived. And with any luck, I thought, excitement buzzing through my veins, that wouldn't be long at all.

CHAPTER TWENTY-SIX

Lily

Now

I could still smell her on the soft cotton, my daughter's newborn skin permeating the fabric, filling me with emotions I didn't have time to give in to. I gripped the material tightly, wondering what Hannah was doing with it, why she'd failed to take the old clothes to the charity shop as she'd said she would. It didn't make sense. None of this did.

I pushed myself up to stand, needing answers, and with Ella's tiny vest still gripped tightly in my fist, I spun, moving towards Hannah's chest of drawers. I yanked the top one open, dropping the vest as I pulled piles of clothes out, throwing them aside. I had no idea what I was looking for, but I needed something to help me understand what was happening. Why had Hannah, my best friend, who had never shown the slightest interest in becoming a mother, suddenly become obsessed with *my* daughter?

I froze abruptly, my hands gripping the edge of the drawer, as I replayed the three months since Ella's birth. Hannah, who'd been conspicuously absent during my third trimester, had reappeared in our lives days after Ella's birth, without so much as an apology. I'd accepted her excuses about work, shoving aside my hurt that she hadn't been there for me. I'd been angry that she couldn't see how much pain I was in. I couldn't tell her about Jon – I'd sworn to him that I would keep his secret – but shouldn't my best friend have known there was something desperately wrong? Ella's arrival had only heightened my fears, though Jon had continued to tell me I was worrying over nothing, but taking care of three children had stretched me to my limit and frayed my nerves.

I hardly slept, and I was constantly letting my imagination wander to terrible scenarios. What if I developed an illness too? I was well aware of the strain I was under, the relentless pressure to get through each day, to meet everyone else's needs. What if I couldn't take care of my children? What if after all this time fighting to get better, Jon relapsed? Who would care for our babies then? I drove myself round in circles in the depths of the night, lying in bed staring up into the darkness with tears streaming down my face, desperate to be able to share my pain with someone, to be talked down from this anxiety-ridden panic.

Hannah should have seen how deeply I was hurting, kept pushing until she guessed the answers I was unable to give, but instead, she'd taken the opportunity to enjoy her freedom, and now I realised she'd been keeping secrets from me too. I hadn't given any thought to her regular visits, simply relieved to have her back in my life, though our relationship still wasn't the same as it had once been. I hadn't questioned why she was always willing to hold Ella, feed her a bottle while I dealt with things around the house, come over after long days in the office to sit with her so I could cook dinner. I thought it was her way of showing she cared, wanted to help, even if she seemed more and more distant. Who doesn't enjoy a snuggle with a newborn? It had seemed perfectly ordinary to me at the time, but looking back now, it felt sinister. Had she been obsessing over Ella since the beginning?

I moved to the wardrobe, shoving aside the hangers, the dresses and skirts, my eyes scanning the space frantically. Reaching up to the shelf at the top of the wardrobe, I moved a basket of silky scarves aside, my hand colliding with something hard. I stood on tiptoe, pulling the cardboard box file forward, easing it down and dropping it onto the bed. I didn't hesitate as I sat down on the mattress, pressing the black plastic clasp down and pulling the box open. It was the kind that was separated by twenty or so transparent pockets, and I looked closer, reading the tabs, frowning as I pulled a sheaf of papers from the first one, spreading them across the duvet. I screwed up my face, lifting a piece of paper, reading the smart turquoise logo.

'Bournemouth Fertility Clinic?' I muttered, scanning the page, seeing Hannah's name clear as day printed at the top.

I picked up another sheet, reading quickly, then another, and another. Dates and times, appointments scheduled, invoices, information. Donor sperm. IVF. Genetic testing. The pile grew bigger as I sorted through the reams of paperwork that contained a secret I had never even begun to suspect. Hannah had never wanted my life. She'd told me that before, said she couldn't imagine giving up the travel and the dinners at expensive restaurants for sleepless nights and tantrums in the supermarket. But when was the last time we'd even broached the subject between us? She'd clearly changed her mind somewhere along the line.

I glanced at the letter on the top of the stack, seeing the date printed above the appointment for an initial consultation with a Dr Larkin at the fertility clinic. It was scheduled for over a year ago. Before I'd even conceived Ella. Hannah had kept all of this to herself for so long.

I slid my hand into the next section of the folder and pulled out a pile of bank statements, scanning them in horror. I saw the dwindling savings pot, the loans, the final demands from the bank. Hannah was in trouble, and had been for a long time. She'd never once come to me. Never asked for help, support, though I'd have been there for her in a second. She was clearly desperate.

I felt tears begin to pool in my eyes and realised this was so much worse than I could have possibly imagined. Hannah had done everything in her power to have a baby, that much was clear, and when it hadn't succeeded, she'd taken mine.

Terror gripped my heart as the reality set in. She wanted a baby enough to give up everything she had, including me. And now that she had her in her grasp, she wasn't going to bring my daughter back.

CHAPTER TWENTY-SEVEN

Hannah

Then

The smile froze on my face as Dr Larkin met my expectant gaze with a resigned shake of his head. I couldn't understand his solemn expression. 'I'm sorry, Hannah. You did everything you could. We all did, but on this occasion, I'm afraid it hasn't worked.'

I clasped my hands to my belly, staring at him in bewilderment. 'I don't understand…'

He sighed. 'The pregnancy test was negative.'

'But…' I shook my head, certain that there had been some mistake. 'I've been queasy every morning for the last ten days. I'm emotional and off my food and my breasts are swollen, for Christ's sake!' I cried, grabbing them as if to prove my point, feeling the unmistakable twinges and tenderness. 'I'm not imagining this. I'm not!'

'I'm not saying you are, Hannah. But my guess would be that your hormones are a bit haywire right now. You've put your body through a lot this past six months, and I'm not surprised you're getting these kinds of symptomatic responses. I know how difficult this is for you to hear – believe me, it isn't the news I was hoping to give you today. But you aren't pregnant.' He scratched a fingertip on the steel-grey patch of hair above his ear. 'It doesn't mean you won't ever be.'

'Repeat the test.'

'Hannah—'

'I want you to do it again. You're wrong. You must have got the dates mixed up. It's just too early or something.'

He looked at me, his expression full of a sympathy I didn't want to see. 'I *could* do it again, but it will only cause you more pain. Look, take some time out. Give your body a break from all the hormones, the stress you've been under, and spend some time focusing on taking care of yourself. You can revisit this in six months – a year even.'

I stood abruptly, my chair falling backwards onto the floor with a clatter. 'You know I don't have that kind of time.'

He glanced down at his desk, and I saw the guilty expression, felt sure that he was only trying to placate me with empty promises. He knew just as well as I did that there would be no more chances for me after this.

'I'm so sorry, Hannah. I did all I could.'

I turned wordlessly, walking out of his office straight past the reception desk without stopping, though I could hear Joan calling me, not wanting me to leave without paying my bill, still set on fleecing me for every last penny. I strode out onto the pavement, slamming the door wide, hearing the satisfying crack as it hit the wall. He was wrong. He couldn't feel what I felt. Only a woman could understand this feeling, this beautiful secret shared between a mother and her unborn child. The daughter I had longed to meet for so many months now. She was there. I couldn't let myself doubt it.

I crossed the road, narrowly missing being hit by a car, holding my hand up in a show of apology as I ran across to the other side, heading into the pharmacy. I scooped up a whole row of pregnancy tests, then, catching the price ticket, put them back, choosing two of the cheapest. I knew they all worked the same way. The result would be identical; it just wouldn't come in fancy packaging. I still had the one in my bag I'd been waiting to take too. I'd planned to take it later today after my trip to the clinic, after Dr Larkin had confirmed the pregnancy first. I'd been too afraid to do it myself, not wanting to upset myself with a false negative result if I took it too soon. But I thought it would be nice to keep to show to Lily when I finally revealed my secret.

I paid for the tests and shoved them into my handbag, walking purposefully to my car. The moment I was inside, I pulled out my phone, navigating to Google and searching for local private ultrasound clinics. If Dr Larkin wasn't going to bother looking fully into the situation, then I would have to take the matter into my own hands. I found a clinic within ten minutes' drive of my flat, and winced when I saw the price of an urgent early pregnancy scan. Biting my tongue between my teeth, I pressed dial and waited for the receptionist to answer. I ignored the fear inside me trying to break free as I booked an emergency scan for an hour's time, managing to stutter my thanks to the man on the phone who'd squeezed me in at such short notice, then dropped the phone in my lap, leaning my head against the wheel and trying to steady my frantic breathing.

He was wrong. He was wrong. He was wrong. Please, *please* let him be wrong.

A minute later, feeling only slightly less shaken, I typed the clinic address into my satnav and turned the key in the ignition. I made the twenty-minute journey on autopilot, my mind spinning.

The clinic car park, when I arrived, was empty. I pulled into a space, and then, as if I'd been holding on the whole journey, threw open the car door and vomited onto the tarmac below. I sat back, breathing hard, and wiped my mouth with the back of my shaking hand before rifling through my bag for a tissue and some gum. I paused, my hand resting on the tests, staring at them, then closed the clasp of my bag and climbed out of the car, stepping over the puddle without looking directly at it.

The clinic was sparsely decorated – white peeling paint and cheap IKEA furniture, nothing like Dr Larkin's place – but I didn't give a damn what it looked like. Only that they could prove him wrong. The nice man I'd spoken to on the phone was still at the reception desk, and he checked me in with a kind smile that made me have to blink back tears. I knew I must look a complete basket case; no doubt most women who rushed in here for an emergency scan were much the same. We all wanted the same thing – to keep our babies safe and do whatever we could to protect them. He directed me to a row of plastic chairs and I sat down, feeling fidgety.

My eyes fixed on the sign opposite for the toilet, and I stood up, making an incoherent sound as I walked towards it. Inside, I bolted the door and pulled the three plastic-covered boxes from my bag, unwrapping them slowly, not needing to bother reading the instructions. I held all three in one hand and squatted over the toilet, closing my eyes. The receptionist had told me over the phone that I should come to the scan with a full bladder, but I couldn't wait another second. I had to see for myself.

I placed the tests down on their respective boxes and stared into the mirror, waiting for what felt like the longest two minutes of my life. I'd taken tests before, but never had one felt so crucial, so monumental. I looked at myself in the cheap rectangular mirror, seeing a terrified woman on the brink of losing everything. Where had the professional, capable version of Hannah Adams gone? Shaking my head, I gripped the edge of the sink.

Suddenly I couldn't wait another second. I looked down at the tests, reading each one in turn. Negative. Every one of them.

'No,' I whispered, my hand reaching out towards them, unable to touch them for fear it would cement their decision. I pressed my hands to my middle. There was something in there, there *had* to be. With a flash of white-hot anger, I swept the tests, boxes and all, off the side of the sink and into the open-topped waste-paper basket, then opened the door and headed back to my seat, staring at my knees as I tried to hold back the onslaught of tears simmering just beneath the surface.

A door opened somewhere along a hallway behind the reception desk, and I looked up, hearing voices, my heart thudding erratically against my ribs as a heavily pregnant woman smiling from ear to ear came into view. At her side, holding her arm supportively, was a beaming man, a strip of black-and-white photographs clasped between his fingertips. He held open the door for her, and I watched, for the first time thinking how much easier this would be if I had someone to lean on. Someone who wanted this as much as I did to hold my hand and tell me it was all going to be all right.

'Miss Adams?'

I stood instantly, my hands curling into fists around the strap of my bag. A nurse with a neat grey bob and narrow glasses held out her arm, indicating for me to follow her, and I nodded, finding I couldn't speak, couldn't swallow against the dryness of my tongue. I walked silently into the dimly lit room, dropping my bag on the chair beside the bed.

'So, how many weeks pregnant are you, Miss Adams? As you might be aware, before six or seven weeks, it's too soon to be able to detect a heartbeat, so we always like to caution our ladies so as to prevent unnecessary worry.'

I nodded, feeling suddenly stupid that I'd forgotten this vital piece of information. It had only been sixteen days since I was inseminated, which by the strange set-up of pregnancy calendars translated to just over four weeks pregnant. It was possible I would see nothing and fly into a panic when I had no reason to. 'Six weeks,' I heard myself lie.

'Exactly six weeks? Every day counts at this early stage.'

I nodded.

'Well, it's right on the borderline, and it may still be too early to detect the heartbeat, but you'll be able to see the yolk sac in there at the very least. It won't resemble a baby quite yet, though. What was your reason for booking the scan? Have you had any spotting? Pains?'

I shook my head. 'Just for reassurance really...' I faltered. 'I had a friend who experienced an ectopic pregnancy and lost one of her tubes. I just need to know everything is where it should be,' I lied.

'I can understand that. Let's have a look then. When you're ready, climb up here and roll up your top, okay? I'll need you to pull your trousers down a bit too. What we'll do first is try to pick the baby up through your tummy, but it may be that we need to use an internal scan to see what we're looking for. Is that okay with you?'

I nodded, climbing up on the table, feeling the familiar anxiety that I'd learned to associate with being in this position. The nurse pressed a few buttons on the monitor, then pulled on a pair of blue gloves and squeezed the ultrasound jelly over my still flat abdomen. I noticed she'd turned the monitor so I couldn't see it; instead, I had to stare up at the ceiling as she moved the wand across my skin, making little murmurs of concentration. After a few moments, she leaned back, passing me a handful of paper towels. 'No sign of the little bean here. We'll have to go for the internal, if you still want to proceed?'

'I do.'

'Right. Pop your trousers and underwear off and you can put this over you for a bit of privacy,' she said in a professional tone, handing me a blue blanket and turning her back, stepping behind a divider that blocked me from view.

I shuffled out of my clothes, folding them in a hurried ball and tossing them towards the chair where I'd left my bag. I arranged the blanket over my legs, ignoring the mounting queasiness that threatened to peak for a second time.

'I'm ready,' I said quietly.

'Lovely. Let's have a peek then, shall we?'

She worked quickly and efficiently, and I closed my eyes, waiting for her to tell me that everything was as it should be. I knew it was too early, but there might be *something* there, a sac, some evidence of my baby, even if it was too soon to see a heartbeat. She gave a tut, and I opened my eyes to see her frowning.

'One moment, love,' she said softly. She smiled, then rose from her stool, heading for the door, and I heard a muffled conversation taking place in the corridor.

'I'm just bringing my colleague in to take a look,' she said brightly. She was too cheerful, her words robotic, practised.

A second nurse came in. She was younger than the first but still older than me, her brown hair plaited over one shoulder in a girlish style. 'Are you happy for me to take over?' she asked, her voice gentle, as if she knew she was about to deliver news she didn't want to have to give.

I gave a short nod, unable to speak, and leaned my head back against the paper towel covering the pillow, waiting desperately for a noise, a sign that they had seen her at last.

Eventually she slid the wand out of me and patted my shin. 'You can cover yourself up now.'

'But... I didn't get to see...' I pulled the blanket tighter around my lower half, sitting up, coming face to face with the two of them.

'I'm so sorry, sweetheart, but it doesn't look like there's a baby after all.'

'I... I've had a miscarriage?'

'I don't think so, no. There's no sign that anything has been in there, and you've not been bleeding. I think, on this occasion, there's been a mistake. Did you take a test?'

I stared at her, unable to answer, my thoughts snapping to the three tests in the bin down the hallway, their results strong and unambiguous, though I'd wanted so badly to prove them wrong. 'Are you certain?' I whispered as tears began to fall, splashing heavily onto the blanket, turning patches of cotton from light blue to dark.

'I am. I'm so sorry.' She sighed. 'We'll give you some privacy to get dressed. Is there anyone I can call for you?'

I shook my head, stunned, and they left quietly, closing the door behind them as if there had been a death. But there hadn't been.

All these weeks I'd convinced myself it was finally happening. That after pouring everything I had into this, I was finally going to have a baby of my own, to hold, to love, to share my life with and show her the world. I knew I'd come for the scan early – too early, perhaps – but I could no longer keep pretending to myself that there was still a chance. The tests should have been enough to convince me, but I'd been so stubborn, put myself through this heartbreaking experience because I hadn't wanted to believe it was true.

It was over now. This had been it. The last chance. By the time I rebuilt my savings pot and paid off the loans, I would have lost the last remaining window of my fertility. I wasn't going to be a mother. Not ever.

With an anguished cry I had no control over, I let my head drop to my knees and gave in to the shuddering sobs, the grief that I'd been trying to brush off all day. My dream was over, and there was nothing I could do about it.

CHAPTER TWENTY-EIGHT

Now

I stood over the bed, watching Ella sucking at her tiny pink fists in the depths of sleep, my heart thudding at the realisation I'd just had. I could take her away somewhere, *keep* her… I had to. I'd burned my bridges now, and besides, the idea of getting to stay with Ella – be a mother to her – was intoxicating. It was everything I wanted in the world. She was my only chance.

Lily's image burned brightly in my mind's eye, and I blinked it away, pressing my hands to my face, my thoughts jumbled and confused. There was a part of me that knew I wasn't in my right mind at this moment. It was as if I'd stepped into some psychological thriller and was going through the motions of the kidnapper. But this was different. I wasn't out to harm anyone. I loved Ella. And if I was honest with myself, I loved Lily too, despite the cracks that had formed between us in the past few years. I would never have chosen to hurt her, but it was too late for that now, too late to undo my impulsive actions and brush it all under the carpet. And given the chance, I still wasn't sure I would take it.

The crushing reality was that I knew this was my last chance. Without Ella, it was over for me. There would be no baby, no family of my own. I'd given it everything I had, every scrap of my energy, all my hope and every penny I'd earned and then some, and none of it had made the slightest difference. I'd been prodded and poked, had multiple people crowding round my naked lower half while my legs were spread open on stirrups, things inserted into me while I closed my eyes and waited for it to be over. I'd had hormone injections, blood tests, so many needles I'd lost count, and all of it had been a waste of time. Nobody could give me a reason for my repeated failure to get pregnant. Dr Larkin said my fertility was dwindling, but I'd had viable embryos during the three rounds of IVF I'd done. My eggs could make a baby. They just wouldn't stick, and each time I had to hear that news, I felt a piece of me break off, my heart hardening against myself, disappointment so visceral I could taste it.

I always told myself not to get my hopes up, but it was impossible not to. That two-week wait was a curious cocktail of dread and excitement. But it was over now. There was no more money. Three days ago, Dr Larkin had sat me down and told me that I should take a break, give my body a rest, make time to do normal things without putting all of my energy into this. He'd made out like this time to press pause was a good thing, but I'd heard the hidden meaning behind his kind words, seen the way he'd looked at me as he said goodbye. He hadn't expected to see me again.

I bent down, carefully scooping the sleeping baby into my arms. She snuffled, her face rubbing against my T-shirt, her eyes flickering, before she lost the fight and let herself sink back into a deep sleep, her head lolling against my shoulder. She was so tiny, so very precious to me. I couldn't believe how oblivious Lily was, how she couldn't see how lucky she was. Time and again I had watched her palm Ella off on me or Jon. I'd seen the total lack of emotion on her face as she went through the motions, feeding and changing her, doing the bare minimum as if it was enough. It wasn't. Not by a long way. She'd never wanted Ella, and now that she was here, I felt sure her feelings about that hadn't changed.

She didn't even want poor Maisy. How many times had I seen her take William's side over her daughter's? Maisy needed more – she needed support, an advocate to demonstrate how to stand up for herself in this world, but Lily had been anything but a good example, always choosing the easy path, never having the energy to get into a conflict or be the leader her children needed. I hated sitting by helplessly watching her go about her duties with a martyred expression on her face, failing her girls and complaining about William and his clinging, intense behaviour every time he left her side. She didn't see that it was her own fault he was like that, how the fact that she always gave in and pandered to him had made him lose empathy for anyone else.

I'd tried to talk to her about it, but she never wanted to hear it, and I was sure the real reason was that she just couldn't be bothered. And her long love affair with Jon had clearly fizzled now, leaving her wanting more, looking outside the home for a spark, for romance. How could she put herself before her family, seek her own selfish pleasures without a second thought for the harm she was causing to everyone around her? She wasn't the woman I'd thought she was.

I cuddled Ella closer, feeling sick with nerves. I could *not* give her back to a mother who didn't appreciate her. Ella deserved better.

CHAPTER TWENTY-NINE

Lily

Then

'And so then,' Maisy said, her face animated, 'William turned into a purple balloon and was floating up into the sky and the balloon had a face and he was smiling and shouting about how he'd always wanted to fly, but *I* wanted to fly too. Then I got a sudden thought and I spun around ten times and jumped as high as I could, and when I looked over my shoulder, I had sprouted wings and I could fly even higher than William! And my way was better too, because balloons don't come back down.'

'You really do have the best dreams,' I exclaimed, smiling at her. Our foreheads were almost touching as we cuddled together on her single bed. 'I always forget mine straight away, but you could write a book about yours.'

'I like dreaming. I feel like I'm someone different in my mind.'

'Different? From what?'

She shook her head, her eyes sliding away from mine, not quite ready to let me in that far. 'Just different.'

I smiled, not put off by her reluctance to talk.

During the last few months of my pregnancy, and after Ella's birth, I had stuck resolutely to my goal of spending more alone time with my eldest daughter before it was too late. There had been evenings, plenty of them, when all I'd wanted to do was crawl into bed and sleep after a long and exhausting day. Jon was still managing to work, heading off on trips for weeks at a time, and when he was home, he was often too tired to be much help with the bedtime routines. There were evenings when William had refused to go to bed or Ella had decided she wanted to feed for longer than usual, or when Maisy had needed to be alone and had turned me away at her door, but despite it all, I had never faltered over my promise to myself. I'd made a commitment to do better, be the parent she needed, and though we were still a long way from her opening her heart to me and showing me the real Maisy – the Maisy who came out in her dreams – we'd come on in leaps and bounds in the past six months. Now she knew to expect a visit from me, an offer of whatever she needed – a story, a cuddle, time to talk or ask questions. Sometimes we just sat together in silence, me stroking her hair as her eyelids grew heavier.

It was something I would never have considered doing before. She was six, not a baby, and she always seemed so independent that it would have felt silly to suggest she might want company to go to sleep. But as it turned out, she often did. I hadn't known how much she would cling to those special moments, how my sitting in silence, just being there for her in a way I'd never found the time to in the past, could become the foundations of us building a very different relationship from the one we'd once had. It seemed Ella's arrival was exactly the motivation I had needed to push myself to try that little bit harder.

After seeing that positive pregnancy test, I'd been desperate to connect with Maisy before another baby arrived, taking up my time and energy. I could see now that if I'd let things continue as they had been back then, she would be even more of a stranger to me now. But those months together, learning to understand one another, had established a stable footing that had given me the confidence to parent her. Even when I was pulled in every direction by each of them, I knew she trusted me enough to interrupt the chaos, to be sure that I would be there to listen to her, even if I didn't always take her side.

Now she shuffled further under her quilt, and I smiled, recognising the subtle signs of drowsiness in her face. She'd told me everything she wanted to, and she was ready for sleep. I felt her reach for my hand, her small fingers encircling mine as she snuggled against my side. 'Goodnight, sweetie,' I whispered. 'I hope you have lovely dreams again.'

'Night…' she murmured. 'Love you, Mummy.'

'I love you too.' I watched her eyes drift closed, traced her smooth cheek with the tip of my finger, so grateful that I had never given up trying.

Leaning back against the headboard, I let my thoughts move to Hannah, the way she'd lashed out verbally in defence of Maisy when I'd let William play with her teddy the other day. Her outburst had come out of the blue, and it had hurt me more than I wanted to let on. After the progress I'd made in my relationship with Maisy over the past year, to be told that I never considered her feelings, that I was letting her down, had stung. If we'd been in a stronger place, had more time to break down our walls, maybe I wouldn't have let Hannah's accusations faze me. I would have been more confident in my relationship with my daughter. But they *had* fazed me. And it had bothered me that Hannah, my best friend in the world, would suddenly point out all my supposed failings.

When she'd left, I'd sat down to think through everything that had happened, wondering if I had made a mistake in telling William he could play with the teddy. Had I been dismissive of Maisy's feelings? Would there always be a barrier between us if I didn't change my approach? I'd gone to find Maisy in the garden and sat down beside her, asking if she felt as Hannah had suggested. Had I made her feel like her space wasn't respected, that her wishes didn't matter? Maisy, tight-lipped and clearly uncomfortable, had refused to answer, but I knew her little signs better now, and I could see that there might be some truth in what Hannah had said.

I had felt awful. Like a failure. I was doing my best, constantly trying to keep everyone happy, but I never seemed to get it right. No matter which path I chose, someone always felt wronged. I'd left Maisy to play alone, feeling her desperation for me to go away and give her some space, and then I'd gone to find William, only to discover he'd got bored of the teddy and was making a den in his own room. Perhaps Hannah had been right, but I didn't understand why she suddenly had such a strong opinion about how I should raise my children. She never had before. Why couldn't she have brought up the topic without being so hurtful? It seemed completely out of character for her to attack me, especially in front of Maisy.

I hadn't bothered to confide in her about the new routine I'd formed with Maisy, just as I hadn't revisited my fears over adding Ella to my family since her cold, judgemental reaction that day on the beach when I'd told her I was considering not keeping her.

The memory made me shudder now, the idea that I might not have Ella, that I could have gone my whole life without meeting her. I loved her with every inch of my being, and had from the very first moment I saw her, but that love didn't cancel out the fears I still carried. But I hadn't told Hannah any of it. The friendship we'd once had was hanging by a thread, and though I couldn't bear to let her go completely, most of the time we spent together I felt lonelier than if she weren't there at all.

CHAPTER THIRTY

I eased Ella down into the soft brushed-cotton lining of the Moses basket, keeping my hand pressed warm against her tummy and holding my breath as I waited to see if she would accept the transfer. She didn't stir as I gently tucked her blanket around her, stepping past the basket and climbing into bed beside Jon. If the routine of the past two weeks was anything to go by, I should have at least two hours before she woke again for a feed, and the thought of snuggling up in Jon's arms and drifting off was pure bliss to me. I slid under the sheets, my cold feet finding his warm thighs, pressing against them, and he gasped, rolling away.

'How you manage to have ice blocks for feet all year round is beyond me!' he exclaimed, shuffling his legs back so I couldn't shock him again. 'You know it's summer, right? Someone needs to tell your circulatory system that.'

'It's a terrible affliction,' I agreed. 'And a husband's duty to provide the necessary support.'

'Is that so?' he said, smiling, though I could see something sad in his expression.

I wrapped an arm round his waist, slipping it beneath his T-shirt, trying not to notice the jut of his hip bone, the xylophone of his ribs where muscle and fat had once been. Now that I was waking up for night feeds every other hour, I had realised just how restless Jon's nights were. I'd slept like a log the last few months of my pregnancy, and somehow managed to miss that he was often in and out of bed all night long, going to the bathroom and not returning for absolutely ages, heading downstairs to watch TV when he couldn't sleep. I didn't like it; it made me uneasy and placed thoughts in my mind I didn't want to address.

The topic of his cancer and his recovery was one I'd begun to avoid like the plague, unable to bear to think of him suffering. It was as if Ella's arrival had made everything more raw, that fragility of our family unit exposed in a way that made me feel real terror. I'd never believed that we might not make it through this, and I still wasn't prepared to. Now, I just needed him to hurry up and get better so we could enjoy our family of five.

'How was today?' I asked, leaning forward to rest my chin on his shoulder, my eyes fixed on his face, watching his expression closely. He had gone to London to have a meeting with his team about an upcoming research trip and hadn't got back until after the kids were asleep. He looked shattered, and I wished there was something I could do to help.

He hesitated, picking up his phone and looking at it. 'It was fine. Long day. How were the kids?' He put the phone down, leaning his head back against the mound of pillows and looking up at the ceiling. I'd been hoping for a bit more than just *it was fine*, but I could see he was tired and I didn't want to push it right now.

I smiled. 'They were really lovely. I've had Ella in the baby sling all day – she loves it and sleeps for hours on my chest, and it means I've got my hands free for the older two. William and I did a science project involving collecting and categorising the insects in our garden, so of course he was in his element, and Maisy came down and joined in too. I think I'm starting to see more interaction between the two of them now, though they've a long way to go before they can consider each other friends rather than just siblings. But these things take time, don't they? It was a pretty blissful day,' I admitted, thinking back to the trip to the park after lunch, the clear blue sky, the shouts of excitement from William and Maisy. I'd put Ella on a blanket on the grass in the shade of a big oak tree, and she'd stared up at the leaves in wide-eyed fascination.

'It was one of those rare days where everything just seems to go perfectly,' I said, smiling as I pressed another kiss to his shoulder. 'We're so lucky to have them.'

'We are,' he replied, his voice heavy with exhaustion. 'You know, Ella is the spitting image of you, except for her eyes. That hazel colour… who do you think it comes from?' he asked softly.

'Oh, I'm not sure. I mean, babies' eyes change after a few months, if I remember rightly. Perhaps they're still not settled on their final colour. They are pretty though.' I looked down. 'I was worried about how we would cope with another baby, I really was, but now that she's here, it feels simple. It's not easy, and I could do with a lot more sleep, but I really feel like we're going to be okay. Don't you?'

He nodded, still not looking at me. 'Lils, with a mother like you in their lives, they'll want for nothing.'

'Don't… don't say it like that. You know I don't like it.' I felt his shoulders stiffen, his eyes fixed on the ceiling. 'I mean it, Jon. The moment you start thinking like that, making little consolation plans for you not being around, you begin to lose the battle. You can't think like that.'

He didn't speak for a moment, then slowly he turned towards me, his head on the pillow, his eyes finally meeting mine. 'Lily…' he sighed. 'Babe, we need to have a conversation. I need to know—'

I pulled back from his hold, my feet on the floor in one swift movement, hurrying towards the bedroom door. 'I think I heard William calling. I'll go and check. He might have had a nightmare.'

'Lily, we can't avoid this forever.'

I didn't answer, didn't even look at him as I rushed from the room, my heart palpitating hard enough to burst.

CHAPTER THIRTY-ONE

Hannah

'Hannah fucking Adams!'

I turned at the sound of the familiar voice, seeing the bulky shoulders and confident swagger of Jack Sinclair, an ex-fling from two years before, approaching from the café across the street. I watched him move, noticing how little he'd changed since I last saw him, his dark hair still thick and meticulously styled, his brown eyes warm and sensual. We'd enjoyed six weeks or so together, going on wild dates, and spent several long weekends in hotels or forever undressed at my place. It had been fun, but it seemed like a lifetime ago now, and I could hardly picture the woman I'd been back then. I was surprised he even recognised me.

I'd gained weight on the IVF, and the sleepless nights and frequent tears had made my once clear skin puffy, my eyes permanently rimmed with dark circles. It had been over a week since I'd discovered the baby I was carrying was nothing but a figment of my desperate imagination, and now, I just felt empty. Numb.

Jack made it across the road and stepped in front of me, and I swallowed down my pain, pasting on a smile. 'Hi, Jack.'

'Hi yourself.' He leaned forward, kissing me on the cheek, and I blinked, overwhelmed by the intensity of his aftershave. 'How are you, gorgeous? Long time no see.'

'I'm okay. Working long hours. What about you?' I said, aware that my voice sounded flat, my words like tar as I forced them from my reluctant lips. All I wanted to do was grab some fried noodles and head home to eat them in my bed whilst watching mindless TV.

I'd refrained from taking a sick day after my catastrophic ultrasound, though going into work this past two weeks had been the last thing I felt able to face, but I knew I was skating on thin ice when it came to Eloise, and I didn't want to draw unnecessary attention to myself by not showing my face. I'd put my head down and tried to focus on my work, though I knew nothing I'd designed this week would ever see the light of day. The whole process of pretending everything was okay had given me a migraine, but at least I'd been there. And right now, that was the best I could offer.

I blinked, realising that Jack was still speaking, giving a monologue on his new promotion and the five-star hotel he'd just been to in Marrakesh. I remembered now why we'd fizzled out. He loved the sound of his own voice far more than I ever had. 'So, what are you doing now? You want to go and grab a drink?'

I shook my head, thinking of the early start I had tomorrow. Why I'd agreed to go to the theme park and tag along with Lily's picture-perfect family, I couldn't begin to understand. Right now, being surrounded by happy, smiling parents and children was the last thing I wanted. 'I'm just heading home actually. I don't fancy crowds this evening.'

'Oh… shall I join you?' His voice was velvet, his eyelids lowering in that suggestive way I remembered from when we were dating. There was no mistaking what he was getting at. I opened my mouth to refuse him, and then closed it suddenly.

'Sure.' I nodded, my eyes meeting his. 'Why not? You remember the way? I have my car. If you have yours, you can follow me?'

He nodded, leaning forward, a rush of minty breath hitting my face. 'Never forgot it. I'll be there in ten.' He flashed me a wink, turning and sprinting down the pavement, and I cast a forlorn look at the Chinese takeaway before turning in the opposite direction and heading back to my car. A reckless, wild feeling had started to spread through me. How many women had I known to drop off the corporate ladder because they forgot to take a condom on a date? How many surprise babies had I bought gifts for?

I'd all but given up hope, and there was certainly no money left for another shot at doing it the clinical way. But why *shouldn't* I be a bit crazy? Have a nice evening with a man I trusted – knew well enough to let into my flat, at least – and who was tall and handsome to boot? He never had to know, and if it worked…

I squeezed my keys in my hand, feeling queasy and excited and guilty all at once. I was ovulating. I'd realised it that morning, cried over the wasted cycle, the missed opportunity. It was as if I'd been offered a gift. Jack was only coming over for one thing, and it certainly wasn't to chat about the good old days. I was under no illusions of romance and happily-ever-afters. He'd be gone before morning, and if I was lucky, perhaps this time…

I didn't let myself finish the thought as I flung open the car door and clambered inside, shoving the keys in the ignition. I would think about the morality of my decision later. Right now, I had a man to meet.

'It's different… from the last time I was here, I mean. Are you moving?' Jack frowned, looking at the empty surfaces, the spaces where furniture had once stood.

I shrugged, opening the fridge, intending to offer him a beer before realising I didn't have any. I closed it, turning to face him. 'I'm trying out minimalism.'

'I'm not sure you've got it quite right.' He laughed, and I followed his gaze, seeing the place through his eyes.

'You might be right. It's pretty bleak. Sorry,' I said, though I wasn't sure why I felt the need to apologise. It was none of his business.

He smiled. 'Hey, I'm not here for the beautiful antique furniture. I'm here for the gorgeous woman standing in front of me. I can't believe how long it's been since we caught up. Too long. We had some fun, from what I remember.'

I nodded. 'We did,' I agreed, though I hadn't thought about it in ages. He stared at me, and I felt suddenly awkward. I wished I still had my stereo, could put on some music and open some wine. It felt strange just getting straight down to business – dirty somehow – and I began to feel uncomfortable. *Suck it up, Hannah. Remember why you're doing this.*

He pushed away from the counter and I tensed, expecting him to come to me. Instead he wandered into the living area, taking in everything – or the lack or everything – as he moved slowly through the room. He poked his head through the bedroom door. 'Still got a bed, then. No futon on the floor? Roll-up mattress?' He smiled, and I was grateful that he was trying to lighten the mood.

'Not yet,' I said, grinning. 'But there's still time to make improvements.'

'May I make a suggestion?'

I nodded.

'Don't.'

We both laughed, and though mine felt hollow, it gave me the boost of confidence I needed to take the next step. I walked across the room, my eyes fixed on his. Reaching him, I didn't pause. This wasn't going to be a romantic, drawn-out thing. I wanted to get it done. It wasn't that Jack wasn't great. He was a decent guy. Nice. Good in bed from what I could remember. But right now, romance was the last thing I needed. I had no room in my mind or my heart for a man, and this… liaison was purely the means to an end. I wrapped one hand around the back of his head, pulling his mouth down on mine, moving to unbutton his shirt with my free hand.

It was all the encouragement he needed. With a strength I remembered hazily, he lifted me up against his chest, carrying me to the bed, throwing me down on the mattress and climbing on top of me. His mouth crushed against mine, his hands sliding up and down my body, trying to find a way in through the long layers of the maxi dress I was wearing. He slid one hand down my waist, and I tried not to flinch as it continued down, pulling at the silky material, hitching my dress up inch by inch. His other hand went to my hair, and he kissed me again, his eyes sinking closed. I shut mine too, wishing I could loosen up at least enough to enjoy this, wondering when I had lost the ability to take pleasure in a night of being swept off my feet.

I was suddenly aware that Jack had frozen, his body heavy on top of mine. I opened my eyes to find him staring at me with a questioning look, his fingers clasped around the tiny baby vest I had kept beneath my pillow for the past few weeks. Ella's vest. It had given me hope, something to focus on when everything seemed utterly impossible, and some nights, holding it close had been the only thing that had stopped me from hurting myself out of disgust for my own body. It had kept the panic at bay.

'What's this?' he asked.

I shook my head, pressing my lips together, my hands shoving against his chest. 'Get up. Get off me.'

He moved in an instant, sitting on the end of the bed, the little bundle clutched between the very tips of his fingers like he'd just discovered a grenade with the pin missing. I reached across and snatched it from him, holding it tight between my hands.

'You didn't have a baby last time we met.'

'And I don't now.'

He nodded. 'Right.'

We sat in silence for a moment, Jack casting covert glances at me beneath his lashes. 'Look, Han... I don't need to know. None of my business, right? But if you still want to do this, I'm cool with it.'

I stared at him. 'No,' I said, realising I was crying. 'I don't. You know what I want? For you to leave. I can't do this. I can't have you here, so please, just go.'

'Hannah, talk to me. Is there something I can do to help? You look really messed up.'

'Just fucking go, all right? Get out!'

He rose slowly, pursing his lips. 'Got it. I'm going.' He walked out without so much as a backwards glance, and I heard the click of the front door as he pulled it closed behind him. I was sure that I would never see him again.

CHAPTER THIRTY-TWO

Now

My stomach growled and I searched through the changing bag, hoping to find something to keep my hunger at bay – a cereal bar or a packet of crisps – but there was nothing. I could have called room service, but the last thing I wanted was to draw more attention to myself. I filled the little plastic kettle with water from the bathroom sink and settled for making a cup of coffee – a treat I'd recently started allowing myself after months of avoiding it – and a tube of Pringles from the minibar, which I knew I couldn't afford. I shoved them in, crunching them between my teeth before my sensible side could talk me out of it, and then gulped down the hot coffee, feeling marginally better.

The room felt smaller than it had an hour ago, the walls closing in on me, and I knew, no matter how safe it had felt on arrival, how sure I'd been that we wouldn't be discovered here, there was no way I would be able to sleep. Every noise in the hall had me jumping up, rushing to the peephole, a wave of tension hitting the bullseye of my heart, radiating out to the very edges and further still, down to my stomach, my limbs, making me tremble with that instinctive fight-or-flight response. I couldn't stay the night here.

I slid my phone out of the back pocket of my jeans and sat down on the edge of the bed, careful not to disturb Ella. I'd switched it off just after leaving the theme park earlier, and now

I was afraid to turn it back on. It felt like we'd been gone days, weeks even, but as I fired up the battered Android I hadn't had the funds to upgrade, I saw the time and realised it had only been four hours. It was ten to nine. I swallowed as the signal kicked in, notifications popping up one after another after another. Voicemails, texts, missed calls. I didn't click on any of them. I couldn't face hearing what Lily had to say to me.

Instead I tapped the internet icon and navigated to the website for Bournemouth airport. Could we fly without a passport if we stayed in the country? Maybe somewhere far up north? I shook my head, sure that there would be a horde of police looking for us in the airport. Maybe we could get a taxi to somewhere a little further away, Southampton perhaps, and then hop on a train from there. We could go anywhere in the country. I loved the idea of a little cottage in the countryside, somewhere lost in the wilderness of Wales perhaps… I clicked onto my online banking, typing in my details with a sense of nervousness, wondering if I might be traced somehow. I'd seen enough detective programmes to know anything was possible.

The state of my accounts was dire. I'd been paid, but the money had instantly been filtered off to chip away at the numerous bills and direct debits I'd accumulated. But there was a payment from my dad I'd forgotten he'd told me he was sending. A thousand pounds from the sale of my old kayak. He'd been reluctantly keeping it for me in his garage for years, and when I'd run out of things to sell in my flat, I had mentioned to him that he might ask around at the sailing club and see if he could drum up some interest for me. I'd taken good care of it, popping by every chance I got to manhandle it onto my roof rack and head down to the beach, and though it was well used, it was a decent one and had plenty of years of use still ahead of it.

It had actually been one of the hardest things to let go of, more difficult than any of the art, the expensive furniture I'd collected over the years. The kayak wasn't pretty, but it had a purpose far more important to me than any table or lamp ever had. I had loved the freedom of taking it out on a calm, misty sea, the air cool and damp against my skin, the quiet of nature never truly silent. Seagulls battling in the distance over a coveted piece of food. The far-off tinkling sound of the masts of the sailboats bobbing gently on the water, the ripple as the paddle cut through the gleaming blue-green surface.

My parents hadn't given me much in life, but they'd given me the freedom of the ocean, taught me how to respect it, understand it and, most of all, become one with it. Some of the few memories I had of being happy, feeling wanted and loved as a child were of days spent out at sea, listening to the wind hitting the sails, my mum and dad talking and happy and teaching me what they considered important life skills. I had soaked it all up like a sponge, determined not to miss a thing, desperate to demonstrate that I was capable of everything they had to show me and discovering a deep sense of joy with every minute that passed. It was where I felt most as home, safe and complete, and even out there by myself, I never felt lonely. The water was all the company I needed, and I loved drifting further from shore, leaving all the stresses and worries of the real world in my wake. It was better than any meditation class. Letting go of that kayak had been like carving off a part of myself, offering it to the highest bidder, and though I'd had no choice but to make the sale, it was the only one I regretted. I hoped that someday soon I would be able to replace it.

I would have given anything to be out there now, surrounded by water, the place I had always felt safest. I'd made myself vulnerable in taking Ella, and right now I didn't have the strength in me to cope with this level of exposure. All I wanted was to hide until it was safe to emerge again. The money for the kayak had been intended to go towards paying off my debts, but right now, it was a lifeline. It wasn't much, but it was far better than the nothing I'd expected to find. I could make this work.

I glanced uncomfortably at the notifications bar one more time, then, making up my mind, switched off my mobile, picking up the room phone instead.

'Hi. Can you call me a taxi please?' I asked, my eyes on the sweet sleeping baby on the bed. 'There's somewhere I have to go.'

CHAPTER THIRTY-THREE

Lily

There was nothing in Hannah's flat to indicate where she might have gone with Ella. Her passport was still in the kitchen drawer, her phone charger plugged into the socket beside her bed. I glanced at the digital clock on the oven and saw it was just gone twenty past nine. Ella had been gone for four and a half hours now. It wasn't that long, not really, but it felt like a lifetime.

Still holding the vest I'd found squirrelled beneath Hannah's bed, I tucked the folder of paperwork beneath my arm, casting one final look around the place, hoping to see an answer, a clue. When nothing appeared, I sighed, heading for the door.

It felt wrong, taking Hannah's private documents, though the irony of feeling guilty over some pieces of paper when she had my child in her grasp didn't escape me. I wanted to show Jon what she had been doing, and it was possible the police would need to see them too. I could imagine what they would think when they realised how desperate Hannah had been for a baby of her own. No doubt it would be exactly what I'd thought: that this was something she had been considering for some time.

Even so, I couldn't begin to grasp how she could do this to me, how she could think of taking my baby. Didn't she realise Ella was the glue that was holding my family together right now? Since Ella had come into our lives, she'd given me a focus, something to take my mind off worrying about Jon. She'd pushed me to repair my relationship with Maisy. She was the reason I smiled every morning, when the two of us would sneak downstairs before sunrise to cuddle up on the sofa. I would feed her, watching her little cheeks as she suckled, her eyes fixed on my face, curious and already full of so much intelligence. The thought that tomorrow morning I would wake up without her by my side made me feel physically sick.

But then Hannah didn't know any of that...

I stepped out into the warm summer evening and walked to my car, still watchful, looking around for anything that might alert me to her presence. They could be anywhere. I got into the car, dropping the file and vest onto the passenger seat, and pulled my phone from my pocket, pressing Jon's name. It rang twice and he answered, his voice heavy. 'Hey, Lils. Any sign of her?'

I sighed. 'No. Have you heard from the police?'

'They called fifteen minutes ago,' he said, and I felt my stomach tense up as I waited for him to continue. 'No news, just some chap asking a load of questions we've already answered. Trying to look like they're on the ball, I suppose, but quite frankly, it's not good enough. I got a bit angry with him, to be honest with you. Told him to read the bloody statements we've already given and try communicating with the rest of the team. He said they were reviewing CCTV at Bournemouth airport.'

'They couldn't have got on a flight. Ella doesn't even have a passport. And Hannah's is still here.'

'Is it? Good. That's something then. I told him Ella didn't have one, but I'm not sure they've ruled it out yet. To be honest, I'd rather they cover all bases at this stage; it just frustrated me that they think asking the same questions over and over again is going to be helpful. It's like they're trying to catch us out or something, though God knows why we'd lie about any of it.'

I nodded, feeling disappointed that he didn't have more to tell me. 'Okay, well I'm coming home now. I found something I want to show you.'

'Drive safely, okay, babe? The last thing we need is you having an accident right now.' His words sounded jokey, but I didn't miss the fear simmering in his voice.

'I will.' I ended the call, dropping the phone and resting my head on the steering wheel. I couldn't stop thinking about Hannah's secrets. How had I not been aware of her desire to have a baby? This was something she'd been working towards for a long time, and yet she'd never said a word to me and I couldn't understand why not. Had I really been that bad a friend that she hadn't felt able to confide in me? I knew I'd kept my own secrets from her, but it hadn't been by choice. I would have loved nothing more than to talk to her about the things going on in my life lately, to ask her advice or just have a listening ear to absorb all my fears.

The knowledge that she'd kept this from me made me feel hurt, question every minute we'd spent together recently. Was this my fault? Had I been too distracted by my own problems to ask about hers?

I couldn't recall the last time we'd had a proper chat. If I was honest, I knew I'd held back from those deep conversations, not wanting to talk about anything serious out of fear that I might not be able to stop myself from letting out everything I'd been hiding. I'd been so sure I knew Hannah inside out, I'd never thought to ask, but now I couldn't stop myself from thinking: if I'd been less self-involved, a better friend, could I have stopped all of this from happening?

CHAPTER THIRTY-FOUR

Hannah

The taxi driver pulled away from the hotel, and I watched as the sun dipped below the horizon, casting a soft orange glow behind the beautiful building. Ella was restless in my arms, having been woken from her sleep, and I sat her on my lap, her back resting against my chest. She stared out at the blurred landscape as we made our way through the country lanes, and I hoped that we would reach the city before it was too dark to see anything. A dark window wouldn't hold her attention, and we had a long way to go before we would reach Southampton.

I'd regretted ordering the taxi the minute I'd put the phone down, sure that if the police managed to track me down to the hotel, they would be able to find out which taxi firm they used, and subsequently ask the driver where he'd taken me. I'd thought about cancelling my request and calling for one myself, but in the end, I'd decided there was no point. I would just have to hope that by the time they got the information they were looking for, Ella and I would be long gone.

The driver glanced at me in the rear-view mirror, and I got the horrible feeling he was about to start chatting. The last thing I needed right now was small talk. I couldn't begin to think of enough details for a cover story to fill the length of our drive. Thankfully, Ella, already fed up with the view of the fields, began to fuss, her tiny fists balling and opening, her legs straightening in a way that always made me feel like I was about to drop her. The noise was enough to cut off any interest the driver may have had in making conversation, but I had no idea what to do to placate her. I raised her against my shoulder, rubbing her back, then fished in the top pocket of the changing bag for her dummy, promptly dropping it on the floor in my haste. I rummaged in the bag for the spare before remembering it had been attached to her car seat earlier this morning. Instead, I made do with a water wipe from the packet, hoping that cleaning the dust and dirt off would be enough. After all, babies were always picking things up off the floor and shoving them in their mouths, weren't they? A few taxi germs were probably good for building her immune system.

I held the partially clean dummy to her lips and she took it. For a second, I almost relaxed, but it would have been too soon. Ella opened her mouth, letting out a furious wail, the dummy dropping straight back down to the suspect carpet in the back footwell. I felt myself begin to sweat, my heart hammering, my body rushing with adrenaline. I'd seen her like this once or twice before, but Lily had always taken her from me, soothed her somehow, making it look easy. This was anything but easy, and I had no idea what to do.

'Try feeding her.'

I looked up, seeing the taxi driver's eyes fixed disapprovingly on the pair of us as he watched in the rear-view mirror.

'I only fed her an hour ago.'

'How old is she?'

I shrugged. 'Three months.'

He scrunched up his face in a knowing smile. 'Yep. S'what I thought. Growth spurt. My littl'un turned into a right milk monster about that age. Go on. Give the poor babe some grub.'

I frowned, wondering if he was hoping I'd whip out a breast, suddenly hyperaware of being out in the middle of nowhere with a baby in the near darkness. There was a sense of vulnerability that came with having Ella here with me, being her sole protector against the world. And even if his intentions were good, there was a part of me that didn't want to take parenting advice from a stranger. Wouldn't a mother know exactly what to do in this situation? But Ella was getting louder, her face red and angry, and I needed to stop the cries. They were making me feel panicky. Reluctantly, I reached into the bag, pulling out one of the bottles I'd made up at the hotel from the tin of formula. I pulled off the lid, positioning Ella in my arms, and placed the teat against her lips. She attacked it hungrily, her hands coming up to the bottle, her tiny fingers gripping mine as she sucked down the milk.

'Told ya,' the driver said, grinning.

'Thanks.' I kept my eyes focused on Ella, waiting for him to turn his attention back to the road. I heard him huff and then turn the radio up, giving up on any hope of conversation. Ella eased into a calmer rhythm, drinking down the milk more slowly now that she had relaxed, her body melting against mine. Babies were so simple to please when you knew what they needed. I loved how quickly she could switch from furious tears to contented cuddling.

I propped the bottle against my chest, then reached into the changing bag to get a blanket to put beneath my elbow for support, and my hand slid into a hidden compartment in the lining. I looked down, seeing the slot where a thin changing mat I hadn't noticed earlier was folded neatly between the fabric. My fingers closed around something hard, and I pulled it out to have a look. It was a hardback A5 notepad, baby pink, with a circular cut-out on the front cover where a photograph of Lily and Ella, both glowing from the exertions of labour, was framed. Lily's eyes sparkled as she stared out at the camera, her arms held protectively around the scrunched-up newborn.

I propped the book on top of the changing bag and flipped the cover open. There were more photographs here, carefully hand-cut and glued to the pages, little captions by their sides. *Your first feed. Your first nappy change. Your first cuddles with your big brother and sister.* I stared at the pages, running my fingers over the photographs, Lily's handwriting so neat and careful as she counted off the milestones.

On the next page was a tiny translucent bag with a tuft of soft downy hair in it. Ella's hair. The caption read: *You love your hair being washed with warm water and brushed. It sends you off to sleep every single time.*

I pinched the edge of the bag between my fingers, feeling tears pool in my eyes. All this time I'd thought she didn't care. That she saw Ella as a burden, the reason she couldn't do the things she dreamed of, another tie holding her back from the career she thought would make everything better. I'd been so angry at her, sure that she was selfishly unaware of her good fortune. Had my own need for a baby made me look at her through skewed eyes? Because this wasn't something created by a mother who didn't care. This was meticulous, made with love. The scrapbook of a woman who couldn't bear not to hold on to every single memory of what could well be her last baby. And I'd snatched that baby away, believing that Lily wasn't a good enough parent to her. I'd wanted to make it okay, justify what I'd done in taking her, make myself believe I could give her what Lily never could. I'd needed to believe that. But this book shattered that illusion. It wasn't true. And as much as I longed for her to be, Ella wasn't mine. And she never could be.

CHAPTER THIRTY-FIVE

I held the baby-pink scrapbook in my hand, wishing I hadn't found it, that I could shove it back in the lining of the changing bag and pretend it didn't matter. But it did. And now that I'd realised how much Lily loved Ella, I couldn't switch off the guilt that had ignited an inferno inside me. She must be out of her mind with worry. Sick with fear, and it was all my fault.

Ella sighed, her head tipping back, finally releasing the bottle from her lips as she gave in to a milk-drunk sleep. My arm was aching, pins and needles spreading through it as the taxi drove on into the darkness. We were on a busy road now, heading towards the centre of Salisbury, cars parked alongside rows of takeaways, traffic fumes still lingering in the air despite the fact that the road was far from full at this time of night. I pulled the blanket from the bag, bundling it under my elbow and feeling instant relief as I found a comfortable position to hold her. Glancing up as a street light illuminated a road sign, I saw that we were about to join the A36. In forty-five minutes or so, we'd be in Southampton. The thought should have given me relief, but it just made me want to cry. What had I done? With each mile that passed, I was taking Lily's daughter further from her.

With a sense of unwilling resignation, I wriggled in my seat, reaching into my back pocket and pulling my phone out. I switched it on, my stomach rolling as it flashed to life, the notifications coming in one after the other. I didn't want to face them, to read the messages, hear Lily's voice, but I needed to. As much as I would have liked to, I couldn't avoid it any longer.

I saw the taxi driver cast another look at me in his mirror and angled my body towards the window, cradling Ella close as I lifted the phone to my ear. The first few messages were from Lily and Jon. He sounded calm, a little confused but confident that there had been a misunderstanding over where to meet. Lily, right from the first message, sounded afraid, as if somehow she knew, though I didn't see how she could when I hadn't even known myself what I was doing. The voicemails that followed were mostly from Lily, growing increasingly angry, demanding I call her, bring Ella back.

Then there was an official-sounding message from a woman who introduced herself as DCI Roberts, asking me to call the station at my earliest convenience. Her voice was clipped, and though I'd known Lily and Jon would have had to call the police by now – what sane parent wouldn't? – hearing the detective's voice now made this all feel so much more real. It brought home exactly what I had done, how serious this was. There were police out there this very minute, looking for me, wondering what my intentions were towards Ella. I hoped they knew that I would never hurt her. I only ever wanted to love her.

I was about to cut off the voicemail when Jon's voice reached my ear again. It was different this time, that easy confidence I'd heard in his earlier messages all gone.

'Hannah,' he said, 'I don't know what your reason was for taking her, but it doesn't matter. Please, I know you must be scared… feel like you're in too deep to turn back, but I promise you, it's not like that. Bring Ella home, Hannah. You have no idea how much we need her, how much we love her. This will destroy our family, and Lily—'

I heard him choke back a sob, my head shaking as if I could stop him, make his tears go away, because I couldn't bear that I was the cause of them. I had never seen Jon cry. Not once. He cleared his throat.

'This will kill Lily, Hannah. You have to bring her back. Please, just—' I heard his voice crack, the call ending abruptly as I tossed the phone aside, unable to stand the feel of it in my hand. I was shaking, I realised, and close to throwing up. I had never wanted to hurt them, either of them; this hadn't been about seeking revenge or teaching them some lesson. It was pure desperation.

But my need to have a baby didn't give me the right to take theirs. I wondered if Jon knew that he wasn't Ella's real dad. If he suspected Lily of having an affair. Perhaps he didn't even care. He was the most forgiving person in the world; I wouldn't be surprised if he'd made up his mind not to punish her for her deception. He would be a good father to Ella no matter her biology. And he was more a father to her than I would ever be a mother. To any baby.

If I turned back now, that would be it. I knew the trajectory my life would take. I would lose everything. I'd probably go to prison. And my dreams of being a mother would be lost forever. I stared down at the sleeping baby in my arms and felt a guttural sob escape my lips.

'You all right, love?'

I nodded, unable to meet the driver's concerned gaze in the mirror, hot salty tears pouring down my cheeks, splashing onto Ella's cotton Babygro. I wiped roughly at my eyes, willing the tears to stop, but they wouldn't. 'I need you to turn back… we have to go to Mudeford.'

'Down to Christchurch? Really? It's going to take another hour from here.'

I nodded again. 'Yes,' I replied, my throat tight. I knew it was the only choice left. I had to take Ella home – and face whatever consequences I'd earned along the way.

The driver flicked his indicator, the clicking sound like a countdown timer on a bomb that couldn't be disabled. I watched as he eased into the left lane, huffing as he reset the satnav and programmed in the new route. I felt an overwhelming mixture of fear combined with relief. I couldn't keep running, playing pretend at motherhood while Lily was falling apart. No matter what was in store for me, I had no choice. I was taking Ella home. It was over.

CHAPTER THIRTY-SIX

Lily

I pulled into the driveway, turning off the engine and looking up at the house. William's bedroom light was off, and I hoped that meant he was asleep. I hated to miss putting him and Maisy to bed, but tonight I didn't have the energy to try and explain to them what was going on. They were both aware enough to realise something terrible had happened, and I knew they needed reassurance from me, but right now, I had none to offer. I didn't *know* what was going to happen, if or when we would see Ella again, and if they asked me at the moment, I was sure it would take all of my strength not to fall apart, to make them believe something I couldn't – that everything was going to be okay.

I squeezed my eyes tightly shut, trying not to cry. Then, with a shuddering sigh, I opened them, looking at the clock on the dashboard. Almost five hours now. Every minute felt like a lifetime, and yet they seemed to slip by faster than I could catch. It was surreal and terrifying.

I swung open the car door, climbed out and went round to the passenger side to grab the file, my phone and the vest I hadn't been able to face leaving behind. The house was quiet as I walked inside, dropping my keys on the table in the hall. I could hear a distant meowing and glanced through the open doorway into the kitchen, seeing Fluffy's disgruntled face pressed up against the window from outside. Ignoring him, I walked through to the living room.

The light was on, the house phone on the carpet beside the sofa, Jon stretched out, mouth open, fast asleep, one arm curled behind his head. I felt a surge of irritation as I saw him lying there. How could he even think of sleeping when Ella was missing? How could he relax? But my irritation quickly transformed to pity as I saw the dark circles beneath his eyes, the jut of his collarbone protruding above his T-shirt. He was still recovering, and though I'd tried not to think of it today, determined to concentrate on the positives of having us all together on a beautiful summer outing, just like any ordinary family, brushing aside our issues and pretending everything was okay, it didn't make it any less true.

When we'd realised Ella was gone, all I'd wanted was to lean on him, rely on his strength – something I hadn't felt able to do since the moment I heard his diagnosis. I'd had to be the calm, unflappable one. To get on with the jobs that needed doing and squash down my fears. But today, I'd needed him to take that role, to be a leader, and to his credit, he had stepped up, stood by my side, taken control when I couldn't. What we'd been through this past five hours was enough to wipe anyone out. It was incredible that he'd managed to keep going so long. I couldn't blame him for drifting off.

I put the file down softly on the carpet and moved towards him, intending to cover him with the throw from the back of the sofa. His eyes shot open as I moved to reach it, and he sat bolt upright, gripping the tops of my arms. 'Is she back? Did they find her?' he demanded, his eyes wide with fear as they fixed on mine.

I shook my head. 'Not yet,' I whispered.

His face crumpled and he pulled me towards him, crushing the breath from me as his arms wrapped around my body, his face pressed against my shoulder. I didn't need to see it to know he was crying, I could feel the harsh unhindered sobs racking through his shoulders, his entire body consumed with grief.

'You can't give up hope,' I murmured, holding him tightly, swallowing back my own tears. 'There's still a chance we'll find her. We *have* to, Jon,' I said, not finishing the thought that filled my mind. That if we didn't, I wasn't sure how I could go on.

He pulled back, his face flushed, soaked with the evidence of his pain. 'I don't know what to do,' he admitted, shaking his head. 'I'm supposed to take care of you, protect our children, and here I am too fucking weak to even stay awake! What help am I going to be to you here? Fast asleep when I should be out there looking for her!' His voice was harsh, full of self-disgust, and I recoiled instinctively.

'You're not weak. You've done everything you can, Jon. You're *recovering*, and that's nothing to be ashamed of.'

He shook his head, his hand reaching for mine, and I didn't pull back. 'Lily…' he said softly. 'I—'

He was cut off by a sudden knocking at the front door. We stared at each other in silence for half a second, and then I jumped to my feet. Rushing out of the room, I flung open the door, and burst into tears.

CHAPTER THIRTY-SEVEN

Hannah

The taxi idled beneath the blue-white glow of a street lamp across the road from the house and I made no attempt to move. Now that we'd arrived, I wasn't sure I had the strength to keep going. My mind was spinning, throwing ideas left, right and centre, but I batted them all away, knowing that it was too late for that now. The driver turned in his seat. 'Well, is this it or not? Because you're spending money sitting here, you know?'

I nodded, not taking my eyes from the house. 'This is it.' I reached into my purse and passed him a handful of notes, wishing I'd found a more frugal way to travel.

He took the cash, pocketing it and handing me a few coins as change. The old Hannah would have told him to keep it, but now I had to watch every penny and I took it gratefully. But still I didn't move. He gave a heavy sigh and opened his own door, then climbed out, walking round the car and opening mine. 'Seems you're not in any hurry. Well, sorry, love, but I am. You need help with the littl'un?' he asked, nodding towards Ella, still sleeping soundly in my arms.

I looked down at her, shaking my head, realising my time was up. With slow, reluctant movements, I clambered out onto the pavement. He reached into the back seat, grabbing the changing bag and blanket and handing them to me. I took them without speaking, and he slammed the door and headed back to the front. He got in and drove off, leaving me standing dumbstruck in the dark. I shifted Ella in my arms, slinging the bag over my shoulder and shoving her blanket inside. The night was still hot, the pavement radiating the heat it had absorbed through the day, and I felt a trickle of sweat run between my shoulder blades. The downstairs lights were on in the house, and my stomach clenched as I wondered if there would be police there waiting for me.

Every instinct screamed at me to run, to go now before it was too late, but I stepped out onto the quiet road, crossing with slow, measured footsteps, and walked up the drive past their parked car. I stood in front of the door, my breathing shallow, and before I could lose my nerve, I knocked. I heard footsteps almost instantly and knew it was too late to change my mind. The door swung back, Lily's hand gripping the frame, her face pale and small. She looked from me to the sleeping baby in my arms and promptly burst into noisy tears.

'Oh, thank God!' she cried, lurching forward, snatching Ella from my arms, bringing her to her chest as she sobbed without restraint.

I stood rooted to the spot, unable to speak, to explain. I looked over Lily's shoulder and saw Jon appear, his face filled with a desperate hope as he rushed forward.

Lily looked up at him, tears streaming down her face, her relief palpable. 'She's back, Jon, she's really here!'

His hands travelled over Ella's face, her body, as if checking for injury. Ella opened her eyes, breaking into a gummy smile, reaching a little hand up as her parents' heads met above hers. Jon gripped her finger, and I saw he was crying too as he wrapped one arm around Lily's waist, their foreheads pressed together in silent relief.

For a moment, nobody moved. There was just the sound of subsiding sobs and my own panic ringing in my ears. I wondered if I should go, leave without a word, but my legs felt like concrete as I stared on uncomfortably, and despite myself, I stayed. Finally Lily lowered her head, kissing Ella one last time then carefully handing her to Jon. Their eyes met, and my bowel spasmed in fear as I heard him mutter her name, a low warning.

She turned towards me, her eyes fire as they met mine, then took two brisk steps forward, raised her hand and slapped me hard across the face.

The pain ricocheted through me, my cheek burning, my teeth catching on the soft skin inside, my eyes watering from the sting of both the slap and her hatred. I could feel it radiating through her as I swallowed a mouthful of blood.

'How could you do it, you bitch?' she hissed, her eyes blazing. 'How dare you take her!'

'Lily,' Jon said, his voice soft, a tremble of deep emotion captured in the single word. He moved beside her, one hand coming to her shoulder.

I didn't speak. There was nothing I could possibly say. I knew she had every right to react like this, and yet for some reason it still surprised me. I'd never seen her like this, blazing with incandescent fury. She looked like she wanted to rip me limb from limb, and I didn't blame her. I knew what I'd done was unforgivable.

She reached for Ella again, taking her from Jon's arms, cuddling her close as she took several shaking breaths. Jon looked at me, his expression serious. 'Hannah, come inside. Clearly, we need to have a conversation.' His voice was calm, as if we were going to discuss something far more benign than the kidnapping of his newborn child.

'You want her in the house?' Lily demanded.

'I want to sort this mess out and try to understand what on earth happened today.'

Lily opened her mouth to speak, then shut it, turning from the pair of us and walking into the living room, Ella clutched tightly against her chest. Jon stepped back to let me in, but I didn't move.

'Jon, I—'

'We deserve an explanation, Hannah.'

I nodded, pressing my lips together, and walked inside. Lily didn't look up as I stepped through the living-room door, remaining standing stiff and awkward beside it. Jon moved past me, and my eyes followed, falling on the box file on the carpet.

'What are you doing with that?' I whispered, my hand coming to my mouth.

Jon frowned at the file, as if only just noticing it. Lily sat on the edge of the sofa and raised her eyes to meet mine, demanding explanations I wasn't strong enough to offer.

'It doesn't mean anything... I never planned to take her,' I whispered.

'But you wanted a baby. You've wanted one for a long time, haven't you? And you never said a word.'

'I couldn't,' I replied.

Jon shook his head. 'I don't understand. What are you talking about?' He glanced from Lily to me, and I felt all the energy leave me.

'It started about eighteen months ago... I thought it would be simple, easy – so many women manage it without any intervention, and I'm healthy, strong, only just thirty-five. I never thought it wouldn't happen.' I sighed, leaning back against the wall for support. 'I tried sperm banks, and when that didn't work by itself, I started IVF too. I've had three rounds,' I admitted quietly.

'And none of them worked?' Jon asked, wide-eyed, clearly confused and shocked by what he was hearing. His face softened and he lowered his voice before asking his next question. 'Or did you lose a baby, Hannah?'

'None worked. The embryos didn't attach. I thought the last one—' I broke off, unable to admit how stupid I'd been, how I'd been so desperate for it to be true I'd managed to convince myself of the lie. 'I've got myself into debt, almost lost my job, sold most of my possessions, and still no baby. I know it's not an excuse for taking Ella, but I wasn't thinking straight. I just… I wanted it so badly, and realising there were no more chances for it to happen, it was hard to cope with.'

I raised my eyes, seeing the two of them watching me. Lily's face was unreadable, her eyes cold, her anger still simmering. I couldn't blame her. I'd terrified her tonight. Jon, however, was looking at me with unexpected sympathy. 'You should have come to us earlier, Hannah. Told us what you were going through.'

I shrugged and looked away, not wanting to lose his compassion by admitting that most of the time I felt like a stranger in their home these days, certainly not comfortable enough to reveal something so painful.

He sighed, rubbing his hands over his eyes, looking to Lily. 'Is she okay?' he asked, nodding at Ella.

'I think so,' Lily replied.

'She's fine,' I said, not missing the defensive tone in my voice. 'I've changed her and fed her. She's had some formula because I ran out of your milk.' I knew Lily wouldn't like that, but at least Ella hadn't gone hungry. 'I took care of her. You know how much I love her, Lily. I would never do anything to hurt her.'

'But you hurt *me*,' she replied softly, finally raising her eyes to meet mine. They were glistening, tears pooling in the corners, her anger transforming to pain, and I nodded, admitting she was right. 'Hannah, when I went to your flat and saw how it had changed… found that box of papers and realised what you'd been going through, I couldn't believe you'd kept it from me. It breaks my heart to think of what you've had to deal with, and I don't understand why you felt the need for all this secrecy.'

'I—' I started, scrambling to find the words to explain, but she cut me off, her tone clipped.

'I'm sorry you've had so much going on, Hannah. I wish I'd known. But if you think that being unable to have a baby of your own gives you the right to take *mine*—'

She broke off as a loud knock at the front door echoed through the quiet house, and my stomach tensed instantly. Jon moved to the window, frowning as he peered through the curtain to see who was there. 'The police,' he said gruffly, stepping back to look from me to Lily.

'Oh.' I nodded. I had known it wouldn't be simple. That the choices I had made today came with consequences I couldn't escape. But now that it was happening, I wasn't sure I had the strength to face them.

'You'd better go and speak to them,' Lily said to Jon. She looked at him, her lips pressed together, and I saw a thousand silent messages pass between them. Not for the first time, I wished that I could understand what they were communicating to one another. I'd noticed more and more over the past year or so that they no longer voiced their feelings out loud, often preferring to share a meaningful glance that made me feel even more cut off from the two of them – an outsider, an intruder. 'Go on,' she said softly, nodding at him, not glancing my way.

Jon dipped his head, stepping past me into the hall, and I concentrated on the sound of his footsteps on the wooden floor, the click as he pulled open the door. I glanced at Lily and saw she was watching me with a curious expression. She looked down at Ella and sighed. Jumbled voices grew louder, and I gripped my hands tightly together as I realised they were coming inside. *Of course* they were coming inside. Jon entered the room, followed by two young uniformed policemen.

'So as you can see, she's back safe and sound,' he said to the two officers, nodding towards Lily, who rose from her seat, the men stepping forward to look at the baby in her arms.

'She's okay?' one of them asked.

Lily nodded, looking over his shoulder towards Jon. I watched the silent interaction between them, feeling the tension course through my veins, wanting to run yet unable to move.

Jon cleared his throat. 'I'm so sorry to have wasted your time. You see, our friend here completely misunderstood the plan.'

The second police officer frowned, and they both turned to look at me with piercing eyes.

'We told her to wait for us while we went on the ride, but she thought we wanted her to take Ella somewhere out of the heat, so she went to her dad's house – it was closer than taking her home. She called after us to let us know, but I guess we didn't hear. A case of crossed wires, it would seem.'

The frowning PC seemed to see straight through the lie. 'So why didn't you answer your phone? And why bring her back so late?'

I shook my head, unwilling to make excuses for myself, unsure why Jon was bothering to. His story didn't ring true, but I didn't think it even mattered whether they believed him or not. The police wouldn't have a case without Jon and Lily's statements. I looked to Lily now, our eyes meeting, and felt the relief before she even opened her mouth, sure of what she would say next.

'I should have remembered she never has a signal there. It's always been that way. And Hannah always falls asleep when she's putting Ella down. Don't you, Hannah?' she said, her voice clipped, strained, though she tried to hide it. 'I should have guessed she'd be fast asleep with her somewhere.'

I stared at her with a mixture of confusion and gratitude, completely lost for words. This was the last thing I'd expected to happen.

Jon stepped forward. 'Please pass on our apologies,' he said, smiling tightly. 'And our thanks. But as you can see, all is well here tonight. I'll show you out, shall I?'

He guided them out of the room, and though I was certain that wouldn't be the last I would hear from the police – they would surely have questions about my flimsy alibi and that awful text I'd sent to Lily – I couldn't help feeling lighter than I had since leaving the theme park all those hours earlier. I heard the front door shut, and Jon stepped back into the room, leaning heavily against the door.

'Why did you do that?' I asked, my eyes boring into Lily's. 'I don't deserve it.'

She sighed, her hands tightening around Ella, her gaze meeting mine, cold and hard. 'No. You don't,' she said, her voice quiet now. 'You have no idea what you put us through today, Hannah. I won't ever forgive you for this. Our friendship is over. The trust is shattered between us. But,' she breathed, 'I don't want to see you in prison. I couldn't forgive myself, no matter how much you might deserve it.'

I nodded, resigned to my punishment. I'd expected her to say it, but that did nothing to mute the sting of her words. She'd never looked at me with such anger before, and knowing I'd lost her was breaking my heart. I suddenly felt exhausted, desperate to leave, needing to climb into my own bed and sob myself to sleep. There was no point in prolonging my visit, nothing I could say to make up for the mistakes I'd made today. I looked at Lily, needing to apologise though I knew it wouldn't make a difference. 'I'm so sorry,' I said quietly, hoping she could see just how deep my regret ran. 'If I could undo it, I would.'

'You can't.' She shook her head, and Jon eased off the door and moved to the sofa, slumping down heavily.

'Sit down, will you, Hannah,' he said, his voice gruff. 'We need to talk about this.'

'I don't think there's anything left to say,' I replied.

'After what we just told the police, I'd say there's a lot more we need to hear from you. And I think Lily deserves more than just a few muttered excuses about you wanting a baby. It's the first we've heard about any of that, and I'm sure you can understand how confusing it all is. I think we've only scratched the surface of why you've done this.'

I stared at him, wanting nothing more than to escape their scrutiny and go home, yet knowing he was right. I owed them this. I sighed, nodding a reluctant agreement, and with both of them staring at me, I sank down into the armchair and waited to be cross-examined.

CHAPTER THIRTY-EIGHT

Lily

I stared down at Hannah as she lowered herself into the armchair beneath the window, still drinking in the reassuring weight of my daughter in my arms. My heart had stopped palpitating wildly now, and the gentle fall and rise of Ella's chest against mine was more calming than any meditation class, any drug. She was back. I could have lost her tonight, and I would never forget how close I had come to it. I tried to keep my voice measured as I spoke, not wanting to disturb William and Maisy sleeping upstairs.

'I can understand your need to have a baby, Hannah. Believe me, I get that. It can drive a woman mad – that raw need becomes all-encompassing, it crawls through your skin, never fully leaves your mind.'

I paused, catching my breath. The truth was, I could feel deep in my gut the agony of what Hannah must have been going through this past year. Ever since I'd slid that box of papers from the top of her wardrobe, I had felt a ball of emotion wedged like a rock in the back of my throat, impossible to swallow or ignore. I *knew* Hannah. At least, I'd thought I did. She was a woman who never did anything by halves. If she set herself to completing a goal, she did it fully, threw herself in head first, and I could just imagine how crushed she would have been when she realised she didn't have control of her future. How the mounting negative pregnancy tests would have broken her spirit, made her feel unworthy. I knew what it would have cost her and I felt her pain as my own, despite her betrayal today. But I couldn't show that empathy now, couldn't risk letting down my guard with her. Despite my sadness, I was too angry to give in to pity. I needed to understand how she could have come to the decision to rip my world out from under me when it became clear that hers wasn't going her way.

I took a deep, shuddering breath, reining in the urge to cry, hardening my expression to protect myself. 'I know how hard the whole process must have been for you – the negative pregnancy tests, the failed IVF,' I continued, hearing the coolness of my tone and hating it. 'I get it, I really do. And if you had let me support you through the disappointment, I would have, in a heartbeat. I understand you were hurting, but what I just don't understand is why you would want to cause pain to *me*. Why you'd hurt me like this. How could you take my child, my newborn baby, and think for a second that was justifiable?'

Her shoulders remained tense, as if she was holding herself together for fear of snapping. I knew how she felt. 'I told you,' she said quietly. 'I didn't plan it.'

'But you *did* it, Hannah! You made a choice, and I want to know why. You're my best friend and you betrayed me. You betrayed Jon.'

She gave a bitter laugh, and I froze, glaring at her. 'Lily, I'm sorry I took her, I really am. And I'm beyond grateful for what you both just said to the police. Believe me, I never expected you to do that for me. But—' She broke off, shaking her head. 'I should go. This isn't a conversation we need to have.'

'Don't you dare!' I said. I could tell there was something more she wanted to say, and I knew I had to push her – it was exactly what I'd failed to do for all these months. 'You owe us this much after what you've done tonight.'

She looked up at me, her lips pursed, her expression indecisive, and I saw a flash of anger in her eyes that caught me off guard.

She nodded, resigned. 'Fine. If you really want to hear it, I'll say it, but I don't see what good it will do any of us.' She took a shaky breath, her hands gripping her knees as she perched on the edge of the seat. 'I think you've got a nerve to talk to me about betrayal, Lily, considering you've hardly been open with either of us.'

Jon looked up from his clasped hands, his eyes meeting mine, questioning. I shrugged, confused. How could she know? It was impossible. We'd been too careful. 'What do you mean?' I asked quietly.

Jon's shoulders tensed as he turned towards Hannah, waiting expectantly. She seemed to falter, her face flushing. 'Go on,' he pushed. 'If you have something to say, let's get it out in the open. It's for the best.'

Hannah stared at him, folding her arms tightly across her chest. She gave the briefest of nods and I watched her, feeling tense and wrong-footed. 'I would have said something sooner,' she began, 'but I didn't want to be the one to have to do it. I don't want to be the reason a marriage fails.'

I shook my head, my arms tightening instinctively around my daughter, a cold feeling spreading through my belly. 'What are you talking about? Jon? What's she saying?' I demanded. He shrugged, and I saw no tension in his expression, only open curiosity. He didn't look afraid of whatever secret she was about to spill, and that made me feel instantly more reassured.

Hannah looked up at me. 'I was waiting for you to tell me. To tell *him*. I think after all these years we deserve that, but clearly *you* don't.'

'Tell me what?' Jon asked, his eyes locking on mine.

Hannah took a breath. 'Lily. *Please*. Don't make me say this. Not when it should be you. Please, just be honest. I wouldn't have taken her if I believed for a second that she was in a happy, loving family. That you put her needs above your wants. I know what I did was wrong, but the choices you've made this past year contributed to what happened today, and you can't make it all black and white when we both know it's not that simple.'

I frowned, leaning my face down to Ella's head, sniffing deeply, trying to understand what Hannah was talking about. It was true, I had kept secrets from her, but that was the nature of marriage. Sometimes there were things that only the two of you knew, things that you had to hide from the outside world because it wasn't your place to reveal them. But secrets from Jon? No. Never. There was nothing he didn't know, no detail I'd failed to share with him. We'd always told each other everything.

I glanced up from Ella, seeing Hannah's rigid expression, her cold eyes waiting for a confession I couldn't offer. 'I'm sorry, Hannah, but I don't know what you want me to say.'

She shook her head sadly, and I saw her eyes glisten. 'I want…' she began, not breaking her gaze despite the tears that began to spill over, running down her cheeks. It was shocking to see. I couldn't ever remember having seen her cry before. Not once, in all our years of friendship.

'I want you to tell us the truth. I want you to admit that you had an affair. Maybe it's still going on – I don't know. I want you to tell Jon that the daughter he's spent the past six hours looking for might not even be his. And I want you to admit that you didn't even want her, that you considered getting rid of her because you're so ungrateful for your blessings you're willing to just throw them away without a care in the world. You have a perfect family, Lily, and I'm sorry, but sometimes it's easy to think that you don't deserve them, you don't appreciate what you've got. So, if you want to know the truth, maybe that's why I took her. Why should *you* get to have her when you don't even want the two you already had?' She sat back, breathing hard, her face soaked with tears, her short blonde hair falling in her eyes.

I stood dumbstruck, my hands shaking against Ella's sleeping body. I was shocked at her words, confused and hurt that she could ever think such awful things about me. This woman who I'd loved like a sister didn't know me at all. She didn't understand who I was, because if she did, even the tiniest bit, she would never accuse me of not loving my husband. My *children*. Didn't she know what they meant to me? I felt frozen, torn between wanting to defend myself and yet wanting to comfort her. It was distressing to see her like this, nothing like the strong, unflappable woman I had always known.

'Well?' she spat, wiping her nose on her sleeve. 'Aren't you going to say something?'

I opened my mouth to speak, but Jon got there first. He rose from his seat, coming to stand beside me, his arm wrapping around my shoulders in a show of solidarity that made me want to cry.

'Hannah,' he said gently, offering a sympathetic smile. 'What on earth has given you the idea that Lily has ever been unfaithful to me? Why would you think Ella isn't mine?'

Hannah blinked, clearly surprised by his calm reaction. 'It's the truth.'

'You…' I broke in, stifling a sob, 'you think I don't love my children? What would ever make you say that?'

She sighed. 'Lily, come on. Be honest. All you ever do is complain about them. You roll your eyes whenever William asks you to play. You're always telling me you're jealous of my life. My *freedom*. Poor Maisy may as well be invisible as far as you're concerned, and you can't pretend you didn't seriously consider an abortion when you found out you were pregnant with Ella. You never say anything about them that isn't negative. A moan, a worry. A regret.'

'Because I'm venting my frustrations with you!' I exclaimed. 'Because I'm *tired*, because they *are* hard work, because being a parent is the greatest challenge of my life! That's what best friends do, Hannah! They vent. They offload their worries, the exact same way you have always done with me. You're always moaning about work – meetings running late into the night, cock-ups with suppliers, missed connecting flights – but do I take that to mean you hate your job? That you don't want to be doing it? Of course I don't. I thought you knew that, Hannah. For goodness' sake, don't you get it? My children are everything to me. Everything!'

'You never said.'

'I didn't think I had to. Yes, William is intense, but I adore him. I love the time we spend together. I love how clever and curious he is, how he always wants to learn more. He teaches me so much and he never holds a grudge. He's the sweetest boy imaginable! And for all the times you see Maisy disappear off into her room, you miss the late-night chats we have when we cuddle up together in her bed. You don't see us baking together, picking berries in the garden or laughing over silly jokes we've made up. Maisy and I have grown so much closer in the past year, and you've missed it because you've not been around to see – haven't bothered to ask. You don't see me at two in the morning, looking down at Ella as I feed her, all of my family sleeping under the same roof, wishing I could press pause because I would do anything – *anything* – to stay in those moments. You don't see it because you aren't there. Because I don't tell you everything. Because I don't want to rub it in your face. And actually, because if I think about what I have right now, it makes me realise how much I have to lose and I can't fucking stand it! I can't…' I cried, hiccupping back a sob, determined to finish. 'I can't even speak of my blessings without wanting to scream. You talk about it not being fair? You have no idea, Hannah. None whatsoever. Because if you knew the truth, you wouldn't swap places with me. Not for a second. Yes, perhaps I talk about the little irritations of life too much. I paint a picture that's far from accurate, but it's out of self-preservation. It's—' I broke off, my throat spasming against a ball of emotion, my entire body shaking.

Jon pulled me into his arms, wordlessly pressing a kiss to my forehead, breathing deeply. Ella snuffled in the space between our bodies. I let myself be cocooned in the comfort he offered, to fall into the familiar blanket of safety I only ever felt when I was with him. For a long moment there was no sound but Ella's contented little sighs, and Jon's breath falling on my cheek.

Finally, he pulled back, his eyes meeting mine. He didn't have to speak. I knew his thoughts as if they were my own. I gave a tiny nod, and he caressed my cheek. Slowly he raised his head and looked at Hannah, who was sitting frozen on the edge of the armchair cushion, watching us with a bewildered expression.

He sighed. 'You've jumped to some wildly inaccurate conclusions, Hannah. But you were right about one thing. I *have* lied to you, and so has Lily. We've kept something from you for a long time, and that's my fault.'

'I don't understand. What do you mean?' she asked, leaning forward. Her hands, like mine, were shaking, and I hated that what we were about to tell her was only going to cause more pain.

Jon looked at me, and I could see how much it cost him to finally admit the truth out loud. We'd barely spoken of it, skirted around the issue for months, and now that the time had come, I wasn't sure I wanted to be here when he told Hannah. And yet, to walk out now would have been unforgivable. He rubbed his hands over his face and gave a heavy sigh that seemed to come from somewhere deep inside the very bones of him.

'There's no easy way to say it, so I won't try and make it sound pretty. I have cancer. I was diagnosed with Hodgkin lymphoma a short time before Lily got pregnant with Ella. I made her promise not to tell you – not to tell anyone – because' – he smiled wryly – 'I didn't want to be looked at with shock and pity – like you're doing right now,' he added, meeting Hannah's eyes. 'I'm sorry we didn't share it with you, and I know my decisions over the past year have contributed to the strain on your friendship.'

'I don't believe this…' Hannah whispered, the blood draining from her face. 'Oh my God, Jon… Lily…' She shook her head. 'It can't be true.'

I stood silently, unable to offer a word of sympathy, the wind knocked from my sails as if I were just hearing the news for the first time. 'But, you're going to get better?' I heard Hannah ask. 'You're getting treatment? Seeing doctors?'

He cleared his throat. 'I…'

I glanced sharply at Jon, saw him pause, sway on his feet. The world seemed to move in slow motion as I watched his eyes open wider, his mouth forming a surprised O, and then, time seemed to flick into hyper-speed as he suddenly pitched forward, collapsing face first into the glass coffee table with a sickening crash. There was a high-pitched ringing in my ears, the blood pumping thickly through my fogged brain, and I blinked, aware of Hannah shouting, crouched on a carpet of shattered glass beside him, his thin wrist clutched in her hand.

'Lily!' she yelled, and I gasped as if my head had been pulled from a bucket of water, the colours of the room far too sharp. Too real. 'Call an ambulance! Now! I'll start CPR.'

I stared open-mouthed, clutching my baby in my arms, her cries rising up around me, as the woman who had stolen one portion of my heart earlier that same day now lowered her mouth over my husband's blue-tinged lips, trying to save me from losing any more.

CHAPTER THIRTY-NINE

Hannah

My mouth was dry, my cheeks aching, the tendons in the backs of my hands throbbing painfully as I pressed down hard into Jon's chest. There was blood trickling down his cheek from a cut above his eye, and I tried not to think of it hot and damp against my own skin. I could feel the bone and sinew beneath my fingers, the muscle I'd always associated with the burly man barely present, and wondered how I'd missed such dramatic changes in him. It seemed impossible that I hadn't noticed before, but perhaps I simply hadn't looked close enough. I had always thought of him as being so strong. Now, I realised that strength was not only on a physical level. The emotional strength he'd needed to keep going, pretending, while his body waged a war against him, was hard to fathom.

He didn't stir as I pushed harder against his ribs, didn't make a sound, and I could feel a churning fear simmering just out of reach, ready to explode, hysteria moments away and getting closer with every breath I forced into his lungs. 'Please, Jon,' I whispered, leaning close. 'Please wake up.' I breathed again into his slack mouth, pinching his nose, wanting to shake him, slap him, whatever it took so that he would open his eyes and everything would be okay. The alternative was unthinkable, but even as I pressed harder against his chest, determined to make a difference, I could feel my hope ebbing away.

My arms shook, my head spinning, but I didn't slow, didn't even think of stopping. I heard movement behind me, and voices, but didn't break my focus. Then, with unexpected yet gentle force, I felt big hands wrap around the tops of my arms, pulling me back. I blinked, surprised, as I realised the person who had moved me aside was a paramedic, already stepping past me as his colleague, a tall woman with a watercolour tattoo of a lion covering most of her left forearm, bent over Jon, making assessments, giving quick, assertive instructions to the man.

I wanted to tell them to move, to let me continue, because trying to save him was better than hearing them tell me it was too late, but I couldn't speak. Instead, I looked up, seeing Lily's ghost-white face as she watched them work on her husband. A thousand stings broke through my consciousness as I became aware of the devastation surrounding me, the broken glass cushion, the angry red cuts on my knees that I had only just acknowledged. I stood slowly, my legs jelly, pins and needles crackling through my stiff limbs as the blood rushed back to my calves, and on unsteady feet, I moved towards her.

I hesitated only for a second before slipping my hand into hers, squeezing tight. She didn't look my way, but her fingers gripped mine as the two of us stood in desperate silence, waiting... wishing. Ella continued to cry, the sound casting a pitiful background to the horrific scene. I didn't offer to take her.

'We have a pulse!' the tattooed paramedic announced, passing something to her teammate, moving around Jon as she adjusted his position. She placed something firmly in his mouth, and I wanted to ask what was happening, if he was going to be all right, but I couldn't seem to find the words.

'Is he okay? Will he be okay?' I heard Lily voice the question I couldn't.

'He's breathing. We're taking him in. Are you coming in the ambulance?'

She nodded, eyes wide.

'You can't bring the baby. No space for car seats, and no time – we need to go now,' the paramedic said, already turning back to Jon, preparing him for the stretcher.

'I'll call my mum. She must be nearly here by now,' Lily murmured, looking at the clock on the mantelpiece, then down at Ella.

'Lil… go. Go with Jon. I can take care of the children until she arrives.'

She stared at me incredulously. 'I can't. How can I trust you?'

I gripped her hand tighter, meeting her eyes with determination. 'I promise you, I won't let you down. Look, I'll call your mum for you, find out where she is, wait here until she comes. I can bring Ella to you at the hospital if you like? Please, I want to help.'

She shook her head, turning to watch Jon being loaded onto a stretcher. The paramedics wheeled him from the room and I could see the desperation in her eyes. 'Lily, I swear to you, I will *not* break your trust again. I made a mistake. This changes everything. I love you. I love Jon. Let me help you.'

'We're ready to leave,' a voice called from the front door. Lily stared down at Ella, and I hated that I'd made this so hard for her when it should have been simple. This was my fault, my doing.

She pressed a kiss to Ella's head, then looked up, her expression wild with panic. 'Promise me? Promise you'll bring her the moment Mum arrives. You have to promise me, Hannah!'

'On my life, I swear it. Now go.'

She chewed her lip, her chin jutting forward, her hands wrapped tight around the crying, thrashing baby. From outside we heard the ambulance engine roar to life. She gave a panicked moan and passed Ella to me, and I saw what it cost her to hand her over. Then she tore her gaze away from the baby she'd only just got back, grabbed her handbag from the coffee table and rushed outside after her husband. I heard the ambulance door slam shut before it drove away, leaving me behind.

I stood, rocking Ella back and forth in my arms in the middle of the pile of broken glass, rubbing circles on her back and staring up at the family portrait above the fireplace, all the smiling faces I couldn't bear to lose.

CHAPTER FORTY

It was gone 11 p.m. when I finally made it through the main doors of the hospital and stared glassy-eyed at the board by reception, trying to figure out where to go. Ella was back in the baby sling, fast asleep, and I tried not to think about how this might be the last time I would hold her. I'd seen how hard it had been for Lily to walk away from her after what they'd been through today. What I had put her through. She'd had no choice tonight, but I knew things wouldn't continue this way.

I rubbed my palm over Ella's back, the action calming somehow as I turned from the sign, heading through the atrium in what I hoped was the right direction. When I'd knocked on Lily and Jon's front door this evening, I'd thought I would never get the chance to see Ella again, let alone be trusted to care for her alone. The idea that just a few short hours later I'd find myself in this position had been unthinkable, but then so had the events that had followed that knock on their door.

There was still a tension curled up in my belly, a fear that though they'd told the police it was all a misunderstanding, they might rethink their decision later. I had felt the anger coming off Lily as she demanded answers I hadn't wanted to give. It broke my heart that I'd destroyed a friendship that meant so much to me.

Being forced to admit what I'd been keeping from her all this time, to explain how I'd failed at the one thing I wanted most, had been utter agony. In the past, when I'd pictured telling her about what I'd been doing, it had always been in a positive light.

Finally getting the chance to see the surprise on her face as I showed her a grainy scan photo of the baby I was carrying. I'd replayed the conversation we might have over and over in my mind, unable to stop myself from smiling as I closed my eyes, seeing the way she would jump up, hold me tight, congratulate me and reprimand me teasingly for keeping such an enormous secret. I'd never imagined it would come out like this. With her hating me, and no baby, not even a scrap of hope left for what might yet come. And Jon…

I blinked back my tears, thinking of how he'd held my gaze so bravely as he'd told me the secret he'd been keeping, the news that had made me want to put my hands over my ears, blot it out because I couldn't bear to hear it. The emotions of the past few hours had been overwhelming, and now I had to fight to keep going, keep moving. There was no time to stop, to rest, not yet.

I walked quickly along the corridor, glancing at the signs as I passed. I was torn between wanting to get to Lily and desperately wanting to run in the opposite direction. I didn't want to hear the news I was sure I was going to hear. Something deep in my gut told me Jon wouldn't be okay, and I pushed it aside, refusing to give in to the fear. His skin as I'd bent over him, breathing my own life's breath into his lungs, had smelled like death. Like decay. It had made me recoil, the rancid fragrance surrounding me, and I'd had to lock my unease in a box in order to keep going. Even now, I could sense it clinging to my clothes, my hair, and I desperately wanted to scrub myself clean.

I rushed along the corridor, through a set of double doors, and glanced around. It was nothing like I'd expected. No activity, no shouting doctors giving urgent instructions, no doors slamming open and shut. A nurse was casually reading some paperwork at a desk, sipping a mug of tea intermittently. Lily had sent me a text instructing me to come to this ward rather than A&E, and it spoke volumes to me that Jon clearly had open access. I had only known it with one person before – my great-grandfather, when he was diagnosed with emphysema after a lifetime of smoking pipes and cigars – and I was aware that the gift of bypassing A&E was something given to only the most seriously ill patients. But did Lily understand that? And if she did, if she had known all this time that her husband was this sick, how had she managed to keep going as if everything was normal? To get out of bed in the morning and do everything that needed to be done, home-educate her children, feed and change Ella, cook and clean and talk like everything was okay?

I felt a sickening wave of guilt as I realised just how self-involved I had been. I hadn't suspected for a moment what the woman I considered my best friend was going through. What kind of friend did that make me?

I approached the nurse at the desk, asking after Jon and seeing the carefully blank expression fall over her face as she pointed down the hall to a room where she told me I would find Lily. I didn't ask how he was. I didn't want to hear the answer.

I walked slowly, seeing the brass plaque that read *Quiet Room*, and with a feeling of trepidation, I pushed open the door. Lily was on her feet, pacing, and she spun to look at me as I entered.

'Hi,' I said, stepping forward.

'Did my mum come? Are the children okay?'

I nodded, taking in her wild eyes and pale face – the picture of sheer terror. I wanted to hug her, but I stopped myself, unsure how she would react. 'They didn't wake up. Your mum is going to sleep in the spare room. I brought a couple of bottles and some extra nappies – didn't know if you'd have any with you.'

She took the refilled changing bag, then held out her arms pointedly towards Ella. I unclipped the straps of the sling, easing her out gently and handing her over, trying not to let myself feel the emptiness created by her absence.

'Did you tell my mum about Jon's cancer?' she asked, cuddling Ella beneath her chin.

'No. I didn't know what I should say, how much you wanted to share. I just said he'd been taken to hospital and we didn't know what was wrong. She wants you to call, but I did explain that it might not be for a while. She was a bit confused at finding me and Ella there, I didn't know if...' I shook my head, thinking of the mess I'd made of explaining the situation to Lily's mum. The poor woman was probably feeling completely lost right now, having driven all evening to help search for her kidnapped grand-daughter, only to find her back and her son-in-law rushed in to hospital. 'I cleared up the glass as best I could and put the frame of the coffee table out in the garage – I told her it got broken so she knows to look out for stray fragments. I didn't want anyone treading on a piece.'

Lily nodded, distracted, looking down at the floor, and I felt my stomach plummet as I took in her expression. 'What happened? Where is he now?' I asked, despite myself.

She looked up at me, her eyes wide and frightened. 'I don't understand what's happening... what they're telling me. The doctor said he's doing pretty badly... I don't understand. Jon told me he was recovering, that this Hodgkin lymphoma is easy to treat – he made it sound like he would be fine; he's always told me that. But now, the doctor said...' She paused, biting down hard on her lip, turning it white beneath the pressure of her teeth. 'He said Jon has leukaemia, Hannah.'

'What? No!' I gasped.

'When he realised I didn't know, he left the room in a hurry, and now nobody will tell me what the hell is going on or when I can see my husband. What is *happening*? How can any of this be real?'

I stood stiff, unbending, unable to relax for fear of falling apart, as Lily sat down on the small sofa, placing Ella on the cushion beside her leg. She patted her daughter's belly, watching as Ella's head moved to one side, her rosebud mouth sucking on air as she continued to sleep, unaffected while the world fell apart around her. Lily edged away a few inches, her head dropping heavily into her hands. I could hear her ragged breathing, the sobs she was fighting not to release, and I recognised that need to be strong, to keep going, to never give in to those emotions, because if you did, the people who needed you, relied on you, would lose their footing and everything around you would come crashing down. But it seemed to me the time to be strong had long since passed. The demolition of her world had already begun.

'Lily,' I whispered. 'Is he... did they say he's going to—'

'Don't!' Her head snapped up, her eyes fire as they met mine. 'Don't you say it. Don't even think it. He's my husband, and he's going to be fine.'

'I—' I broke off as I heard the door open behind me and stared, gobsmacked, as a man I recognised stepped into the room. The red Honda man. Up close, he was even more handsome than I'd realised, his dark hair thick and shiny, his blue eyes expressive, set in a warm, kind face with a strong jawline. Lily moved instantly, jumping up from her seat and rushing into his open arms, clinging to him, his hands wrapping around her. She gave a low, guttural moan, pressing her face into his shirt.

'I came as soon as I got your message,' he said, not making any move to let her go.

'You've got to be fucking kidding me!' I heard the words leave my lips, the venom intertwined with absolute disbelief. I stepped forward, my eyes wide, my hands shaking as I pointed a trembling finger at the pair of them. 'Your husband is here, fighting for his life, and you invite *him* to come and wait it out with you?'

Lily pulled back, her face soaked with tears, her brow furrowed. 'What?' she breathed, clearly feigning confusion at my anger.

'I know who he is, Lily!' I hissed, trying not to give in to the urge to yell, determined not to wake Ella. 'I know he's been at your house when Jon's been away! I've seen his car on your driveway, the long-drawn-out hugs you think nobody can see. I saw him leave just before you announced you wanted an abortion, and don't think I haven't put two and two together! I knew it!' I said, hearing the shrill rise of my voice, despite myself, furious that I hadn't had the nerve to confront her sooner. 'I knew all along, but I didn't think you'd sacrifice Jon, after everything he's done for you. Don't you think you could have had enough respect to wait for him to die before moving on to the next one? Or is your happiness too important to you?'

Lily gasped, her hands flying to her mouth, fresh tears welling in her swollen eyes. The man, taller than me by a long way, furrowed his brow, stepping back to look at me, one hand still on Lily's shoulder, as if he were supporting her. I narrowed my eyes, staring at him. 'And *you*, coming here when her husband, the man she's spent the past twenty years with, is at death's door! How dare you!'

'Hannah,' Lily said quietly. 'Is that really how little you think of me? You don't know me at all, do you? You really have no idea about anything.' She shook her head, wiping her eyes with the back of her hand, and I felt suddenly uncertain, my shoulders slumping as if the air had been sucked out of my body. An awful crawling sensation of guilt began to spread through me as I took in her reaction: sadness, not guilt. Disappointment where I had been expecting shame.

The intruder reached down to the coffee table, plucking a handful of tissues from a small square box and handing them to her. She took them, offering a watery smile in return. He stepped towards me. 'Um, perhaps I should introduce myself,' he said, extending a hand.

I glanced at it but didn't take it, and he withdrew it, slipping it into his pocket.

He looked at Lily and then back to me. 'My name is Joseph Fox. I'm a volunteer with the hospital's cancer support unit.

I've been helping Lily and Jon over the past year, though admittedly, Jon has refused most of the support on offer. But Lily has needed someone to talk to throughout these past months, and I've been able to provide that. And,' he said, smiling wryly, 'I can assure you that my relationship with *both* parties is purely professional.'

I shook my head, confused. 'Ella isn't your daughter?'

He gave a little cough, his eyes meeting Lily's before returning to me. 'No. She isn't.' He paused, as if he wanted to say more, but stopped himself, turning away with a flash of emotion I didn't miss. There was more to his story than he was letting on.

'You seem upset about that,' I pushed, still not believing I was being told the whole truth.

'Hannah.' Lily's voice carried a warning edge that compelled me to dig further, to uncover whatever secrets they were hiding. 'Drop it. Now.'

'Why? Why not get it all out in the open? Everything else is on the table. Why not this?'

Lily folded her arms. 'Because Joseph doesn't need to get caught up in our drama. That isn't why he's here, and you have no right to grill him like this.'

Joseph turned back to me with a small shrug. 'No, it's okay. I mean, if it helps clear things up, I don't mind.'

'You don't have to explain yourself to anyone,' Lily insisted, touching his arm with a familiarity that made me uncomfortable.

'I know. But I've heard a lot about Hannah from you, and I know how close you once were. If I can help you regain that closeness, I will.'

He gave a deep sigh, and I suddenly wondered if I really wanted to hear whatever he was about to say. I stepped back, folding my arms tight across my chest as if to protect myself.

'Hannah,' Joseph said softly, 'the reason your comment about Ella made me emotional was because my own daughter died five years ago from leukaemia. She was just two at the time and it remains the most heartbreaking experience of my life. It's why I went into this role, why I'm prepared to come out at all hours to offer support. I understand how hard it is to watch the person you love most in the world slip away. It was an experience that broke me, reshaped me, and taught me more about myself than anything else could have had the power to do, and in some ways I'm grateful for it, because it led me to this path of helping others through their own pain.' He turned to face Lily. 'I didn't know about Jon's secondary cancer. When I got your text just now and saw the word leukaemia, my heart just stopped. I thought, like you, that he was getting better. He never told me anything to indicate otherwise. Of course, I couldn't have broken his confidentiality if he had, but I want you to know I wasn't keeping anything from you. I'm so sorry he's here now, and I'll do anything I can to support you both.'

'Thank you,' she whispered, glancing over her shoulder to look at her sleeping baby.

I felt dumbstruck, completely lost for words as I absorbed what this meant. The conclusions I had jumped to about Lily were so far from the truth that I couldn't blame her for feeling I didn't have the faintest idea who she was. I didn't. We hadn't talked for so long, not properly, and in the absence of truth, I'd filled in the blanks with catastrophic conclusions. The mistakes I had made were unforgivable. Taking Ella, accusing Lily of adultery… I'd acted on assumptions, and now it was clear to me that nothing I had thought about my best friend was true. She *did* love her family. More than I'd ever imagined.

'I'm so sorry,' I said, seeing what it had cost Joseph to tell me his story. His mouth was pressed into a tight line, as if he were holding back a tsunami of emotions and I wished I could help ease his pain.

'It's okay.' He smiled, his eyes creasing with genuine warmth, and I didn't doubt that he meant it.

I looked to Lily, wishing I could have been a better friend to her. 'Lily, I... I'm sorry,' I said, my eyes welling up as they met hers. 'I got it all so wrong.'

She turned away, walking over to the sofa, her shoulders stiff and brittle as she gazed down at her sleeping daughter. I watched, wanting nothing more than to go back in time, start again, be more honest and less self-involved. I'd been so wrapped up in *my* life, *my* worries, *my* hopes that I'd missed all of Lily's, and I'd let her down badly.

Joseph cleared his throat. 'You both look dead on your feet. I'm going to go for a wander, see if I can find somewhere to get a decent cup of coffee. I may be a while. You two should talk.' He flashed me another smile as he dipped out of the room as quickly as he'd appeared, leaving the two of us alone.

CHAPTER FORTY-ONE

Lily

'I really put my foot in it there, didn't I?' Hannah said softly as Joseph disappeared out of the door.

I turned from Ella, still sleeping peacefully on the sofa, shaking my head incredulously at the monumental understatement.

Hannah clicked her tongue against her teeth, eyes still on the closed door, then sighed, turning to look at me. I could see the embarrassment lingering in her expression at having got things so wrong about my relationship with Joseph. 'I'm glad you've had someone you could talk to about Jon,' she continued. 'I'm just sorry it wasn't me. I wish you could have told me, Lil.'

I glared at her, seething with rage. 'You know, Hannah, if you'd bothered to look closer, spend some real time with me, ask more than surface questions, you would have guessed what was going on in a matter of weeks. I promised Jon I wouldn't tell you, but I never expected it to stay a secret. Not between us. We were best friends before this all happened, I loved you like a sister, but now…' I shook my head. 'You weren't there for me when I needed you most, and now you come in here accusing me of having an affair with the only person who has been by my side through this whole nightmare. Joseph has been great, but I don't see him often, and when I do, it's hard to tell him everything I'm feeling. He's a friend, and he understands what I'm going through, but it's not the same as having the support of the people who love you. I've been so alone this past eighteen months, Han. So desperately alone, and yes, I get it, you were going through your own stuff, but you cut me out. You could have told me all of it, but you chose not to, and that put a wall between us. Jon didn't want you to know he was ill, I *couldn't* tell you, but what stopped you from opening up to me?'

She lowered her head, looking at her shoes. 'Lil…' She gave a shaky sigh, and when she looked back at me, I saw that she was crying again. 'I know how badly I've messed everything up. I wanted to tell you about my baby plans, but I couldn't. At the start, it just felt so private, and I knew how much of a shock it would be for you to hear what I was planning. I've never been the maternal type, you know that, but I've realised now how much of that was because of my relationship with my own mother. I didn't want to be like her, repeat her mistakes and inflict the kind of childhood I had on a child of my own. That loneliness is a cruelty no one should have to endure. *I* shouldn't have had to, though I never understood that until very recently. I blamed myself for not being good enough, interesting enough, clever enough, but it was my parents' fault, not mine. I see that now. But I'm *not* the same as them, I'm really not. I would never treat *anyone* the way they treated me. If I'd managed to have a baby, they would have been—'

She broke off, choking back a sob, wiping a shaking hand across her damp eyes. She held the back of her hand to her closed eyelids, breathing deep, her voice cracking as she continued. 'They would have been so loved. They would never have doubted how much they were wanted.'

I stared at her, shocked at what she was admitting. I'd always known that as a child, she'd craved more from her parents, needed more than they were willing to give. We'd talked about it, but never in much depth, and now I realised that we'd barely scratched the surface. I'd assumed she didn't even think about it anymore;

she was always so focused on the future, it was hard to imagine her still carrying the scars of her past.

She pulled a crumpled tissue from the pocket of her shorts, blotting her bloodshot eyes with it with a shrug. 'I always pulled away from the idea of starting a family of my own, not because I didn't want to, but because I was afraid. It was out of fear that I chose my work first, that I refused to consider an alternative path.' She shook her head. 'I suppose I might have been oversensitive, but I didn't want you to think I was being silly, going through some mid-life crisis or something. I thought that if I waited until I was pregnant to share the news with you, not only would it be an amazing surprise, but I wouldn't have to convince you how much I really wanted it. But it never happened for me, and by the time I realised how difficult it was going to be – the hormones, the IVF, the realisation that it hadn't worked month after month after month… by the time it got that far, it felt too late to tell you.'

Her eyes met mine and I folded my arms, feeling dazed and vulnerable, sensing she was about to shine a spotlight on my own faults. She lowered her voice, and I looked away, trying not to cry. I always found it hard to keep my composure when anyone else cried, but seeing Hannah like this – strong, unshakable Hannah – was tearing me in two.

'I knew there was something you were keeping from me too, Lil,' she went on. 'Although you're right, I jumped to the wrong conclusion and never guessed about Jon being ill. I felt like we couldn't share things the way we once had, and the baby stuff, it was so raw… such a vulnerable part of myself, that to tell you would have taken real trust, something I could feel breaking between us. There were secrets tainting our relationship, and the more you kept your mouth closed, the more I stepped back, watched you and Jon for clues. You never hold his hand anymore. You don't hug. He's constantly trying to get close to you and you're always pulling away. After seeing you and Joseph together, knowing Jon was away, and then hearing the news that you were pregnant, it was hard not to think you were going behind his back. You seemed so cold with him, and you've always been such a close, intimate couple.'

I nodded slowly, then moved towards the sofa, my legs shaking with exhaustion, the adrenaline that had carried me through the day long since gone. 'I had no idea you'd noticed,' I said softly.

Hannah moved around the coffee table, taking a seat at the opposite end of the sofa, Ella positioned between us, still sound asleep on the middle cushion. 'I did. I knew something was wrong. Something serious. But I thought it was because you were unhappy in your life. You're always talking about how you wished you could retrain and have a career, how often Jon's away with his work, how you don't have any money to take up new hobbies or go on holiday. I thought you'd gone looking for happiness elsewhere.'

I nodded, realising how it must have looked without the context. 'You're right, I know. I *have* been cold with Jon. But it's not because I don't love him. It's because I do. Too much. I can't bear the thought of losing him. Behind closed doors I can let myself go a bit, but in public, I can't trust myself not to fall apart if he hugs me, holds me, reminds me what I have to lose. I needed to be strong, to show the kids that everything is okay, keep Jon's secret for him. Bursting into tears every time he touches me, because I'm reminded of what he's going through and what I have to lose, is not the way to do it. I can't be a strong mother and wife if I give in to my fears. I haven't had a choice.'

Hannah shuffled across the sofa cushion and reached over Ella, taking my hand in hers, squeezing tight. I could feel her trembling, the cool, damp sweat coating her palm. 'You can choose to share the burden of his secrets,' she said softly. 'I know now. And if you let me, I'll be here for you both. I want you to be able to lean on me.' A tear ran down her cheek and I resisted the urge to comfort her, the old habit of trying to fix everything, even when I knew it was impossible.

I shook my head, sliding my hand from hers, though part of me wished it could be so simple. I didn't feel angry now. I was too wiped out to feel much of anything. My body felt like jelly, my head thick and dizzy, and I knew that despite my deep exhaustion, I wouldn't sleep. Not tonight. I understood more now about why Hannah had done what she had, and I felt empathy for her, but it didn't change the fact that she had betrayed my trust and broken my heart. 'You stole my daughter, Hannah,' I whispered. 'We can't just wipe that out.'

I looked up as the door opened and the ward sister stepped into the room. 'Jon's awake,' she announced quietly, smiling as she saw the sleeping baby between us. 'He wants to talk to you.'

'Oh.' I looked down at Ella, wondering if I should wake her.

'Lily,' Hannah said, and I heard the worry in her voice. 'Please, go to Jon. I'll stay with Ella. She's safe with me.'

I bit back a comment, a flare of anger rising up in me, but then I thought of Jon waiting for me and pushed the feeling aside.

'Just for tonight. I don't have a choice, but that doesn't mean—' I broke off with a heavy sigh, unsure what any of it meant now. What would become of the friendship I'd once cherished so much. I couldn't deal with those questions right now. 'I'm not going far. And I don't want you to leave this room. I need to know you'll be here when I get back.'

The ward sister raised an eyebrow in surprise as Hannah nodded. 'We'll be right here. I promise.'

I stood up, feeling my bowel twist painfully. I was terrified to step out into the corridor and walk down it to where Jon waited. I didn't want to hear what he had to say, but I couldn't pretend anymore. I had to know the truth.

With a final glance at my daughter, I followed the sister out of the room, pulling the door shut behind me.

CHAPTER FORTY-TWO

I stood outside the door to Jon's room, breathing in deeply, trying to steady myself before pushing it open. When no wave of calm came, I sighed and stepped quietly inside, squeezing my hands into tight fists by my sides to try and stop them from shaking. Jon was lying on his back, head slightly raised on the hospital bed, an intimidating stack of pumps attached to a tall metal stand beside him, each one connected to a clear line that ran across his body, attaching to a cannula on the inside of his wrist. His eyes were only half open, and his skin had a bluish, waxy sheen that frightened me, made this all far too real.

I closed the door quietly behind me and stepped forward, seeing that at least his chest was rising and falling. He opened his eyes slowly, and I stood, glued to the spot as our eyes met.

'I thought I was going to lose you,' I whispered, hearing the crack in my voice as tears spilled from my tired eyes, blurring the image of his face. I lurched forward, bending over the bed, holding his head between my hands, kissing him hard on the mouth. 'Jon, I thought you weren't coming back to me! I was so scared. And the doctor – he said you have leukaemia, but that can't be true. I don't understand what's happened... what's going on?'

'Lils...' His throat sounded raw and scratchy. 'Babe, the doctor shouldn't have told you that.'

I felt relief sweep through me and nodded vehemently. 'I knew he couldn't be right, I knew—'

'He shouldn't have told you because it was *my* news to break.'

My heart seemed to stop in my chest. 'No.'

'I wanted to tell you before. I tried, but… well, the crux of it is that I was nearly at the end of my chemo – I thought this whole nightmare was almost over, but then, some blood tests came back a few months ago showing some issues and, well…' He closed his eyes as if he couldn't bear to finish the sentence. I waited, not wanting to hear it any more than he wanted to say it. Finally, he opened his eyes, fixing me with an intense stare. 'The short version is, I've developed something called acute myeloid leukaemia. It's rare and they said I was really unlucky to get it, but it's aggressive, Lily.'

'Is that why you collapsed tonight?'

He nodded. 'They say I've had a bleed in my lungs. Acute pulmonary haemorrhage.'

'Jon!'

'I know. And if I'd thought it was all going to fall apart this quickly, I would have tried harder to tell you. I hate that I put you through that tonight – I know how terrifying it must have been for you.'

'I thought you were getting better.' I pressed my head to his chest, hearing the reassuring beat of his heart. 'We can fight this together. You should have told me, but it's not too late. You aren't going anywhere. You can't.'

There was a pause, the feel of his fingers moving slowly up the back of my neck, strong and steady. They slid into my hair and I heard him sigh. I raised my face from his chest to meet his eyes.

'I'm so sorry, babe, but it would seem I am.'

'What?' I gasped, the moisture evaporating from my mouth. I clutched at the hospital gown he wore, panic coursing through my veins.

He shook his head, looking up at the ceiling, and I got the horrible feeling he was trying not to cry. 'I tried to tell you, I really did. I think you know it too. But you didn't want to hear it, you weren't ready, and I didn't know how to make you listen. It seemed harsh to put you through it, especially when you already knew about the Hodgkin's. You were seven months pregnant with Ella when I found out, and so stressed already. You knew I was getting treatment – it didn't seem so important to give you all the information when it would only frighten you.'

He paused, breathless, and I watched as his lips turned a deeper shade of blue, wondering if I should call someone to come and help. He coughed then leaned back on his pillow, clearing his throat.

'I still had hope. I thought I could fight this. The thought of leaving you and the kids… I couldn't bear it. I know how scared you were to have Ella when we were going through such a period of uncertainty, and at the time, I felt sure that we should be grateful for such a gift. I know she wasn't planned, but we had to have conceived her just before I started that first round of chemo, right after our anniversary party. I had this feeling that she might be the last opportunity, our last chance to make a baby together, and as it turned out, I was right. The chemo has destroyed my health, my fertility, though it hasn't made a dent in the leukaemia. For every reassuring blood test I get back, a far worse one will follow a few weeks later. It's taken hold of me, Lils, and I can't seem to slow it, let alone stop it. I know how much harder things are with a newborn, but Ella will get you through this. She'll give you the strength to keep going when I… when I'm not around anymore.'

'Jon, don't you dare talk like that. She's not our last, because you're going to get well. We're going to raise our children together. Have more if we want to. We're not letting you leave us!'

'I tried so hard, Lils. I did everything I could to make this go away. I had to lie to you about some of it. When I was away earlier this month, it wasn't for work. I went to a treatment centre in California where they put you on a detox. Coffee enemas. Fasting. The lot.'

'And did it help? Will it work?' I asked, shocked that he'd lied to me and I hadn't even suspected. He'd been in America while I'd assumed he was on a ship off the coast of Norway, researching locations for filming the melting ice caps for the documentary he was so passionate about. How could he have been on the opposite side of the world without me sensing it?

He shook his head. 'The last tests show that the cancer has progressed even further. None of it made the slightest difference.'

'But you will get better! The doctors can keep trying different treatments. You can go to another detox centre. You have to keep trying, Jon!'

He shook his head. 'No, darling. I'm sorry, but it's gone too far. I...' He choked back a sob, and my hand gripped his, my knuckles turning white as his tears began to fall. 'I can't fight this anymore. It's what I've been trying to find the words to tell you this past month. I'm dying, Lils, and it's happening more quickly than I can keep up with.'

I shook my head, staring into his eyes, knowing he meant it. That he believed it. And Jon wasn't a man to give up. Not unless the odds were stacked too heavily against him.

'I can't lose you,' I whispered. 'I just can't.'

'I'm so sorry.'

He pulled me close, and for the first time in as long as I could remember, I let myself go completely, held him fully with every last ounce of my strength, as if I could transfer it to him. The time for putting up walls, for self-protection was over. It hadn't helped. I'd lost him anyway.

CHAPTER FORTY-THREE

Hannah

I had no idea what to expect as I walked slowly down the corridor towards the room where Jon and Lily waited. The nurse had told me that they wanted to see me, that was all. I held Ella awkwardly in my arms, walking as if I were heading to the executioner's block. Every time I closed my eyes, the image of Jon's lifeless body slumped on a glittering blanket of glass burned bright against my retinas, and I felt a shudder travel through me. It would be a long time before that image would fade, before the memory of the taste of his mouth left me.

I pushed the door open, stepping inside the small, clean-smelling room. The blinds were open, and outside the moon was high and bright in a cloudless inky sky. Jon smiled unexpectedly as I met his eyes, holding out his arms, and I moved towards him, lowering Ella for him to hold. Lily, watching him, gave a choked sob from the chair on the opposite side of his bed, pressing her face into her shaking hands.

'Hi, Hannah,' Jon said, breaking the tense silence.

'Hi,' I replied, wishing I knew what to say next. Lily looked distraught, but Jon was resolute and calm.

'I hear you gave me CPR,' he said softly, his gaze flicking between my face and Ella's. 'Thank you.'

'I couldn't save the coffee table, I'm afraid.' I tried to keep my voice light, but just one look at him screamed that this wasn't the time for jokes. 'Jon… tell me. I need to hear it.' Our eyes met and I saw the pain in his, the resolve as his jaw set.

He gave a small nod and I knew it was going to be bad. 'I'm dying, Han. Bloody quickly as it happens. Funny how the days seem to stretch on forever, how you think you have decades left to do all the things you'd hoped to, and then, out of the blue, you realise the sand is slipping through the gap in life's hourglass and you can't plug the hole. I never thought about my mortality, about checking out early, but now that it's happening, I wish I'd been more aware of how little time we get. I might have done a few things differently. Spent more time with the people I loved.' He glanced at Lily, held out his hand towards her, and she grabbed it, pressing it to her damp cheek.

I stood awkwardly at the side of the bed, unsure how to even begin to respond to his admission. His words made it all real, and though I'd known it instinctively since the moment I'd watched him collapse, to have it said out loud made it feel final, like the beginning of a new stage. A goodbye. I felt a sick emptiness deep inside me at the idea that soon Jon and Lily would be a thing of the past. I could only imagine how this must be tearing her apart.

Jon caught me glancing her way and pursed his lips. 'Today has been eventful. It's pushed us all to our limits, shattered illusions and revealed the secrets we were all so desperate to keep to ourselves. The trust has been damaged. But look,' he said, smiling down at Ella. 'She's back. We're all here together, as we should be. Hannah, you made some bad choices today, and I won't deny that you broke our hearts. You terrified me, to put it bluntly, and when I thought you'd gone for good, taking Ella with you, I won't lie, I wanted to hunt you down and tear you limb from limb.'

I looked down at my feet, guilt coursing through me at what I'd put them through when they were already struggling so much with the effort of simply making it through each day.

'But you came back, and if you hadn't, I might not have had the opportunity to have this conversation now. You saved me tonight, Han, gave me a chance to say the things I needed to before it was too late. That means something, it really does. It's going to be hard going forward, and Lily is going to need your friendship more than ever before. And you'll need hers too. You've always been so close, and it was my fault the cracks formed in your relationship, my insistence that nobody should know about any of this.' He gestured to the hospital bed, the drip stand. 'Lily, I should never have asked it of you. It wasn't fair to make you deal with this without Hannah's support.'

Lily didn't look my way as she spoke, her cheek still pressed against Jon's outstretched hand, her fingers clasped tight around his as if afraid he might pull away. 'I don't know if I want the support of a woman I can't trust,' she said through a veil of tears.

I shook my head, knowing she was entirely justified in her reaction, yet wishing she could see how sorry I was. 'Lil, I made a mistake, a stupid, selfish mistake, and I'm sorry. If I could undo it, I would.'

'But you can't. And, Jon, please, stop this awful talk of death. You can't give up – you owe us more than that. You aren't going anywhere!' she cried, her voice suddenly shrill.

I could hear the panic behind her words, the hysteria so close to the surface, and I wished I could do or say something to make it easier for her to accept.

Jon, his face set in a blank mask, unwilling to give in to his emotions right now, fixed me with a knowing stare, as if he too would have given anything to help Lily survive this. I had never doubted his feelings for her in all the years I'd known him. His eyes locked on mine, asking the silent questions he needed answers to. *Will you be there? Will you stick by her when I can't?* I knew exactly what he needed from me, and I nodded, determined to do whatever it took to be the friend she would so desperately need in the coming months.

He seemed to relax as he understood my commitment. He leaned back on the stack of pillows, Ella snuffling against his chest. 'I won't give up on life, Lils. I never have. If there's a chance, I'll grab it with both hands. But you need to prepare yourself for the worst, because unless you do, this is going to be so much harder on you.'

Lily's eyes widened, her hands coming to her mouth, stifling an animal moan that sent shivers through me. Her body slumped over in the hard plastic chair. 'I can't do this, Jon, I can't!'

Slowly, I walked around the bed, coming to stand behind her. 'Lily…' I said, unsure how to even begin to help. I reached out slowly, placing a hand on her shuddering back, and she shot up and spun around, kicking the chair over in her fury.

'Don't you *dare* try and comfort me – don't even think of it! I want you to leave! You have no right to be here, none whatsoever! How can you think you can just wipe out what you did to me and become the friend I thought you were? You're a fake! A liar! It's over, Hannah. You've killed whatever pitiful excuse of a friendship we were clinging to. I've lost you, and now I'm losing my… my…' She turned, slamming her palm hard against the wall, and I jumped, shocked.

I had thought we'd shared a moment back in the waiting room, that there might have been the slightest shift in her feelings towards me after we'd both spoken so frankly about the secrets we'd been keeping from one another. I had held her hand, and though she'd let mine go, she hadn't been filled with the same sense of rage I saw now. I knew that hearing the words from Jon's lips would have broken her heart, and I could see just how much she was hurting, how she needed to shout and lash out to protect herself from the true crushing reality of her feelings. After all she'd endured today, this would be the final straw, and

I was racked with guilt at how much pain I had caused her on top of everything else.

I glanced towards the door, wondering if anyone would come to investigate the noise, but heard nothing. Perhaps I should go now. Give her time to process everything without me getting in her face. Maybe she was right, and we'd gone too far to come back to one another. I'd rendered the trust irreparable.

I stepped back, then stopped as I saw Jon slip out of bed, leaving Ella asleep on the mattress, her arm pressed against the rails that ran along the side. I watched in silence as he approached Lily, feeling increasingly awkward at still being here. He moved behind her, snaking an arm around her waist, turning her to face him. She melted into his chest, her arms tight across his back. In his hospital gown, he looked diminished, a tiny fragment of the brawny man I'd always pictured when I thought of him.

'She took Ella. She kept secrets. But she brought her back to us, Lils. She never would have stayed away, and you know it as much as I do. She didn't do it to hurt us. She did it out of desperation and pain. We all do stupid things when we're desperate, don't we?'

He eased away from her, though his hand still clasped her arm as if for support, and I resisted the urge to rush forward and help him back to the bed, though I knew that was exactly where he needed to be. He straightened his spine with what looked like considerable pain as he turned to face me. 'Hannah, I don't fully understand what happened today, but what matters most is that you realised your mistake. You turned back and brought our daughter home to us, and that took courage. We can't just gloss over what happened – it will take time to repair the cracks that formed between us today – but we *will* get there, I have no doubt about that.' His eyes were filled with soft sincerity. 'You're too important to us not to try.'

I bit my lip, determined not to cry again as I nodded, overcome with gratitude at how gracious he was being.

Lily pulled back from him, her expression incredulous. 'You can't be serious?'

'I am. You'll need each other in the coming weeks and months. And whatever you think right now, I know you can get through this and become as close as you once were. That's what I want. I have to know you're not going to be alone. That you'll have someone who'll be here for you when I can't be.'

Lily stepped back, shaking her head wordlessly, and I saw him wobble without her for support. He placed one hand on the wall, but Lily didn't see. She was already walking out of the door, slamming it hard behind her.

CHAPTER FORTY-FOUR

Lily

I ran along corridors, down stairwells, through doors, hardly seeing where I was going in my need to escape this crushing claustrophobia. The hospital seemed to weigh heavy on me, the expectation of despair, the loss pulsing through the walls. I made it to the front of the building and didn't slow as I rushed outside into the blissfully cool night air. I gasped in lungfuls of the clean, fresh air, only slightly tainted by the smell of cigarettes being smoked by pyjama-clad patients with drip stands and determination.

I crossed the path to move away from the little group and walked towards a row of empty benches, collapsing onto the first in the row and tipping my head back. The moon was glaringly bright, full and glowing, blocking out the light of the stars in its closest circles. I stared up at it, the sound of my own heart thudding in my ears, Jon's words swimming through my mind incessantly. I wished I could unhear those words, that I could do something to make them untrue, because I couldn't lose him. I couldn't even think of it.

My thoughts travelled to all the times he'd approached me recently, a grim, serious look on his face that had the effect of making me jump up from whatever I was doing and rush from the room. He was right that I'd been impossible to pin down. I'd known he wanted to tell me something I didn't want to hear. But not this. Never this.

I pulled my feet onto the edge of the bench, hugging my knees tight, and saw a figure moving towards me, illuminated by the lights of the hospital. 'I thought I made it clear I didn't want to see you.'

Hannah nodded, though she didn't slow her pace. She reached the bench and sat down beside me. Her fingers knotted together, but she didn't speak, and that irritated me enough to make me break the silence.

'Did you leave Ella alone with Jon? What if he passes out?'

'I asked a nurse to come and sit with him. It's quiet on the ward and she didn't mind. Besides, he's not likely to fall asleep not knowing if you're okay, is he?'

'Of course I'm not okay.'

'I know.'

Her eyes met mine, warm and comforting, and I suddenly felt tired of fighting her. My head slumped forward, my throat tight with emotion as I pressed the heels of my hands to my eyes, squashing back the tears, though they came all the same. 'How am I supposed to do this, Han? How do I keep going without him? This is *Jon*. He's the most incredible man, he deserves a full life, years of happiness ahead of him. He works so hard, and when he comes home, he's the best dad the children could ever wish for. He's going to miss them growing up. He's going to miss everything. It's not right!' I cried.

She handed me a clean tissue from a pack in her bag, and I took it, balling it in my fist.

'It's not going to be easy. But you will get through this, Lil. You have to, for your babies. They're going to need you to be strong for them.'

'And who's going to be strong for me?' I whispered.

'I am. I know I don't deserve your forgiveness, and that's fine. I don't need it. But I will be there for you through this, Lil. Whether you want me or not, I'm not going to let you go through it alone. I'll be with you for all of it and I'll make sure you don't crumble. I'll do everything in my power to help you keep going.'

I blotted my eyes with the balled-up tissue and looked at her. 'I just don't know, Han… I don't know anything anymore. This morning, heading through the gates of the theme park with the sun shining and the sound of children laughing all around us, seems like another lifetime now. Another world.'

'I know. If we could go back—' She broke off with a sigh. 'You have to know, I would never have kept Ella. I just went a bit mad for a minute. I let my fantasy take over. My hormones have been crazy. There's no excuse for what I did today, but I know she's not mine and I would never have kept her, even if bringing her back meant being put behind bars. I'm so sorry. For her. For Jon.'

I nodded, certain that she meant it, though I didn't have the energy to decide what that meant for our friendship. 'I don't know what to do now,' I admitted. 'How to get through these next weeks, months, waiting for the moment it will come. How does anyone keep going, knowing that death is lurking on the periphery of everything you do?'

'One minute at a time. And without thinking of the future. You know you have *this* moment. *This* minute. It's all any of us ever truly has, it's just that you have the raw reality of Jon's mortality staring you in the face. But in this moment, he's here, he's alive. And he's upstairs, waiting for you to come back to him.' I felt her hand wrap around mine, and this time I didn't pull back as I let her words comfort me.

'You're right.' I gave a shaky sigh. 'I have to go and talk to him.'

'I think so. Do you want me to take Ella home?'

I shook my head. 'No. I need her with me tonight.'

'I understand.'

I stood, sliding my hand from hers, and for the first time in as long as I could remember, I felt the fragments of that sisterly bond between us.

She smiled. 'Call me as soon as you wake up. I'll come and see you – here or at home, whichever you want.'

I nodded. 'Thanks, Han.'

I turned, glancing up at the moon one last time, and then, feeling calm and ready, I held my head high and walked back inside to go and be the wife my husband deserved.

'Hi.' I stood in the doorway, watching Jon as he ran one finger over Ella's cheek as if he were drinking in the moment, saving it up to take with him. The nurse, sitting unobtrusively in a chair by the window, rose to her feet, offering me a warm smile and then heading past me, leaving us alone. I stepped into the room, closing the door softly behind me. 'Jon, I'm sorry. That was unfair of me to run off like that. It's you who should be throwing a fit and yelling about the injustice of it all. I'm just—'

'You have nothing to apologise for, Lils. And believe me, I've thrown a fair few fits myself since this all came to light. I wasn't always this stoic about my impending doom. I might not be later on. But right now, I feel like I've reached a point of acceptance, and now that you know the truth, it will be easier for me. I've hated having to pretend. I've never lied to you before, in all these years of marriage, and it's felt awful.'

'You should never have been forced to do it.'

'If I'd really wanted to tell you, I could have found a way. But I guess I wasn't ready to say it any more than you were ready to hear it.'

I nodded, still standing by the door. I felt such a rush of love for him, baffled by how he could be so kind, so caring, even with what he was dealing with. Without making a conscious decision, I moved towards him, clambering up onto the bed, mindful of the drip attached to his wrist, Ella bundled against his other arm. I burrowed into his side, breathing in the scent of him, feeling his arm wrap tightly around me, comforting and strong, as it always had been. 'Do you remember that time we decided to borrow my parents' boat and sail to Land's End for the weekend?' I asked suddenly, my ear pressed to his heart.

He gave a gruff chuckle. 'Oh, how could I forget? It started out as the best weekend of my life. Eighteen years old, out on a crystal-clear ocean with a gorgeous woman beside me. You were stunning. I remember thinking how incredible it was that you just knew what needed doing, how to hoist the sails, gliding across the waves. You remember swimming? Those dolphins that came over to investigate off the coast of Cornwall?'

'They stayed so long I was afraid they wouldn't leave.'

'I've still never met anyone else who has a fear of dolphins, in all these years.'

'Hey, if sharks are afraid of them, I'm taking no chances. Besides, they're all slippery and weird, and far too friendly for my liking.'

'That's why I got Fluffy for you – I knew you'd love a cantankerous pet with a fierce sense of independence.'

'He's certainly that!' We both laughed. 'That trip was when you first talked about getting married. When I really knew it was always going to be you and me,' I said softly.

I heard him sigh. 'I would have asked you that night if it hadn't been for the storm. I had the ring with me.'

'You never told me that!'

He shrugged beneath me. 'It wasn't the right moment. But I knew from your reaction that you'd say yes – *if* we made it home,' he added wryly.

'I would have.'

It had been a freak gale-force wind that hit us seemingly from out of the blue. One minute we were drinking sparkling wine and cuddling up on the deck, watching the setting sun cast gold and orange streaks across a clear sky. The next I was fighting a losing battle against a torn sail and Jon was making a mayday call to the coastguard. It was my own fault. The careful rules I'd always followed out at sea had seemed so unnecessary with Jon there to keep me safe. I hadn't checked the radio or noticed the subtle changes happening around me. It had been a miracle when we'd managed to save the boat, and it had taken a long time to convince my parents to trust me with it again.

'I never felt scared,' I whispered, turning to look at him now. 'I knew that whatever happened, even if the boat was wrecked or we were flung into the sea, you wouldn't leave me. You'd be by my side and together we would save each other. But now I can't save you. And you won't be here to save me.'

'You've saved me more times than I can count already.' He smiled softly. 'The first being all those years ago when you let me sit with you in maths class and I felt like I'd walked into a dream. You know, the first day of school is supposed to be torture. But it wasn't for me. I got to sit with this sexy pirate girl who talked incessantly about boats and adventures and made me feel like I'd stepped into a new world.'

'Sexy pirate girl? *Me?*' I giggled despite myself, feeling his ribs shudder beneath me as we began to laugh uncontrollably, remembering how young and free we had both been, the great adventures we'd shared. We laughed until tears streamed down our faces, and then, without us realising how or why, the laugher dissolved and we were sobbing breathlessly in each other's arms, gripping tight as if we could hold on to this moment as it slipped through our fingertips.

EPILOGUE

One year later

I shielded my eyes with the back of my hand as the sun beat down on my bare neck, watching William and Maisy on the shoreline, their life jackets zipped up securely, their little Oppies at their sides, waiting to be rigged and sailed. It was a beautiful day for it, and I saw William place a protective hand on Maisy's back as he guided her forward into the group of children, making sure she didn't get left out. He was different with her now, gentle to both his sisters in a way he'd never been before, always checking in with them, bringing Ella her sippy cup and helping Maisy with her shoelaces or a complicated maths problem.

Jon had spent a lot of time talking to him about the importance of thinking of others, encouraging him to look closely at each situation to see how he could find opportunities to be kind. William, always quick to learn, had taken it to heart and transformed from the somewhat self-obsessed, needy boy he'd once been into a selfless and caring brother and son. He'd always been sweet-natured, but those talks with Jon had channelled his energy and given him more direction about how to showcase that side of his personality. He and Maisy played together daily now, something they had rarely done before, and I could see how deep a friendship they'd developed in the past six months.

Ella, dressed in a purple and green glittery swimsuit with a ruffle round the tummy, crawled through a little patch of sand, then spotted a pebble a few metres off, its shiny red exterior standing out amongst the collection of black, brown and cream. She manoeuvred herself into a downward dog position before slowly rising to stand on two unsteady bare feet caked in sand. She took a tentative step forward, then looked up at me with a dribbly smile. I beamed at her, watching as she took another careful step before wobbling backwards and landing on her bottom. She gave a little grunt of surprise, then, deciding it was easier, shuffled onto her knees and crawled lightning fast towards the pretty red pebble, holding it up for inspection.

It was hard to believe it was almost a year to the day since that momentous trip to the theme park. The abduction. The revelations. Jon's collapse. A day that had changed my life forever and opened doors I would have preferred to remain closed. So much had happened in the months since then, that day almost felt like another lifetime, a different family.

After Jon's admission to hospital that day, I'd held on to my hope that things would get better, that we would make it through, battered and bruised perhaps, but alive. But as the weeks passed and I watched the life seep from my husband in incremental drops that I couldn't ignore anymore, I'd been forced to accept that he was right. It was too late to fight. This monster had taken hold of him, and as much as we wanted to destroy it, it was too strong to overcome.

I thought I would break; that I would fall into an irretrievable depression once I'd accepted his fate, but I'd surprised myself, and Jon too. Those last weeks of his life had been the most special, most connected we'd ever been. There had been no barriers between us, no resistance. We'd talked for hours, opening our hearts fully, and though some of what I heard had hurt deeply, there had been no anger between us.

Jon revealed that he'd known far longer than he'd ever let on that he was ill. That his fear over what was happening inside his body had prevented him from going to see the doctor at the beginning, though he couldn't be sure that it would have ultimately made a difference. He'd told me after our anniversary party that he'd suspected something might be wrong for around six months. At the time, I'd been horrified, but the truth was far worse. It had actually been more than a year after his first suspicions before he'd finally admitted to himself that he needed to see a doctor. His symptoms, though he'd refused to acknowledge them out loud, had triggered a panic within him that had him convinced he couldn't leave me without knowing I'd be secure. We'd never really discussed financial matters, and I felt stupid when I realised I didn't even know what Jon's income was, but he told me that he'd been putting money aside for years since being promoted at work, and after he became ill, he'd been overpaying the mortgage massively. He'd also increased his life insurance just after he got his promotion, long before he knew how much we would be grateful for it now.

As it turned out, the tightening of our belts – no expensive clubs for the children, no holidays, hardly any days out – was not due to a lack of money but down to Jon carefully planning for a future where he might not be around. By the time he was too unwell to work, the house was paid off and I was set for life. He told me he wanted me to be free to choose. That now, if I wanted to, I could afford to retrain and go back to work. Hire a tutor for the children, or send them to a small private school. He said he never wanted me to feel trapped, and perhaps it was being presented with a world of opportunity, but I realised as he spoke that what I most wanted, as it turned out, was exactly what I already had.

I wanted to raise my children myself, be with them every moment I could, because if there was one thing Jon's illness had taught me, it was that life is over far too fast. That these moments with my children, having the privilege of watching them grow and change before my eyes, to see their first steps at each new stage of life, was something I wanted to cherish. Perhaps in the future I would be a fancy career woman with a hand-stitched suit and a personalised briefcase, but not yet. Not now.

There was one other thing Jon brought up as he'd explained the truth of our financial situation to me, and it had made my heart burst with love to realise how much thought he'd already given the matter before mentioning it. He told me he wanted to give Hannah a gift – a final round of IVF and another shot at having the baby we knew she so desperately wanted. He explained how he couldn't bear to turn his back on her and how he truly believed that if she were to conceive a baby, it would be the start of a new beginning, a catalyst to repairing the friendship we'd once valued so much.

There had been trepidation on my part. I had still been so angry, bitter even – the emotions of that traumatic day intertwined with the memories of seeing Jon collapse and hearing that I was going to lose him had made any chance of reconciliation seem quite impossible. Hannah, though she'd kept her promise to support me whether I wanted her to or not, had still been someone I had needed to keep at arm's length. I hadn't wanted to let her close, hadn't been able to trust her, though I knew she was sorry and hurting for her own reasons. I'd been resistant, confused, but in the end, I couldn't deny Jon his wish, and so I agreed to put forward the offer to her.

Her expression when I'd sat her down to have the conversation had told me everything I needed to know – how much this chance meant to her, how much she'd been pushing down her grief to be able to step up for *me* – and the moment she gratefully accepted Jon's gift, something had begun to thaw between us. I'd enjoyed seeing the smug smile on Jon's face as he watched us begin to rebuild what I though was broken beyond repair. I knew he was relieved, and though I never said it, I was too. I had missed her more than I dared to admit.

William finished rigging his dinghy, deftly tying a final knot before turning to help Maisy with hers, her little fingers struggling with the rope. I watched him tie her sail to the boom, securing the mainsheet, with the instructor's keen eye checking it was all completed safely. Maisy picked up her rudder, confidently attaching it and smiling up at William, who gave her an enthusiastic high five. He passed her the daggerboard and together they secured the elastic strap then stood back, bouncing on their toes as they waited for permission to launch.

I grinned, thinking back to the day Jon had led us all outside to the driveway, pointing a skinny finger as a jovial man unloaded the two little Optimist sailing dinghies, Jon breathlessly telling me that he'd paid for a year of lessons upfront at the local kids' sailing club. The smile on his face and the squeals of our children would be imprinted on my mind forever. Watching them on the water, living the adventures of the childhood I'd adored, free as the wind, made me feel that everything would be okay. And I was sure that it had been healing for both of them.

Jon had lived just long enough to see their first lesson. I'd brought him down to the beach and he'd refused a wheelchair, though I knew he needed one, insisting he wanted to hear the crunch of the shingle beneath his feet, that he wanted to walk right up to the water and feel the waves cool on his toes, though it was well into autumn by then and I knew how the cold seeped into his bones, racking his body with convulsive shivers. I'd held my tongue, refusing to spoil the moment, supporting his elbow as he walked.

Hannah, true to her word, always there for us, had supported his other, and the three of us had moved slowly down the beach, listening to the sounds of the circling gulls, the excited screams and shouts of the little group of children all keen to get out on the water.

Maisy, turning to see her dad approaching, had dropped her life jacket on the ground and rushed over to wrap her arms around his waist, whispering, 'Thank you, Daddy. I always wanted to do this,' before sprinting back to the group.

I hadn't missed the tears that streamed freely down Jon's face as he watched our sweet girl move with more confidence and self-possession than we'd known she had in her. It seemed that like me, she was made for the water.

'Are they wearing sun cream? It's going to be scorching this afternoon.'

I turned my head, squinting, to see Hannah waddling across the shingle towards me, one hand held protectively across her enormous bump, the other clutching two lemonade lollies she'd bought from the van on the road.

'Smothered,' I said, grinning as I took the lolly she offered, tearing open the packet before it could melt. 'Don't you wish we were going out there today?' I sighed, smiling as William began sharing sailing facts with the instructor, his voice reaching us loud and clear as he told the fascinated group about Viking longships and how ahead of their time they were.

Hannah laughed warmly. 'Have you *seen* me lately? If I dared to get in one of those dinghies, I'd capsize it in half a minute. I have literally no balance.'

Ella, hearing Hannah's voice, turned in the sand and held up her arms, babbling loud comical instructions.

Hannah smiled. 'You want a cuddle, baby girl? Come here then, you sandy little urchin.' She grinned, scooping my daughter into her arms and kissing her cheek.

Ella patted Hannah's round belly with a gentle open palm. 'Baba soon?' she said, repeating the words she'd been told, her little face serious and knowing.

Hannah nodded. 'Yes, very soon.'

Our eyes met, and I felt so much love for the woman who was still my best friend, my closest support and my source of strength when I'd no longer been able to find my own this past year.

Since she'd accepted Jon's offer, diving head first back into the nerve-racking waters of IVF and donor sperm, I had gone with her to every one of her appointments. I'd seen first-hand what she'd had to go through all those months by herself. The fear. The hormone injections. The tests and physical examinations. I couldn't believe she'd done it all alone. The two-week wait after the fertilised embryos had finally been placed was beyond unbearable, and to think Hannah had endured it so many times before with nobody to lean on had given me a fresh sense of empathy for her, and helped me see how she'd been driven almost to the point of insanity when she'd taken Ella. I could understand now how frayed her emotions were at that low point, how hard the repeated losses had hit, and that helped wipe out any bitterness I might have been holding on to.

Jon had held on just long enough to see Hannah through the twelve-week scan. He'd held the grainy photograph of the baby in his hand, his breathing laboured, his skin waxy and pale, and he'd smiled, his eyes filled with joy, though by then he didn't have the energy to speak. Three days later, he'd fallen asleep at home, in the bed we'd shared our entire marriage, and when morning came, he was gone. His last moments were filled with love, surrounded by family, and though I'd sobbed, I hadn't felt angry that he'd been stolen from us. I'd felt lucky to have known such a man.

Ella wriggled in Hannah's arms, and she lowered her down to the sand to explore. She slipped an arm round my waist, and I hugged her back as we stood watching the children launch their boats out to sea, the sun sparkling on its clear surface, the smell of salt and sun cream all around us.

I missed Jon a thousand times a day, but I wasn't alone, and I knew I never would be. That was something to be grateful for.

A LETTER FROM SAM

I want to say a huge thank you for choosing to read *Save My Daughter*. If you enjoyed it, and want to keep up to date with all my latest releases, just sign up at the following link. Your email address will never be shared and you can unsubscribe at any time.

www.bookouture.com/sam-vickery

The idea for this story came about whilst thinking of all the times we, as individuals, create our own stories, our own version of events when faced with challenges, and how despite our best efforts, we can so easily fall into the trap of pushing those stories onto others and misunderstanding a situation entirely. In *Save My Daughter*, the consequences are severe: an abducted child, a suspected affair, and the potential loss of a lifelong friendship. But those little misunderstandings and miscommunications can happen to all of us, causing us to assume the worst and jump to conclusions about the motives and intentions of our friends, our partners, our families.

If only Hannah had found the courage to tell Lily about her desire to have a baby, it would have opened the door to a closer friendship. If she had sat Lily down and spoken to her about her concerns, rather than pulling back, how much sadness would have been prevented?

If only Jon had allowed Lily to seek comfort when she needed her friend, or Lily had communicated this need to him and been more aware when it came to the changes Hannah was secretly going through, all of the drama could have been avoided.

Admittedly, these communications would have made for a far less interesting story, but learning to be open with one another, speaking the truth even when it required trust and vulnerability, was what ultimately brought Lily and Hannah back from the brink. And when they really listened, heard the story from each other's mouths rather than filling in the blanks with their own assumptions, they were rewarded with a closeness that made it all worthwhile.

I hope you enjoyed reading *Save My Daughter* as much as I enjoyed writing it. If you did, I would be very grateful if you could leave a review. I'd love to hear what you think, and it makes such a difference in helping new readers to discover one of my books for the first time.

I always enjoy hearing from my readers – you can get in touch at www.SamVickery.com or find me on my Facebook page.

Until the next time,
Sam

SamVickeryWrites
www.samvickery.com

ACKNOWLEDGEMENTS

Thank you so much to everyone who has had a hand in bringing this book to market. To my wonderful editor, Jennifer, for such lovely feedback after receiving the first draft of this story, and for all your hard work and support, thank you.

To Debbie Clement, the talented artist who designed such a stunning cover for this book, thank you! It's absolutely beautiful and I love it.

To my publicist Sarah Hardy for organising blog tours, and all the behind-the-scenes work you do, I am beyond grateful.

To my beautiful cousin, Stephanie Bennett, who, when I told her I was writing this book, shared with me her own story of her journey to conceive via sperm donor and IVF, offering candid details that helped make this story so much more accurate, thank you so much. You are going to be an incredible mother!

To all the talented and hard-working people at Bookouture, I am so grateful to all of you.

To my family, my friends, my children and my husband, thank you for your support and love.

And as always, to my readers, those who have been with me for years and those who are just discovering my books, thank you. I'm glad to have you with me.

Made in the USA
Middletown, DE
06 April 2021

37120798R00168